TIMEWYRM: REVELATION

With thanks to:

Miles Booy — Criticism and structural advice.
Jean Riddler — Rune lore.
Tony Gallichan — 'This is a dead chapter...'
Penny List, Wendy Ratter, Marion Barnes — Moral support.

And to all my friends, for their love and patience.
And thanks to Mum and Dad, for Bread and Butter and Honey.

Thanks to the Estate of Aldous Huxley for permission to quote from *The Doors of Perception*, published by The Hogarth Press, and to Elaine Greene for permission to quote from Arthur Miller's *The Crucible*, published by Penguin Books.

THE NEW DOCTOR WHO ADVENTURES

TIMEWYRM: REVELATION

Paul Cornell

First published in Great Britain by
Doctor Who Books
an imprint of Virgin Publishing
338 Ladbroke Grove
London W10 5AH

Cover illustration by Andrew Skilleter

Typeset by Type Out, London SW16
Printed and bound in Great Britain by
Cox & Wyman Ltd, Reading, Berks.

ISBN: 0 426 203607

For Jackie Marshall

Prologues: Hymn From a Village

> *'But if it wasn't for the snow, how could we believe in
> the immortality of the soul?'*
> *'What an interesting question, Mr Wilde. But tell me
> exactly what you mean.'*
> *'I haven't the slightest idea.'*
> Oscar Wilde, escorting an over-earnest lady into dinner.

They say that no two snowflakes are the same. But nobody ever
stops to check. Above the Academy blew great billows of them,
whipping around the corners of the dark building as if to
emphasize the structure's harsh lines. Mount Cadon, Gallifrey's
highest peak, extended to the fringes of the planet's atmosphere,
and the Prydonian Academy stood far up its slopes.

From within the fortress, chanting could be heard, as young
Time Lords were instructed in the rigours to which biology had
made them heir. Trains of scarlet-robed acolytes made their way
about the towers in endless recollection of protocols and procedures. From the courtyard came the sounds of mathematical
drill, as instructors demanded instant answers to complex
temporal induction problems. In high towers, certain special
pupils were being taught darker things.

But behind the Academy, somebody was tending a flower.

The bloom was a tiny, yellow blossom, sheltering in a crack
in the grey-green mountainside. Near it stood a blasted tree,

1

and under the tree sat a robed figure, regarding the flower. It was just a simple bloom, but hardy. The Gallifreyans called it a Sarlain, but the Hermit knew of people who would have called it a Daisy, or a Rose, or a Daffodil. It was complex and strange, the edges of its petals notched and striated. It was very beautiful, but to understand it, they would have to label it as something, the Hermit knew.

This, to him, was the most urgent issue in the universe.

The acolyte dashed up the hill, panting, his breath boiling away in the cold. Tears were freezing on his cheeks. He approached the hooded man almost angrily, as if to demand something of him.

'They're fools! Blind, uncaring fools! They can't see the way it's going, they won't —'

'Sit down.'

Calming himself, and wiping his face on the cuff of his robe, the acolyte sat, and bowed to the dark figure.

'I am pleased that you wish to continue your . . . other studies. Have you prepared the verse?' The voice from beneath the cowl was a whisper.

'I have. I have fasted for three days and three nights, I have made supplication to . . . to the powers you named. I was discovered.'

'They will not punish you.'

'I don't understand much of what I've written.'

'Of course!' The old man laughed. 'That's the point. Much of it you are too young to remember. Read.'

So, shivering in the breeze and the billow of time, the acolyte began to do so.

The head beneath the hood nodded, one eye glinting from the darkness.

It would be several centuries before the acolyte grasped the meaning of his work. And as for understanding it —

Perhaps he never would.

It was the Sunday before Christmas 1992, and the churchgoers of Cheldon Bonniface were wrapping up, shutting the doors of their houses and stepping out this fine Norfolk morning. Distant

2

bells were ringing. Those who lived in the more distant cottages, near the marshland, had bicycled or driven in, and were buying Sunday papers from the little shop on the village green.

The chill in the air was pleasant to the old folk, who remembered their youth, before there was any television, when they'd build snowmen and run through the forest, following each other's tracks. It certainly smelt like snow was on its way.

And with the snow, something else. It was muttered in many versions, along the road that led to the small hill where St Christopher's stood. Old men wondered if they would see another Christmas, wives said that this was unusual weather for the time of year, and blamed it on that ozone, and little boys wondered if they were growing up, because, somehow, things were different.

Inside the little church itself, the same conclusion had been reached. The Reverend Ernest Trelaw, vicar of St Christopher's, was pacing up and down the aisle, debating.

Nobody stood with him amongst the seasonal decorations and the piles of food for charity. The organist, Mrs Wilkinson, was ill. But Trelaw was not alone.

Saul was with him.

Saul was a voice, a presence, that Trelaw had been introduced to by his father, the previous vicar. He inhabited the church in the same way that Trelaw inhabited his body, and had been on the site, in various guises, down the centuries. Trelaw could communicate with him silently, but the cleaning ladies had heard him humming hymns, and had named him as the ghost of old Saul Bredon, who had died asleep in the pews sometime last century.

But Saul was not a ghost. He was an accumulated wisdom, an intelligence formed from the focus of so many dutiful minds over such a long time. The Celtic Cenomanni had called him Cernwn, and each succeeding people had their own name for the spirit of the hill.

Saul had hardly been surprised when the Christian missionaries had tried to exorcize him. But he had been taken aback when, failing to do so, they came up with a typically pragmatic answer to the problem.

3

They built a church around him and declared that he was an angel, or the Grace of God. Or something.

It had taken the first Reverend Trelaw, Ernest's great-grandfather, actually to talk to Saul rather than pray at him. Upon realizing that the church was an independent entity, and not actually divine, old Dominic had set about teaching it, both in scholastic and spiritual terms.

In 1853, at a midnight ceremony, Saul had been baptized in his own font, splashing the water around with his psychic muscles.

Save Trelaw, there was only one witness, and he claimed to have little knowledge of religion. He was a traveller, known as the Doctor. A wise, hawklike old man with a mane of silver hair and an eccentric nature, he had made his way up the hill and entered just as the ceremony was about to begin. He had, he said, left his companions in the village, having known that there was a happy occasion afoot.

Without quite knowing why, Saul had trusted him instantly.

Over the years, Saul had met the Doctor on a handful of occasions, always as part of some hectic adventure, some heroic quest. That was what the church and the vicar, having swung the morning bells together, were considering now.

'Something is different,' chorused Saul, in a voice like an infinite church choir. 'The fabric of reality has changed.'

'It could be that the Doctor is returning,' Trelaw muttered at the rafters. 'I thought last time was too good to be true.'

'Indeed. I must admit that when he walks through my doors, I expect all hell to break loose.'

Trelaw smiled. Saul could be quite charmingly innocent at times, particularly in his choice of metaphors. For his own part, he didn't know whether he looked forward to the Doctor's visits or not. On the last occasion, the Doctor, in yet another new form, had simply brought his niece Melanie to Cheldon Bonniface to enjoy some brass rubbing.

'Perhaps it's just the weather Saul, getting to both our old timbers —'

Trelaw broke off as the church doors swung open. Standing there were those new people ... what were they called?

'Hutchings,' Saul informed him silently. 'Peter and Emily. And Peter heard you.'

'Ah, good morning, you're here a bit early, you caught me rehearsing my sermon.' Trelaw shook hands with the man and wished for a verger.

Peter Hutchings was in his early thirties, tall and solid, but with the slight stoop of somebody more used to the desk than the playing field. He wore his suit uncomfortably, and had cultivated a beard that would have done a hermit proud. 'Pleased to meet you, reverend,' he muttered, seeming slightly abashed. 'This is my wife, Emily.'

'Ah yes,' Trelaw took the cool hand offered him. Younger than her husband, Mrs Hutchings had the face of a great beauty. The reverend, who noticed these things more than he cared to admit, imagined her as a carefree student, riding some mythical Oxbridge bicycle. Her features were almost aristocratic, but it was an aristocracy mocked by the humour inherent in her face. Her russet hair was cut in a bob.

'Hello,' she murmured and wandered further into the church, absently. Resisting the urge to stare after her, Trelaw turned to Peter.

'Well, what brings you to Cheldon?'

'A change of scene, really. I'm on a leave of absence from Cambridge, and I thought it was time to put the savings to good use and settle down somewhere.'

'Cambridge?'

'I'm a professor of mathematics. I've got a new paper brewing. Knot theory. It's all a bit abstract.'

'I'm afraid my maths doesn't stretch beyond O level,' Trelaw smiled. Other parishioners were starting to enter the church now. He made his excuses and attended to the preparations.

'She is very sad,' opined Saul silently, indicating Emily Hutchings with a mental gesture. 'But there is something very meaningful about her. She is a character in a very big story.'

'Indeed,' replied Trelaw in the same fashion, studying the faces of his flock. 'I wonder where the Doctor is now?'

From the pew where she had sat, Emily suddenly looked up, as if she had half-heard something.

'I think somebody just walked over my graves,' muttered the living church. 'All of them.'

Christmas decorations brightened the windows of St Benedict's School, Perivale. There was a chill in the air, and a smoky taste. In the playground, groups of howling children whirled and weaved. By the main building, Miss Marshall was supping a steaming cup of coffee, blowing into her hands. If only she had their energy.

By the edge of the crowd stood Dorothy. Oh dear. Still all alone, trying desperately to be part of the games, but not knowing how. The little girl was gazing in panic at a circle of her peers, who were skipping in a circle, hand in hand. She was waiting for a place to be offered her, but none would be forthcoming. Miss Marshall knew well enough that she couldn't interfere. That would only make things worse. Still, Dorothy needed a friend, somebody who'd look after her.

At that moment, little Alan Barnes grazed his knee, and the teacher was distracted with the business of disinfectant. It was just as well. Something fundamentally important was about to happen.

Outside the school gates, a dark figure stood, watching intently. Its eyes were worried, sweeping the playground for a particular child.

Dorothy.

Somehow aware of all this attention, the little girl in the patched anorak looked around her. She was scared, as well as angry and confused. Somewhere, there was danger.

With the boys, a little way off, sulked Chad Boyle. He was eight, full of venom, with a little army of followers and a horrible itch in his head. He was carefully listening to some internal voice, his brow furrowed in concentration. He'd seen the teacher retreat into the school, and had instantly picked up a half-brick from the pile where the builders were constructing an extension. He was just obeying orders.

'Whatcha doing with that?' asked an awed admirer, pointing to the brick.

'That creepy Dotty. She's got it coming. I'm going to kill

her,' Boyle spat with relish. The gang cheered. They knew that they'd get hurt if they didn't. Like most bullies, Boyle had a few worried followers, who liked to watch him do things that they wouldn't have dared to do themselves. They supported him with their silence, their unspoken agreement. But they didn't really like Chad. He knew that, somehow, and this made him more angry than ever.

The day before, Boyle had stepped on Dorothy's toe in assembly. Quite offhandedly, Dorothy had pushed her elbow into his stomach and sent him flying with a trip. And the Head had told him off for messing about!

She was strange, anyway. Nobody would play with her. She said she wanted to be an astronaut, which was crazy, because girls couldn't be astronauts. Everybody knew that.

He skipped over to the staring girl, and while her back was turned, raised his hand.

The brick was cold, gritty and hard through his mitten. His raised hand was silhouetted against the low sun, so perhaps it was the sudden shade that made the girl turn.

She screamed.

Boyle savagely swung the weapon down, splitting Dorothy's skull and killing her outright.

The law was called in. Miss Marshall didn't actually tell Chad off. She didn't know where to begin. The whole concept of scolding a child for murder seemed somehow farcical. The boy's peers, his gang, withdrew from him with a kind of superstitious awe.

A decision was made that the child be tried before a juvenile court, and would remain in the custody of his mother until then. The Head took it upon himself to visit the victim's parents. Instead of covering the matter up, he called a special assembly, and delivered a lesson on the taking of life.

For once, everybody listened.

Mrs Boyle could feel the shame of it every time she pulled open her living room curtains in the morning. Initially she'd been tearful, asking Chad time and again how he could do such a thing. She'd beaten him with her old slipper, the one that her husband used to use, but Chad just accepted the pain silently, as though it were a minor inconvenience.

All the time he'd looked at her with a kind of puzzlement, as if the answer to her demands was obvious. Finally, on being shaken, he said:

'The Angel told me to do it.'

This did nothing to improve Mrs Boyle's state of mind. She convinced herself that her son was insane, that from now on it would be a matter for psychiatrists. She had spent some time in their hands herself, and knew that the neighbours knew it. 'Inherited,' they would say. 'The sins of the fathers . . .'

She was unable to sleep. She wished Eric was still here. Perhaps he could have been a better influence on the child, a stronger hand. Through the bedroom wall, on occasion, she heard Chad talking to himself, laughing and mumbling.

One night Mrs Boyle heard something stranger still.

It was 3 a.m. by the clock radio, and she was huddled up into her pillow, worrying. Next door Chad was mumbling away, increasingly excited.

The noise started softly, then rose to a crescendo. A galvanized suck, like something organic being ripped apart by machinery. It rang out through the wall, vibrating the wooden cross that hung above Mrs Boyle's cold bed. Then, with a thump, the sound died.

Mrs Boyle jumped up, stifling a cry. Shaking with fear of the unknown, but brave with concern for her son, she padded to the door of her room, and looked out into the darkened hallway. A blue light was flashing under Chad's door, and she could hear the sound of boyish chuckling.

'Chad?' she called, her voice pitched high with fear. 'What are you doing?'

Sobbing, she made herself walk to the door and push it open.

What she saw convinced her of her own madness.

Hand in hand with a strange little man, Chad was stepping into an old-fashioned police box. The man's eyes were closed, and his head was tilted to one side, locked at an odd angle. But he was leading Chad away.

The little boy turned back and smiled at his mother.

'It'll be all right, Mum. The Angel sent him to get me. We're going to kill Dotty again.'

They stepped into the box, and it faded away with the same hellish roar.

Mrs Boyle collapsed to the floor, screaming.

1: Step On

O God! I could be bounded in a nut-shell, and count
myself a king of infinite space,
were it not that I have bad dreams.

Hamlet William Shakespeare.

Ace sat bolt upright in bed and didn't cry out. She did what she'd done since she was little, looking around her room to make sure that everything was as it should be. Of course, this was a strange kind of room, a dormitory in the TARDIS. Still, with her Happy Mondays posters, hi-fi and cool box full of explosives, Ace felt more at home here than she had anywhere else.

And, of course, everything was fine. The room reacted to her waking, brightening slightly so that she could see every corner.

She had dreamt ... what? Home stuff, probably, wishing she could go back and use a crate of nitro-nine where it most mattered.

But still ... she rubbed her face with her hand, well naff dream. Ace was in her early twenties, but had wisdon beyond her years, the instinctive wisdom of a wanderer in the fourth dimension. She had a face that could be soft and beautiful, but would suddenly frown in a dangerous anger, an anger that could blow the world apart for its sins. Which was sometimes how she felt. Ace held certain things to be important. These, in order, were loyalty, street cred and high explosives. So maybe she was a couple of pounds over fashionable, but it was all muscle, and she liked her bacon sarnies too much to care. 'Sides, if she ever met Tim Booth, he'd love her for her mind, wouldn't he? There'd be trouble otherwise.

She heard it then. Far off in the darkened corridors of the TARDIS.

Somebody was crying out, low and distant.

'Old fella? Look out, man. It's inside!'

'Professor?' the young woman from Perivale called, but no answer was forthcoming. Throwing back the covers, Ace went exploring in her nightie.

The TARDIS was some weird kind of craft, huge on the inside, containing literally miles of gleaming corridors, a swimming pool, even a gym which Ace had set about customizing. But outside, the TARDIS looked as cute and old-fashioned as something in a museum. It looked like a police box, and Ace had had to look that one up, because the idea of a copper rushing around the corner to use a phone rather than a walkie-talkie was really strange. She supposed that the Doctor hadn't changed the way the thing looked because he liked it. Or not. He was, after all, an alien, right? He talked about a place called Gallifrey, a home that he didn't feel good about returning to. That suited Ace. If he didn't want to go home, he wouldn't make her go home either.

In the evenings, the Doctor would serve a mug of something hot, and he and Ace would talk about history and politics and science. Then he would say that he had some loose ends to tie up, and bid her good night.

These 'loose ends' Ace supposed to be the preparation work for the Doctor's tricks. During the night, she would wake up at the distant sound of landing, and be concerned. After the first time, she had asked the Doctor what he did at night.

'Putting props in place,' he had said, 'making sure people know their lines, sometimes leaving notes on the script. All the universe is a stage, Ace. Acting's not enough for me. I like to direct.'

These little touches, the night moves in the Time Lord's game, were not apparently dangerous. They consisted of such things as moving items of furniture, research on when things happened, and making sure certain couples never met. Bit mean, that last one.

However, in the time between adventures, when the Doctor was planning his next campaign, this activity usually ceased. They had only just left Kirith, and with his search for the Timewyrm drawing a blank, Ace had thought that the Doctor would actually get some sleep, or do whatever he did. Still, the activity continued.

Only these days, when Ace asked him about it, he'd only say that she must have imagined, it, that he'd been in his room all night.

As she proceeded through the darkened labyrinth, Ace realized that she had only assumed that the Doctor slept. Sure, he locked himself in his room at night, but this was a man who didn't need to shave, right? Coming to his door, she knocked softly. 'Professor? Are you okay?'

After a moment, the door opened a tiny crack. The Doctor, still fully dressed, glared at her like she was some dreadful thing, come to kidnap him. The little-boy face was hardened with loathing, the kind of fierce disgust that only a tremendous innocent could show. An optimist who had been wrong too many times.

That look had always comforted her when the Doctor applied it to his enemies, because it was real attitude. Now she understood why. It made her feel awful, tiny and weak, and thus angry.

'Doctor? It's me! You were shouting!'

The Time Lord blinked, realized where he was, and grinned at her, which was always beautiful to see, strange and quite funny, like some old cartoon. He opened the door a little wider.

'Oh yes. Sorry. Nightmare.'

'Me too. You were shouting out. Didn't sound like you, though.'

'No. That's the trouble with time travel. Difficult to keep a routine. Cocoa.'

Tossing Ace a robe, he strode off in the direction of the console room.

When Ace got there, the Doctor was circling the console, checking readings and flicking switches. His expression was dark, as worried as she had ever seen him.

'Where are we going, Professor?'

'Nowhere. Everywhere. The TARDIS is waiting. Waiting for me.'

'There's something wrong, isn't there?'

The Doctor seemed to consider, and for a moment Ace felt like a kid at Christmas, about to discover that there wasn't any Santa Claus. Then he smiled again, and ducked out of the room. Ace sighed, and stuck her hands deep into the pockets of the robe.

Her foot touched something. On the floor of the console room lay a pressure hypodermic, empty. Ace sniffed the despatch end quickly, but she couldn't recognize the tang as anything familiar.

The Doctor returned, and Ace quickly pocketed the syringe. The Time Lord was carrying two mugs of cocoa on a tray. Ace carefully took one. Perhaps she would have said something about the hypo, but the Doctor launched into one of his rare explanations, and it was never a good idea to miss those.

'I'm worried. Ever since Kirith. The Timewyrm has vanished from the TARDIS's tracking equipment, which means it's in hiding. That's always the way with evil. Devious, subtle . . .'

Ace realized with a sigh that the Doctor was talking more to himself than to her. Their course over the last few days had been erratic, a series of desperate attempts to detect temporal disruption. The had landed in Lewisham in 1977, and visited a pub called the Rose of Lee. They had prowled the streets of Rome in 1582, they had sat and meditated on the Eye of Orion. It was as if the Doctor was trying to see a pattern, divine some meaning in these varied events. He seemed desperate.

'Dreams are the reason for sleep, Ace. There's no point in sleeping unless you dream. Do you ever get the feeling that somebody is trying to tell you something?'

'No.' Ace was going to say something about the Doctor's general lack of consultation, but he was off again, returning with what appeared to be an ancient glazed pot.

'King Wen's gift. The *I Ching*. For services rendered.' He overturned the pot on the floor, and out fell a jumble of sticks.

'Professor, what −?'

'Shh. A simple macroscopic oracle. Reflects the universe in a small action. Our perceptions depend on scale. As above, so below.' He set one stick aside and divided the stack into two piles, then he proceeded to speed through a complex procedure, holding the sticks in his fingers, throwing them back into the pile and swiftly counting. Finally, he leapt up, and fed a series of numbers into the TARDIS computer. 'The combination of the sticks suggests a series of numbers. 541322, in this case, and let the rest sort themselves out randomly.'

The central column began to rise and fall with new purpose, locked on to a course.

'So, what are we heading for now?' Ace stood up.

'Adventure. Conflict.' The Doctor smiled his secretive smile, and Ace grinned back.

'What, deadly danger?'

'Yes. You'd better get dressed.'

The TARDIS spun through the vortex, its exterior reflecting the spiralling purples of the time corridor.

By the time Ace had pulled on some leggings and a hooded Farm T-shirt, and grabbed her jacket and rucksack from the bedside cabinet, they had landed. The Doctor plucked his umbrella from the hatstand, adjusted his own headgear, and walked straight out into the unknown, not bothering to look at the scanner.

He did that a lot these days. Following, Ace hoped he knew what he was doing and was not just showing off. He always seemed to, but, a bit like a stage magician, the Doctor didn't like to reveal how his tricks worked.

That was fine if you were in the audience, but scary if you were the rabbit waiting in the hat.

A full moon blazed over a snow-covered landscape, a dense

forest and marshlands beyond, where sheets of ice reflected the moonlight. In the distance shone the lights of a village. The air was crisp and clear, with a bite of frost, and the countryside lay silent, expectant. Ace zipped up her jacket.

'Countryside. Nasty.'

'Do you think so?'

'Yeah. Bad things can happen to you out here, and nobody knows. There's nobody around to help.' They started to trudge through the snow, the Doctor licking a finger to estimate the wind direction.

'I remember Sherlock Holmes expressing similar sentiments.'

'Yeah?' Ace was interested. 'Did you meet him? Oh, right, he wasn't real, was he?'

'Just because somebody isn't real, it doesn't mean you can't meet them,' murmured the Doctor with a sly smile.

Ace paused for a moment as he carried on.

'Right,' she said, and followed.

They came to a ridge overlooking the village, and the Doctor nodded to himself. A cluster of thatched buildings huddled around a village green. A little way off lay a blacksmiths, and a coaching inn beamed with welcoming noise and light.

'Cheldon Bonniface. Norfolk. England. Earth. Middle nineteenth century, by the look of the buildings. Hmm, I had better be careful.'

'Careful? Why?'

'I might be here. I visited this place on several occasions.'

Ace frowned, boggling at the concept of two Doctors in the same place.

'Would that be so bad?'

'Potentially catastrophic. No such thing as coincidence. No, somehow I think we're playing a different game this evening.' And suddenly, as if he had revealed too much, he changed the subject. 'Do you know where the word Ace comes from?' They started to descend the hill.

'No.'

'From the Latin, as a unit of weight.'

'Cheers, Professor.'

15

'The French usage came to be applied to a pilot who had shot down ten enemy aircraft . . .' He carried on this conversation until they reached the inn, a jolly-looking place with horses tethered in a stable. The painted sign that creaked outside named it as the Black Swan. 'And of course, there's the expression "to bate an ace".'

'What does that mean?'

'It means giving your opponent an initial advantage. Making yourself appear equal.'

'Nothing to do with using an ace as bait, then?'

'Not at all. After you.' He waved her into the inn.

It was the noise that hit her first. The landlord, a huge, portly chap with bushy sideburns and a ruddy complexion, was struggling to reach a table, carrying a tray brimming with foaming tankards. The crowd that surrounded him, merry-looking villagers, travellers still in snow-covered boots and various musicians and beggars, were making a huge, joyous, row, singing carols.

Ace felt like joining in. Then she realized, with a start, that things wouldn't be as easy as all that. Her leggings weren't really the height of chic in the last century. Was she going to be fending off drunken toerags all night?

'It's all right,' muttered the Doctor, closing the door behind them. 'Nobody will notice.' He squeezed his way to the bar, and called out to the plump woman who was slopping hot mead into mugs.

'Martha! What time is it?'

The woman looked up and beamed, laughing. 'Doctor! We haven't seen you in years! But you always ask that question! It's just past ten o'clock on Christmas Eve!'

'Really,' the Doctor yelled back. 'Is there room at the inn?'

'Now, don't you be quoting scripture at me,' Martha laughed. 'We've got two rooms.' She winked at the Doctor. 'Will you be needing both?'

'Ah. Yes . . .' the Doctor seemed shy for a moment. 'As well you know. I must have a word with George.'

'Well, when 'e's got a moment. George, look who's here!'

George, who turned out to be the landlord, looked up from his discussion with a ragged tinker. For a moment, Ace thought, he seemed worried. Then he broke into a laugh.

'Doctor! From the family of Doctors! How's the young lad?' The Doctor found his hand pumped a little too heartily.

'Oh, he's fine. Still playing his cricket. I need your rooms.'

'You have them. You're the sort of guest I like in an open house, not like that lot . . .' he nodded at the group of tinkers, taken in out of the cold on this special night. 'Half a trade between the lot of them. To tell you the truth,' he leaned closer, 'I've been wanting a word with somebody who has a bit of book-learning. Fancy a game of chess?'

The Doctor nodded, intrigued.

Ace had quietly ordered herself a mug of mead, and had sat down amongst the tinkers, grinning. With their moppy hair and carefully-bound packs, they reminded her of the anarcho-punks she'd known in her own time.

'Hi, I'm Ace.' The hardy men regarded her with amazement.

'Well, you're a bawdy lass. A bit lickerish, I fancy,' began a man with an ocarina. This prompted general laughter. Ace glared.

'I dunno what that meant, toerag, but it didn't sound friendly.'

'Oh, don't be insulted, madam.' The interloper was an Irish-man in a dusty top hat. 'We're just enjoying the hospitality before George closes the place down and ushers us off to church at midnight. I'm Rafferty. This is the missus, Brigid.' A lean, rosy-cheeked woman nodded at Ace. 'For myself, if a bit of praying gets me an inch of hospitality in this world, I don't mind.'

'Into God, George, is he?'

'A fearing man.'

Ace supped the mead gently, relishing the honey taste and the herbs floating on top. The Doctor tapped her shoulder discreetly, and spoke in a low murmur.

'Having fun?'

'Yeah. Well historical.'

'I'm off to do a bit of research. You've got the room at the top of the stairs. Meet you there in half an hour.'

'Okay.'

He moved away, but returned on an afterthought.

'And no more mead.'

Ace sighed and placed her elbows on the table.

'Well then, who's for a sing-song?'

The Doctor climbed the stairs beside George, who carried a candle. The light flickered around the stairwell, and the shadows that crossed the landlord's faced emphasized what the Doctor had suspected. The man was scared. Scared of the dark.

He opened the door of the little upstairs parlour, and lit a lamp, checking the shutters over the window. Then he produced a chess set, and set it up on the old oak table.

'Your customers will miss you.' The Doctor sat, showing only curiosity.

'Not this late. Martha can put some more pies and ale down 'em. Been practising, Doctor?'

'Not against a worthwhile opponent,' the Time Lord replied, allowing himself slight relish. 'White, please.'

They began to play, the Doctor holding back, waiting for George to attack.

'There's been some bother at the church,' the landlord began after a while.

'Bother?'

'Reverend Trelaw, acting odd, like. He thinks the place is haunted.'

The Doctor smiled slightly. 'It night be.'

'But he's been seeing things around the place. Demons, he says.' The Doctor's face assumed the aspect of a hunter who has sighted game. George took a pawn. He was developing a strong position.

'And you're going there, tonight?'

'For midnight Mass, as always.'

'Good. We'll come along.'

'Yes,' George looked up, smiling, having taken another of the Doctor's pieces. 'I was hoping you would.'

Ace was getting tired. Her biological clock, she reasoned, thought it was about four in the morning. And the mead hadn't helped. She stood up.

'Leaving us then?' Rafferty called.

''Fraid so. Not exciting enough for me down here.'

'And will it be exciting up there?'

Ace slapped her forehead with the palm of her hand, exasperated, and headed for the stairs, making a mental note to wedge a chair behind her door. Martha called after her to be back down for midnight, and she nodded.

The room, it turned out, was cool. A big old bed, and a jug on the dresser. Ace dropped her rucksack on to the bed, and opened the shutters on the window, noticing that the room was lit by a lamp.

The forest rustled in the moonlight, deep and silent.

That was another reason she didn't like the countryside. Too quiet. She needed the hum of traffic or the TARDIS to get to sleep. Not that that was going to be a problem here. The Doctor would be up in about twenty minutes, full of plans and strategies. Ace hoped that for once he was wrong, that this calm place held no clue to the Timewyrm's hiding place.

She lay on the bed, hands behind her head. Well, maybe she would just take a rest. She'd locked the door, after all.

Within a minute, she was asleep.

'I'm afraid. Afraid of these demons. They're beyond my knowledge, and what's beyond – well, that frightens us all, eh, Doctor?'

The Doctor had been intently scrutinizing George's face, as if looking for something in the innkeeper's expression. His concentration had so left the game that he was in danger of losing.

George glanced back at the board, moved a piece, and made that potential loss into a real one. 'That's the first time I've beaten you,' he grinned.

'Is it?' the Doctor frowned. 'But what about the time –' he glanced up at the innkeeper again, and smiled his giddy smile. 'Yes, of course, you're right.' His expression hardened, his eyes seeming to pierce the vale of space and time. 'Don't worry,' he whispered. 'I'll rid you of your demons.'

George's expression, which had become suddenly tense, eased. 'Yes, Doctor,' he sighed. 'Of course you will.'

The Doctor and George descended the stairs once more. The inn had quietened a little, and the Doctor noted that Ace had left to keep their appointment. He ordered a mince pie and sat down with the villagers.

'Come on lads,' called George, 'there's still a while before midnight. Let's have another song!'

Ace was dreaming about school. Rows and rows of desks, all the same, and she was using a chisel to slam her initials into one. The teacher, an uptight fascist with a juddering lip, was yelling at her to stop, and in his hands he held a box. A musical box. Wound up and ready to play. But this box could hide a secret inside, can you guess what is in it today?

Oh, it's the Doctor. Where are you going, Doctor?

I see, you're going out into space, to battle alien monsters. May we come with you?

But as the Doctor was nodding yes, a boy at the back of the class stood up, and marched forward through the chattering ranks. He stopped at Ace's desk, and glared at her.

Chad Boyle. The motherless creep who'd nearly ... who'd ...

'Dotty,' he grinned. No, this was her dream, she ought to be able to control it. 'The first thing that you learn in school is that evil is not just the absence of good. Evil is real. The second thing you learn is that you —' he grabbed her by the hair and raised his blood-dripping brick, 'will never be an astronaut!'

And there was an astronaut, bending over her desk, his helmet reflecting her face.

She shouted. Woke up, so she thought, but there was still her own face, distorted, inches above her.

A pressure hypo slammed up into the vein under her chin, and Ace fell back on to the bed, shuddering.

The astronaut was short, only about four feet tall. It looked around the bedroom, as if impressed, then reached out and touched Ace, checking her pulse. With a rough movement, it scooped her up in its hands and stepped smoothly towards the window. The leap carried it slowly to the ground, like an alien snowflake gently descending.

A light, chilling breeze fluttered the curtains with its passing.

Much to Martha's consternation, George had started to sing. He was soon accompanied by the beating of tankards and the purr of a squeeze box.

From out of a wood did a cuckoo fly,
Cuckoo!
He came to a manger with a joyful cry,
Cuckoo!
He hopped, he curtsied, round he flew,
And loud his jubilation grew,
Cuckoo, cuckoo, cuckoo!

The Doctor yawned, and stood up, stretching. 'It's getting late. I think I'd better check on Ace.'

George laughed, perhaps noting that the Doctor's expression had once more become alert. 'She's probably not used to the mead. Come on, you haven't even touched your pie.'

The Doctor relaxed, picked up the pie, and was about to take a big bite. 'What time is it, anyway?'

George glanced at his wrist.

The Doctor dived for the stairs. The villagers leapt up and rushed after him, their hands catching at his coat tails, ripping the fabric. The Doctor fended off a few with his umbrella, tripping the leader.

'Seize him!' shouted George, incensed.

'Why? Why?' Martha was calling. 'What's he done?'

The Doctor broke free and sprinted up the stairs, cannoning off of Ace's locked door. He looked around, then jumped into the parlour, shoving the big table up against the door. Heavy thumps rang from the other side.

He pulled open the shutters and examined the window. Old-fashioned leading. He couldn't break it.

He paused, suddenly calm.

'Or perhaps,' he murmured, 'I can.'

Closing his eyes, the Doctor shoved at the window blindly, and it came free, falling into the night. The door gave way, sending the table across the room, and the Doctor threw himself out of the window.

A moment's drop, and then he was rolling in freezing snow. Villagers burst out of the front of the inn, and he sprinted off into the forest.

The wild-eyed villagers' cries followed him.

'Wait,' instructed George. 'We don't want him damaged. He'll come back.' George's brawny hands ripped apart the pie that the Doctor had been about to consume, and searched for something in the moist mixture of fruit and pork. He quickly found it.

Mistletoe.

'The kiss of death,' George smiled, and held it above his wife's head.

Eyes full of fear, Martha kissed the thing she thought had been her husband.

The tiny astronaut bounded across the countryside, carrying Ace in its arms. The leaps it took were high and long, arching above the shining white ground, and landing with graceful impacts and little snow flurries. All was silent. The being kept looking down at its burden, and shaking its head, as if it couldn't quite understand the situation either.

Ace was dreaming the same old dreams. Rings of children, either distant and unyielding, or around her, kicking, hair-pulling, spitting on her. 'Dirty Dotty, Dirty Dotty . . .' And all because of Mum.

Chad Boyle had been a curse to her then, a name that she couldn't be rid of. At home, in her little bedroom full of moon posters and music (and listen, her music had always, always, been better than the crap they liked at school), she wouldn't even think of the name. It meant dirt in your face, and the burn of tarmac against your skin. It meant having to fight for everything, for every ounce of respect. And fighting didn't achieve anything. No matter how good you were at it. The other kids knew the rules. Girls didn't fight boys, boys didn't fight girls. Dotty didn't belong.

Of course, Chad broke the secret rules too, by picking on Dorothy in the first place. All she would have had to do was say 'what's the matter, fancy me, do you?' and he would have been shamed away.

Or maybe not. Maybe he had fancied her, and that was what drove his stupid, underage brain to go beyond all the rules. Meeting her outside the door of her house, tormenting her in lessons, not caring if the teacher saw. The whole time, these awful years, were just pain and chalk dust to Ace now. She'd got out, grew up, made new friends in Seniors. Friends who were outsiders too. She had become a real person.

Or maybe not.

Ace opened her eyes, and saw the white countryside rushing up to meet her.

This was real. Good!

As the astronaut compacted his legs for another leap, Ace jerked violently in his grasp. They both fell in a plume of snow, rolling over, and the woman dived on her abductor, punching him in the chest. A moment later, she was free of his grasp, and just had time to glimpse the slight stature of her opponent before turning and sprinting away towards the forest. The first thing to do was to get some trees between them. At least the astronaut had obliged her by bringing her rucksack along.

Jumping into some bushes, Ace turned to see what the enemy was doing. He was climbing to his feet, and clutching his helmet in agony, yelling with pain.

She hadn't hit him that hard.

Then, suddenly, the pain appeared to cease, and the astronaut looked around, the snowy slope and trees reflecting in his face plate.

Ace ducked down. She was starting to realize just how groggy she felt, her head swimming with strange dreams and fractal patterns of splintering time.

This was turning out to be an interesting Christmas.

Carefully crossing the marshes, the Doctor had slowed to walking pace. His face was a picture of concentration, and no little worry. Eventually, he came to the small hill atop which was St Christopher's church.

'Saul!' the Doctor called, with a hint of desperation. 'I need your help!'

But no answer came, the church was dark and silent, sullen before the trees that protected it from the blast of the wind.

The Doctor grasped the handles on the ancient doors, and threw them open. Frozen dankness greeted him from within. The pews were cold and damp, and the smell of rot was everywhere. Dead flowers lay like sticks in their vases. Frost had claimed the golden eagle of the lectern.

'Saul!' called the Doctor again. 'Are you there?' Quickly, he ran up the aisle. There was no psychic residue, no sign of the presence in the church.

The Doctor's face darkened as he prowled the building, examining the brickwork and almost offhandedly checking a certain piece of masonry. Finally he rushed back to the threshold.

Closing the doors, he stared back towards the village. That way fear lay. Fear, and a very real threat of insanity.

'Evil must be confronted,' he muttered. It was as if he was trying to convince himself.

The Doctor took a deep breath, and marched off to deliver himself to his enemies.

In modern-day Cheldon Bonniface, Reverend Trelaw was having a hard time with his sermon.

'And in these troubled times, we must take heart from the more eventful periods in the life of our lord on Earth ... umm, well, that is to say, eventful isn't quite ... oh dear.' The vicar fumbled with his spectacles.

Peter Hutchings was frowning in the way that people do when they actually want to burst out in thunderous laughter. He was biting his cheeks so hard that it hurt. At the start of the sermon, he had been silently musing on knot theory, but Trelaw's extraordinary delivery had caught his attention. Besides, his brain seemed reluctant to discuss mathematics with him this morning. Every time he started to formulate a nine-dimensional knot equation, things seemed to get out of hand, and he lost track.

It was as if something was undoing his knots.

He glanced at Emily. Thank God, she was enjoying the sight too. He was only here for her sake. Neither of the Hutchings was particularly religious, but in a towny sort of way, Emily had thought that the local church was the best way to really integrate with the community. Or that was what she had said. Another one of her hunches. It was a bit out of character for a woman whose interest in religion went only as far as weddings — and christenings. Lord, she was beautiful, even after all she'd been through. Peter remembered her face when she'd lost Thomas, the echoing pain of it. Then the vacuum that had replaced it when the doctors had told her that she'd never be able to have another and live.

If not for him, she might have tried anyway.

Feeling his laughter turning to tears, Peter gently touched his wife's hair.

Trelaw looked up at the baffled faces of his congregation. He was angry with himself. It was the feeling of expectation that was getting to him, the taste of change that had come with the frost. It had given him stage fright after years of perfect performances. It made his audience restless and he himself a bad orator.

'And, well, I'll leave you to draw your own conclusions,' he muttered. 'Now we'll ... ah ...'

'Hymn number sixty-four,' whispered Saul.

'Yes, that one,' Trelaw told the audience. There was a puzzled murmur. 'Hymn number sixty-four, I mean,' the vicar added, wishing that he had decided to become a plumber.

Ace had picked up a stout log and was swinging it comfortingly before her as she picked her way through the woods, back towards where she thought the village was. A different kind of light illuminated the trees ahead, and she hoped it was the first sign of habitation. Now that she thought about it, there was something awfully familiar about the spacesuit that the creature wore.

It was exactly the same as the ones that the Doctor had showed her at the dusty end of the TARDIS wardrobe room.

They had been looking for things to wear to a costume party in High Barnet, and Ace had suggested the spacesuits. The Doctor had declined, saying that they didn't want to upset the Edwardians, and that he was saving the suits for a . . .

Snowy day. Oh shame.

It jumped out of the trees in front of her, helmet gleaming in the snow. If Ace was honest with herself, this dwarf astronaut was shaking her up. The way its face just reflected hers, the way it scampered with a kind of insane glee, not quite afraid of what she might do. Just wanting to see. Her head was so full of dreams now that moments came and went where the creature was just a figment, a sweet little phantom. The thing's gloved fingers curled and uncurled, and it moved from foot to foot, sizing her up.

Ace gripped the log more tightly.

'Come and get it, shorty,' she called.

The small being leaped at her, feet first. Ace stepped aside, allowing it to crumple in a heap on the icy ground. Hard as she was, she wasn't callous enough to smash the log down on it, so she just tried to threaten the creature as it regained its feet.

'I'm not afraid to use this, pal.' Heedless, the astronaut pulled open a buttoned pouch, and drew a gun. Too far to smack it aside, Ace feinted with the log and ran, scrambling up the hill.

A blast of scarlet light blew a nearby tree into spraying liquid pulp. Clear shot, that was, Ace reflected. If the little squirt was trying to kill her, he was an awful shot. She dived into a bramble bush, regretting it almost instantly, and, the thorns tearing at her, wrestled to keep moving.

She had a vague impression of reaching the edge of the forest. Glancing behind her, she ripped free of the bush and sprinted for freedom. Into the light.

The blazing light.

Her feet scuffed a huge cloud of grey-brown dust. For a moment, Ace was too stunned to comprehend what she saw.

She had reached the edge of the forest all right. There it lay behind her, covered in snow, and the village and the marshes and all.

In a lunar crater.

Above her shone not the moon, but something impossible, something that long ago had stared down from her bedroom wall. Clouds and seas and greenery.

The Earth as seen from space.

The last vestiges of atmosphere trailed away from the momentum of her run, and her last footstep sent her sailing up off the surface.

'DOC—' burst from her lungs, and then she found that she couldn't draw another breath.

The last thought that Ace managed as she spun into the lunar surface was that she'd made it after all.

One small step for man.

One giant blunder for the girl from Perivale.

It seemed as if she could see her own face again, smiling in death.

2: Art And Articulation

To see a world in a grain of sand
And a heaven in a wild flower.
Hold infinity in the palm of your hand
And eternity in an hour.

William Blake.

The Doctor opened the door of the Black Swan and walked in. A chill breeze followed him, and the villagers, who were drinking and carousing once more, hushed. A candle guttered and died.

'Where's Ace?' growled the Time Lord, advancing on George.

The landlord grinned. 'Away from here, in a place of safety.'

'It don't seem right, George,' blurted Martha, looking around at the other villagers wildly. 'What are we doing, all of us? Have we been possessed?'

George sighed, and bid his wife come to him. Timidly, she did so.

'We haven't been possessed, Martha. Let me show you why.' Softly, he stroked the back of her hair, and, taking it as a sign of affection, Martha leaned closer to him. Gradually, as George stroked, a soft grey powder began to form at the back of her

28

skull.

She blinked, concerned, and reached up to her neck. The other villagers looked on in horror, crossing themselves.

'George, what're you doin' to me?' She examined the powder in her wrinkled hands.

'I've decreased the power that's holding your form together,' George smiled. 'In a moment, you'll cease to exist.'

The Doctor stepped forward, but two burly tinkers seized him. 'You've no reason to do this,' he argued desperately.

'I've no reason not to,' George winked. 'Watch this.'

Martha was desperately looking around the room, seeking help. The trickle of powder had become a steady stream, the back of her head dissolving into a river of grey dust. Whirling round, she reached out to grab the bar, and her arm exploded into a cloud of powder. Her legs gave way, and she sank to the floor, imploring her husband to help her. Gradually, the woman twitched and jerked into a pile of dusty clothes. Then the very clothes themselves became a pool of expanding dust. Finally, there was no sign that she had ever existed.

'It's a fitting end,' George murmured, 'for someone as concerned with dusting.'

The Doctor glared at him, sickened. 'Spare me your obscene humour.'

'Doctor, calm yourself. She was never alive. Fictions cannot feel pain.'

'Fictions?'

'Indeed. This village, these people. These are illusions.' He waved a hand at the window. 'Their lives matter no more than the lives of snowflakes.' The villagers looked at each other, amazed. 'Don't you understand yet? This is a trap. The master of the game has been outplayed.'

The Doctor narrowed his eyes, seeming to come to a conclusion. 'Who are you?'

With a dramatic gesture, George reached up and grabbed the back of his own head. He pulled, and with a ripping of soft material the whole face came away, revealing the silver blank of an astronaut's helmet. The face fell to the floor, spasming, and dissolved into dust.

'A simple biological construct,' laughed the astronaut, producing a gun from an inner pouch of his spacesuit.

'But there wasn't room,' cried out Brigid, the tinker's wife, hysterically. 'That thing couldn't fit inside his head.'

'It didn't,' murmured the Doctor. 'Our perceptions are being interfered with.'

'Indeed.' The astronaut activated the catches on his neck lock and removed the helmet.

A mop of black hair, over an angular face that smiled with grim intellect, was revealed. 'Lieutenant Rupert Hemmings of the Britischer Freikorps. Your servant, sir.'

The tiny astronaut had dragged Ace back inside the atmosphere bubble and carried her up the hill to the darkened form of St Christopher's church. He kicked open the doors and strode inside, placing the young woman's unconscious form on the altar.

Then he stepped back, and removed his helmet. A mass of red hair dropped down over a tightly-jealous little face, every muscle taut in a sneer. Piggy eyes looked out from over a squashed nose and thin, murderous jowls.

Chad Boyle wasn't very pretty. If she had been awake, Ace would have wondered why her childhood bully was still only eight years old. For his part, Chad wondered why Dotty was still alive when he'd killed her years ago. Nobody had explained that to him yet.

The boy shuddered, his whole expression changing from malice to cold calculation. He rubbed his eyes and blinked, flexing his muscles experimentally. Then there was a jerk of pain, and, for a moment, he doubled up, squealing. Then, with what seemed to be a great effort of will, he straightened up.

'Don't fight it!' he snarled to himself. 'It only hurts when you fight! S' for your own good.'

He popped open a pocket on his suit, and pulled out a tiny, mechanical creature. Resembling a spider, it whirred and preened, extending microscopic probes to sense its surroundings.

'That's a pineal manipulator,' he grinned. 'Very special. Put her through a lot of pain inside her head.' Stepping forward, he reached out and placed the creature on Ace's forehead, brushing back her hair. 'You've grown up,' Boyle chuckled. 'Think you're so old now. This'll show you.'

He stepped back as the creature began its work. It seemed to feel its way about Ace's skull, adjusting its position slightly. Then it extended a hair-thin probe, which reached out towards the woman's skin, just above her nose.

Ace, just coming round from oxygen starvation, reached up to brush away whatever was irritating her forehead. But at that moment, the probe pierced her skin. Her whole body jerked, her eyelids flickered, and then she lay still.

'Wake up, Dorothy,' giggled Chad Boyle. 'You're dead.'

The Doctor nodded, grimly. 'Yes. That explains a lot.' The Doctor had met Hemmings on an Earth changed by the actions of the Timewyrm, an Earth where the Nazis had conquered England. The man was a torturer, a minor player in that game. It seemed that he was to be centre stage here.

'I can't tell you everything, of course.' Hemmings waved a conciliatory hand at the Doctor. 'I'm working for the gods, following my destiny from the point where you interrupted it.' Hemmings put the helmet down on the bar.

'Gods?' The Doctor frowned, seeming interested.

'Oh yes. The ancient Norse gods. Or so I assume. They are the ones I believe in, and I doubt that any other would appear to me. Perhaps they are the gods of Ragnarok, the hosts of the end of the world.'

'No,' muttered the Doctor, smiling. 'Please go on.'

'I wouldn't be so flippant if I were you,' Hemmings warned. 'I've been fortunate enough to glimpse the unseen world that I've always suspected existed. In the face of that experience, you, as my enemy, assume a very dangerous role.'

'A trap. Typical.'

Hemmings ignored the knowledge contained in the Doctor's grimace. 'Well, a trap with artistic merit at least. I mean to say, the acting was strictly schoolboy, but the mistletoe has a kind of buzz to it. Loki tricked the god Balder into chancing his arm

31

and used mistletoe, Balder's only weakness, to finish him off. Apt, I thought.'

'What interest can you have in me now? Why are you here?' The Doctor's eyes were alive with interest, burning into his opponent's brain.

'In you? Precious little. But my master seems to regard you as worth hunting and I, having worshipped the gods through my life, my art, can hardly ignore divine guidance. I'm aware of only a part of the overall plan, Doctor. Your companion has been abducted, and you are in our power. That much makes universal sense.'

'You're working for something that you fear, aren't you?'

'I don't fear anything.'

'Yes you do. That speech about demons wasn't just an act. You're afraid that whatever you're working for will regard you as expendable.'

'Quiet,' Hemmings snapped, gesturing at the Doctor with his pistol. 'I'm quite aware of your methods, Doctor. This time you face an enemy who is prepared for you.'

'Are you?' the Time Lord smiled. 'Your research didn't extend to wrist watches.' The smile vanished. 'Or anachronistic carols. Cuckoo. How appropriate.' Suddenly, he coughed, bending double. 'The air. What's −'

Hemmings jumped for his helmet. The Doctor sprang up, wrenched free of his captors and headed for the door.

'Stop him!' called Hemmings. 'We need him now.'

As the villagers poured out of the door after the Doctor, Hemmings reflected on how easy they were to control. Puppets. Mere organic creations, but with minds of their own so that they didn't have to be ordered to perform every simple action. They thought that they were alive and free. The Doctor had been correct in that one thing at least. The obvious analogy scared him. He quenched the fear. His life mattered little beside the will of the gods.

Clambering up out of the village, the Doctor headed straight for the TARDIS, a baying horde of villagers behind him. Through the woods he ran, as a blinding snow gale raged about him. The moon still blazed down over the forest, and he took advantage of the light to hide behind drifts of the glaring whiteness. Skipping from one tree to the next, the Doctor confused his enemies to such an extent that by the time he reached the TARDIS, they had split into many different groups, hunting all over the forest.

All but two of them. They were standing in front of the TARDIS.

Cautiously, the Doctor stepped from cover, watching their reactions. They were the tinker couple, in carefully-patched clothes, Rafferty and the woman, Brigid. They hadn't yet noticed him.

'Hello,' he murmured, stepping forward. They reacted, about to shout and detain him. 'No!' The Doctor raised a finger. 'Listen. George is controlling your minds. But you are free. You have free will.'

'I . . .' Rafferty shook his head. 'Don't understand all this, but I do know that I have to take you back to the inn. I'm sorry about it and all.'

'So am I,' whispered the Doctor, and spoke a word that sounded like glass breaking. At the sickening effect of the sound, the two villagers screamed and tried to embrace, but as they stumbled towards each other, they exploded, collapsing into clouds of flailing silver dust that settled slowly on the lunar surface.

'Ashes to ashes,' the Doctor murmured.

Shuddering slightly, he stepped over them, and opened the door of the TARDIS.

The Doctor slowly walked around the TARDIS console, checking readings, reaching across with his umbrella to recalibrate instruments.

The year, it seemed, was 1992. He hadn't looked, hadn't even bothered to check. He had walked straight out into the snow. That was hardly out of character, but even so . . .

The spatial location was surprising also. The *Lacus Somnorium*, on the earthside of the moon. This game was getting deeper every moment.

He leaned on the console for a moment, and then began to work frantically.

Preparing for the battle to come.

'Is memory drain completed?' mumbled Boyle, stretching his arms over his head. The pineal manipulator chirupped in response, one multi-faceted eye glowing green. 'Your memory, Dotty, everything you are . . .' Boyle reached out and plucked up the metal insect in his stubby fist. 'I could kill you, right? Just like that.'

The pain came again, snapping his head up from his prize. 'But I won't. Course I won't. That'd be stupid.' The pain eased. Boyle rubbed his head. It was just like somebody was knocking a pin into the top of his skull.

He knew who it was, too. It was the Angel.

The Angel had first visited him one night when he had gone to bed. His Mum had told him that she wasn't going to read him a story any more because he was old enough to go to sleep without one. That was rubbish, that was, because everything in his room was scary in the dark, full of monsters that might sneak up on him in the night. The story was only a good reason to have her there, a trick to get himself to sleep.

So, one Perivale night, when the wind was whistling through the maze of paths that surrounded the deserted factories, Chad Boyle had been awake. Something had tapped on his window, and he put his face into his pillow, afraid to look up.'

'Mum!' he had called weakly, but his mother hadn't heard, or more likely, had decided to ignore him.

Then the Angel had called his name. Nicely. Like in some stupid fairytale. He'd looked up, and saw that there was a light outside the window. A little, hovering butterfly light, that seemed to be folding away into itself like . . . well, like all sorts of grown-up words that he was going to learn some day when he was a scientist.

The Angel talked with a gentle woman's voice, saying that she had come from long ago and far away, and had felt his pain and loneliness.

'I ain't lonely,' Chad had sobbed. 'I'm strong.'

The Angel had agreed, and told him that he was being wronged. Other children should like him, because he was cool and told good jokes. Then she asked him if he would like to go away on an adventure.

Chad had said yes, and she said that she would send someone to get him, sometime soon. The person she would send was actually a bad man who the Angel was at war with, but when he slept, the Angel could make him do what she wanted.

Chad thought that was a radically cool idea.

In the meantime, he could be as bad as he liked to the stupid kids that made fun of him. They weren't nearly as important as he was. Chad knew that was true. In particular, there was a certain girl that she knew annoyed him. Well, the Angel had plans for her. She would whisper in his ear about them tomorrow.

The Angel had kept her promise, but it hadn't really been quite as the boy had imagined it. The Angel sometimes talked for him, and made him do things before he had really agreed to do them.

If he was really bad, she caused him pain.

Still. He glanced down at Ace's motionless form. There were good bits too. He brought his thumb down on the back of the metal insect, and its transmitter light flicked on. The air filled with the burble of transmitted information.

Ace's mind was blowing away on the wind.

Finally, the sound ceased. The creature buzzed and looked up at the boy, awaiting its next task.

Boyle ripped its wings off, threw it to the floor and stamped on it, laughing.

The Doctor rubbed his brow, irritated by a sudden pain. It went as quickly as it came. He reached out and touched a control.

Ace swam up in a stream of butterfly bubbles, powering up out of a sea-black pit at the heart of the whirlpool. It wasn't water she was swimming through, but words, language. All around her rolled and broke phrases and meanings, and sometimes it seemed that she was part of the tide, her sense of self being only the ridge of a wave, about to crash and die on the beach, sweeping her back into a totality of nothingness.

'The universe is not Newtonian anymore,' said the sea, 'but prone to a synchronicity built on a very dense web of seemingly unrelated events.'

'Knights and squires, doctors and dicers −'

'You're twisting my melon, man!'

With the words came images, though she had no eyes to see them. Glyphs of talking heads, symbols, iconic gods. They all swirled and blended, saying their piece and departing.

It took an effort of memory to keep any idea of Ace together at all, but she was used to fighting for her name, from Dorry to Dotty to Dorothy, Dorothy to Ace, she had learnt who she was by being continually tested, and she wasn't going to give it up now to this tempting sense of community.

Sometimes she'd woken up at nights, hearing noises through the wall, thinking that maybe she should go into school the next day and like that stupid music, those stupid girly clothes, just to get some friends. But always something inside her had said no.

And here was the choice again, in much more direct terms. She could suffer pain and rejection and guilt as Ace, or she could slip away into the crowd of words and become nothing, floating loved in nowhere.

Ah well, pain it was.

A great rush was whirling through the language, a rush of something being born or being taken home. Ahead was a freezing point, like a library or dictionary, which the language dreaded, and so, for a moment, Ace dreaded it too. But then she heard the words that attended it:

'Impulsive, idealistic, ready to risk his life for a worthy cause . . . hates tyranny and oppression . . . never gives in . . . never gives up . . . believes in good and fights evil . . . Though often caught up in violent situations, he is a man of peace. He is never cruel or cowardly.'

And Ace knew that here was something beyond herself which she cared for terribly, and painfully. Something that could never be part of a crowd.

The symbol for this awful goodness was a rose with a colour beyond colour, a rose covered in thorns that could pierce and injure any who approached too closely.

Ace grabbed the rose and hung on, feeling identity fill up her form once more, memories and smells and tastes and ancient, half-forgotten touches.

She looked at her hand as it appeared before her. The rose was gone, and she was unharmed.

Standing, she saw that she was on a beach, a very normal beach. A dark sea-front with a pier that stood skeletal and black with rust. The tide hissed and sighed about her. Shaking the water from her hair, she set out for the pier.

In situations as weird as this, Ace had learnt that action was often more useful than words. Still, an awful idea nagged at her. The last thing she remembered had been a clenching of her lungs, a horrible, cold attempt to draw a breath when there had been none to draw. She looked around.

'Nah . . . it's Cromer.'

A light was flashing red at the entrance to the pier, so she headed for that. Black stick-gulls soared in the sky, crying deathly cries. There was a town up on the sea front, but it was full of closed shops and deserted arcades. Must be the off-season.

She clambered up onto the promenade, and reached the entrance to the pier. The red light rotated on top of a small carousel beside which stood a startlingly beautiful woman, clad in a long grey hooded robe.

'Oh, hello,' she said brightly, her eyes a beautiful blue. 'You rather caught me on the hop.' She skipped off the ride and popped into the ticket booth that formed the front of the pier. Picking up a pen and an ornate book, she smiled down at Ace. 'Now, first of all, any questions?'

'Yeah.' Ace bit her lip and tried for the easiest option first. 'Look, I haven't, I mean, by accident eaten anything or — have I?'

'No, no,' laughed the woman. 'Your reputation on that score remained clean to the end. Oh dear, I've let it slip, haven't I?'

Ace's eyeballs bulged. Her fists clenched. She wanted to

37

hammer on the booth and shout her head off, but that would have been too uncool to contemplate. After a moment, she handled it.

'You mean I'm dead?'

'Yes. Sorry. I'm in charge of getting people used to the idea. I'm not very good at it, I'm afraid.'

Ace looked around her. The wind on her skin felt real, the tiny drops of rain in the air were wet and cold. Everything but the woman was such a normal grey. The place reminded her of that time she'd hitched up to Morecambe to go to a thrash metal gig.

Dead.

'How did it happen?'

The woman checked her book. 'Oxygen starvation, brought about from finding yourself on the moon having believed the place to be Norfolk. I do believe that's unique.'

'So, what do I do now?'

'Well, I've entered your name on the lists. That means you must proceed to the Gate, where you will be judged and ah, sent on.'

'What's this place, then?'

'It has been called limbo, generally by mystics who pop in for tea and stickies then go away again. All this,' she waved to indicate the surroundings, 'is what I believe you would call an icon, a representative image. I can change it to anything else that suggests angst and melancholia, but I rather like it this way.'

'I can't stay, can I?'

'Do you really want to?'

Ace looked around, at the beach and the gulls and the grey retirement homes. The air in this place smelt of longing, the same smell that wafted down the London Underground at the start of winter. The taste of dead dreams and unfulfilled wishes. Well, that was the whole point of growing up, wasn't it? To stop wishing and start doing.

She'd lived as fast as she wanted to, but had died far too young. At least somewhere on the moon there was a good-looking corpse. Lots of regrets, too.

'No,' she said finally. 'Can't smile. I just got the idea that

– this isn't a joke, is it?'

'No. You're really dead. The, ah, Doctor miscalculated, I'm afraid.'

'You what?' Ace looked up, startled.

'He was betting on you surviving that few moments of decompression, I gather.' The woman pointed to a tiny black and white television installed in her booth. 'I'm rather fond of his programme, actually.'

'The Professor got me killed,' Ace whispered, and then shouted. 'He finally went and did it!'

'Don't be angry,' warned the woman. 'That might not augur well for you in what is to follow. Are you ready for divine judgement?'

'Yeah,' smiled Ace grimly, shouldering her rucksack. 'But is it ready for me?'

The Doctor was looking at the scanner, trying to see through the lie of Cheldon Bonniface.

'The energy required ...' he muttered. 'The depth of the illusion. Gravity, even. How is that done?'

He pulled a fob watch from his pocket, and checked it quickly, like he was hiding it from someone. It was gone again, just as quickly.

Hemmings paced the inn, kicking chairs. He was surprised that this continual Christmas atmosphere, the eternal expectation, was irritating him. Perhaps it was because Christmas in his household had been such a joyful time. His father would prepare a mammoth breakfast, and they would exchange presents before the hearth.

Time was less of a secular concept on the moon, where it wasn't kept by festivals and routines but by the slow decay of rock under radiation. There would be a dawn, of course, eventually, but a bit of snow and a few maliciously chosen decorations wouldn't make it Christmas morning.

So why did he want it to be real, anyway? Wasn't he concerned with destiny?

Well, some distant, unmoved part of his mind replied, destiny is a very boyish thing. He had toys enough in the villagers. But what happened when Santa came calling?

He aimed at a horse-brass that decorated the bar, and blew it into moondust.

Mr and Mrs Hutchings were singing along to a hymn from their pew at the back of St Christopher's, both trying to mime the words that they couldn't remember.

... yet in the dark streets shineth,
The everlasting light
The hopes and fears of all the years
Are gathered here tonight.

Emily could hear the somewhat tense voices of the community around her, and that of her husband at her side, but there was someone else singing, high and beautiful. A male voice, but one that contained a kind of female potential. Emily remembered hearing something similar when she was a teenager, getting over a fever. She had told her mother that a pile of clothes on a chair was actually a rhinoceros. Mum, of course, had laughed, and Emily, in her delirium, had been hurt. The clothes had, after all, just charged the mantelpiece. She had shivered, afraid for her life, and had heard something half-blurred that she had rationalized as being from a TV downstairs, but that sounded like it had been transmitted over light years.

'Fear,' the voice had muttered, 'makes companions of us all.'

And in this church was something like the same voice, evocative of those years of study and tears.

Emily fervently hoped that this wasn't God. If she ever met him she had the awful feeling that she'd ask him to go away because she didn't actually believe in him, to be completely honest, and she didn't want to be the kind of person who chatted to deities.

'That is certainly hypocritical of you,' said the voice, pausing between verses.

'Hold this for a minute,' muttered a small Scottish man, handing her a baby.

Emily did something she'd never imagined doing. Something very old-fashioned. She fainted.

40

Chad Boyle was kicking lunar stones in the church, fed up with waiting.

'It shouldn't be long,' the internal Angel murmured to him soothingly. 'We've sent her into the systems our presence cannot reach. He let down his defences quite unconsciously, because she was such a familiar personality. The plan is well in motion.'

'Dunno what you're on about,' complained Chad. 'I'm hungry, and I want to do horrible things to Dotty.'

'Horrible things like what?' asked the female voice.

'Fill her mouth up with worms, or pull out all her toenails. Really horrible things.'

So the Angel showed Chad some pictures of really horrible things. She showed him war, and grief, and torture, genocide and cruelty. She showed him that these things were universal, and universally ignored when there was profit to be made or advantage to be gained. She showed him what the universe was like in her eyes.

It was almost a test, to see just how well suited her little partner was to her grand intentions. Or perhaps it was some frustrated search for communion. Chad had started to cry with the revelation of it all, and muttered nightmare words.

When it was over he opened his eyes, shaken and a little older.

'Those too,' he whispered. 'Those things too. But first I want to find some worms.'

'You will have your chance,' the voice calmed him. 'At the right time.'

Ace had wandered down the length of the pier, having serious doubts.

She had never really stopped to think about believing in anything. All she had ever believed in was her friends. That wouldn't go down well. Neither would how it was with her and Audrey, her mother. She swallowed hard and kept walking.

Too late now.

At the end of the pier stood a theatre, its hoardings blank and grey, the remnants of posters having rotted away. The great empty spaces invited graffiti, but Ace felt that she should be on her best behaviour.

The door of the place was open.

Cool as a pint of milk, Ace stepped inside.

With a little leap of consciousness that felt like a TV must feel when it's switched off, Ace found herself in the centre of an auditorium. In banked seats, an expectant audience looked down at her. She couldn't see who was up there, but it was almost like being amongst old friends, a bunch of familiar sounds and smells that hovered, unknown, at the edge of recognition.

Her head felt dozy, too, like she had wandered into some fuzzy dream. A spotlight blazed onto her, and she threw up a hand to protect her eyes. The crowd clapped and cheered.

'It's not supposed to be like this,' shouted Ace. 'What happened to the Pearly Gates?'

'Times change,' muttered a female voice from behind the spotlight. Well, that was one suspicion confirmed. God was a woman. 'You must pass on to your first destination.'

'Wait a minute! I've got to ask you —'

'No answers. Nothing here is that simple. What you are required to do must remain a mystery.'

Ace was about to argue very fiercely, but then she was, just as suddenly, elsewhere again.

Behind her, the dark audience shifted and stirred. They would see her again, they knew, for they knew more of this matter than anyone. They sat muttering in pleasant anticipation.

Anticipation smelt of brimstone and roses.

3: Pepper And Architecture

The man who comes back through the Door in the Wall will never be quite the same as the man who went out.

Aldous Huxley.

'Where is he?' the Angel demanded. 'Hemmings should have brought him here by now.' Chad simply shrugged. He didn't understand what was going on at all. 'I wish I could see through the eyes of my prey,' the Angel continued. 'Then I could tell where he was. Still, we can take steps to reduce our power output . . .'

Before he realized what he was doing. Boyle had his hands raised. It took him a little while to realize this, a little shake of his head to free it from the cobwebs. These days he seemed to be waking up every five minutes. Maybe this really was a dream, and soon the alarm clock would go off. Time for school, time for hitting children until they liked him.

He tried to remember how he'd got here. There had been that time in the playground, with Dotty and the brick. Red brick, rough in his hand. He'd been talking to his gang, swearing about her, when he'd got the idea that this was the moment his visiting Angel had referred to. He'd picked up the brick and crept in her direction, watching that little blonde head, the intense stare of her eyes.

He'd raised the brick, not sure what he intended to do.

And then the back of his skull had been pierced by a four-dimensional probe. This had impaled him through the cerebral cortex and peppered his brain matter with hyperspatial reference material. It had hurt like a drill bit. The whole process was over in seconds, and, in the second he brought the brick down, he was a different creature to the boy who had raised it.

Something had bravely jumped out of its lair in daylight, slithered through hyperspace and captured the child. Just as quickly, it had vanished again.

Mum! Make this dream go away! Chad would have started to weep, but something dark flooded through his mind and made him hate instead. He looked down at Ace on the altar. Even now she wasn't helpless. Even now she looked confident. He hated her for that. The hate gave the thing in his mind sustenance, and it overbalanced his consciousness once more, taking control.

With a shudder, Chad Boyle brought his raised hands together. The concussion sang out through the church, impossibly across the lunar vacuum, booming in the endless night.

The bubble of atmosphere that sustained Cheldon Bonniface in the *Lacus Somniorum* ruptured. Molecules flew apart, air becoming void as dust exploded upwards in a silent lunar hurricane. Those few earthbound astronomers who were still interested in the moon gestured excitedly to colleagues to come and see. A plume of dust was blossoming out across the lunar disc, obscuring the light with a wave of darkness.

At the heart of the storm, Hemmings stumbled, swiftly fastening the safety catches of his spacesuit. He pulled on the helmet with the speed of one who had no real idea of what vacuum could do, but didn't mean to find out. Sometimes he wondered how he had come by the spacesuit. He had come across the strange device, the blue box. He remembered that. London Freikorps headquarters. He'd given the Doctor the slip. He had stepped through the blue door. And then a figure had

44

appeared behind him and placed something on his neck.

He had woken here, in the spacesuit, and had talked to a god. The god had been a tiny ball of knotting light, something that was hard to watch and remain sane. The god had asked if he knew where he was.

'The moon?' he has guessed, reluctantly. He had always been fascinated by astronomy, the grandeur of space, how it set up a model of serene order for life on Earth. Horbiger, whom Hemmings had read at his father's knee, had said that the moon was made of ice, and would crash down upon the world, releasing the ancient gods imprisoned inside the planet. Hemmings mentioned this to the deity before him.

The god had been pleased, indeed had laughed, and had asked him if he wished to serve in return for special honour.

The Freikorps man had replied that he would serve without reward, that he had dreamed of this moment, subconsciously anticipated it in his paintings. Jung, whose works had been suppressed but still held wisdom for the few who could be trusted to read and understand, had spoken of archetypal gods. A warrior must accept what is before his eyes as real, as must a learned man. Hemmings was both. He bowed to the god.

In a blink the god had filled his head with information. George the landlord, seen through somebody's eyes, data on the history and geography of Cheldon Bonniface.

Information on the terrorist known as the Doctor.

It was then that Hemmings realized why he had been chosen. He had met this infamous criminal, had nearly brought him to justice. The gods had watched him fail in his destiny, and had given their child another chance.

Hemmings smiled in his reverie as the inn was dissolved into a blizzard of dust. He raised his arm to cover his faceplate, falling against the bar which gave beneath his weight, becoming a mass of silver particles.

When Hemmings lowered his arm, the Black Swan was gone. The pillars, crossbeams and furniture had fallen into mounds of lunar material which was spreading away and settling slowly in the low gravity. Hemmings took an experimental step, and found that indeed the natural gravity had reasserted itself.

The power it took to do that had indeed scared him. A psionic weight had been placed on every footstep taken by every being in the mock village, and the perceptions of the Doctor and his companion had been altered to take into account the differences in momentum.

Hemmings remembered the construction of the place, how he had stood on the lunar surface, barely having been there for an hour, lectured to by a midget avatar in a spacesuit. The small being had described a grand and powerful plan of the gods, a plan to trap and use the Doctor. Most of it had been over Hemmings' head, but, asking certain guarantees, he had agreed. One of the guarantees included oxygen, which was, it seemed, piped magically to his backpack from the blue globe below.

It took vast power to do that, power in hiding. And given two chances, he had failed to carry out its orders.

The lunar plain stretched out before Hemmings under hard Earthlight. He checked the gauge on his atmosphere pack, and shivered despite himself.

All that remained of the bogus church of St Christopher was the altar, carved from lunar rock, the reality beneath the illusion. Ace breathed on, sustained by a renewing envelope of atmosphere. She was still of use.

'Well,' murmured the Angel, 'I am pleased at my skill with the spectacular. Now then, some changes can be made. Would you like to go inside?'

'Inside where?' asked Chad, nervous at the businesslike tone in his internal voice.

'Why, to fairyland, to my playground. Where Dotty is.'

'Will it hurt?'

'Just a little, then nothing will ever hurt again. I promise.'

The thing in Boyle's skull felt the boy panic as his hands reached up to unclip his helmet. The child's own fingers fumbled at the catches, and his eyes bulged with fear and terror.

'Trust me,' the Angel hissed, but the fleshthing continued to shiver as the headpiece was removed.

'It's space! There's no air!' And then Boyle found himself gulping, his face freezing as he felt the ultimate cold of vacuum.

He didn't care that this was exactly what Ace must have felt, all he wanted to do was regain control of his arms before it was . . .

Too late.

A blast of life-support chemicals and oxygen geysered out of the spacesuit, and it was all the alien could do to stop its puppet from flailing about and screaming.

It was pure aesthetics, of course, mere vanity, but being confined in such a clumsy form annoyed the Angel. It had found a forward base here, a place from where it could psionically hold together its illusions using its new source of psychic power. The main host had not suspected a thing. Now the need for the trap was gone, it could induct the consciousness of the boy to the main base inside the host, and make use of his physical body more directly.

The creature worked artistically as the gases plumed around the boy's face, using the psychic energy it had tapped (so much, and put to so little use!) to chisel away at the flesh with the rushing gases, depositing here, eroding there.

Boyle's nerve endings squealed with the pain of it, but the creature smoothed a cool wing over his mind and hushed the flesh creature as his face changed. Finally, it let the boy's consciousness go, flitting away back to the Angel's main base. The action was like a human releasing an insect.

What emerged as the last wisp of gas departed from the helmet link was much more to the Angel's taste. Metallic blue, an angular jaw stuck forward from a flared snout and shining smooth brow. Long, tapering ears of aluminium curved upwards into vicious blades. The general impression was that of a carnivore, a ravenous dragon, but for one detail. The eyes were still those of a frightened child.

The Doctor's gaze swept the console of the TARDIS carefully. His hands remained clasped behind his back, and he seemed almost at peace, a man in the eye of the storm. Only two things disturbed this picture. His eyes were those of a suspicious animal and, hidden, his fingers were playing complex, jittery, games.

47

Ace had woken to find herself lying on a polished floor, her muscles aching. This death lark was certainly a strain. It was also nothing like anything anybody had ever told her about the afterlife.

But then, who would know?

She tried to take in her surroundings. It was, fairly obviously, a library. Endless wooden shelves, the smell of polish, and a ponderous quiet filled the place. Well, libraries were cool. You could get away from the world there and read the new volume of *Chemical Abstracts*. She looked at some of the books. Homer's *Odyssey*, *The Adventures of Sherlock Holmes*, and *Fly Fishing* by J. R. Hartley. The books were in some kind of strange chaotic order that it would have taken a genius to comprehend.

The floor, Ace noticed, was tiled, an immensely complex pattern that curled and knotted around itself, patterns within patterns, full of little pictures of people and places. The pictures changed as you followed a loop of the pattern, and formed some sort of a plot.

Here was a cowled figure shaking his fist at a dark castle, and in the next picture he was cowering from something huge and fearful. Then he was running. But this plot seemed to connect with others. A schoolteacher, a nice-looking one for once, looking puzzled at his class, then sitting in his car outside a junkyard, together with his companion.

Plots within plots, wheels within wheels. Ace shuffled across the floor, trying to find a continuation.

A footstep clicked onto the smooth surface.

Ace stood up, slowly, eyes ready for battle.

Chad Boyle had spun through the ocean of language also, maintaining his identity through hatred, through laughing at any other definition than his. When he'd come to the end of the journey, he had heard the same declaration of principles that Ace had, and had laughed at that too.

It sounded great, but if you behaved like that, everybody else would start hurting you, because nobody liked a keener.

He reached for the rose, and snapped if off at its stem.

The thorns drew blood.

The beach disappointed him, because this was almost exactly opposite to what he regarded as a good time. Still, he saw the light at the end of the pier and proceeded towards it.

'Hey!' he shouted up at the woman in the ticket booth, who was reading from her book. 'Where's the ice cream?'

Seemingly surprised, the robed figure looked down at the child.

'Ice cream?'

'The Angel told me I'd like it here, and that means the whole planet must be full of ice cream.'

The robed figure smiled an ancient smile. 'Yes, of course. The ice cream is that way . . . ' She pointed down the pier. 'Do you intend to hurt anybody?'

'Course I do, Here I can do whatever I want, and nobody can stop me. Even the Angel's not inside my head now!'

Her eyes excited, the woman watched the boy stamp along the boards of the pier.

'I'm afraid she is,' she whispered, 'and you're not.'

Through the flesh of her hand ruptured a single metal claw. She used it to change the channel on her television.

The picture now was of a library.

Something was moving behind the shelves, something glimpsed between books, a sinister figure. Ace moved slowly backwards, checking behind her. There were others all around her.

Ace did what she always did in stress situations. She reached for her nitro-nine. Three cans left. The things were vaguely humanoid, but she couldn't get a hint of features or costume.

'All right, scumbags,' she called, holding a can of her favourite substance aloft. 'Explosive death on sale. Who's buying?'

Then she backed into something.

She spun around, expecting to have to fight it off hand to hand. When she saw who it was, she relaxed slightly. It was an old man, his silver hair swept back. Yeah, he looked like a librarian as well in his red robes, peering at her down his long, hawklike nose.

'That is scarcely an expression suited to a young lady, hm?' he muttered sternly.

'Who are you calling a lady?' Ace backed off slightly, and he raised a hand.

'Oh, don't be silly, child. I'm not your enemy. Indeed, I'm here to help you. Yes. I have some control over the Library. Don't take any notice of the clowns . . .'

'Clowns?' Ace had suspected, but was shocked to discover that that was what the figures were.

'Yes. Totally inappropriate in a place such as this. Go on, shoo!' With a theatrical gesture, he waved away the clowns that lurked behind the bookcases. The elaborate ring that he wore glinted in the reflected light. 'Shoo! Hah, that showed them, eh?' He giggled, and put an arm around Ace's shoulders. Ace didn't mind. He was like a kindly grandfather, and he smelled of roses. 'Their whole purpose, my dear, was to get you to where you are supposed to go. I can do that in a much more civilized fashion. Follow me.'

He gave her shoulder a little squeeze and was off, suddenly authoritative again.

Ace smiled. Maybe she had an ally.

The librarian led her to a doorway, which bore a plaque saying: 'Special Collection. Staff Only.'

'Am I allowed in there?' Ace asked him.

'Hm? Of course, child, of course! I never give advice, never! However, in this particular case, yes, I think I shall make an exception. I detest being ordered around, especially by both sides —'

'Sides?'

'Yes, my dear. Now listen. All is not lost. Do not give up. That is all I can tell you.' The sinister figures were milling in the near distance.

'Thanks. Are you going to be okay?'

'Okay?' The librarian's voice took on an offended tone. 'I live here. Now be off with you.' And he ushered her through the door.

Once Ace had gone, the old man chuckled, and fished a pair of pince-nez from the pockets of his robe. He selected a book on gardening from the stacks and began to read.

'Hmm,' he muttered. 'These youngsters. Such games they play.'

Ace leaned on the door, inspecting the room in front of her. It appeared to be a dead end. A small study, oak-panelled, and with a sense of personal use about it. Like a staff room. She made her usual instinctive check of the resources available to her. An astronomical globe, heavy enough to smash the door. And, yeah, the door had been locked as well. Funny how she could anticipate the tricks of this place, like it was a friend she was playing a game of Spoof against. The walls of the room were lined with bookshelves, and a few obvious titles caught her attention: Blinovitch's *Temporal Mechanics*; *Le Morte D'Arthur*; *The Wizard Of Oz*.

Great. At least she'd have something to read. Maybe she didn't understand much after going to sleep in the inn, and maybe death was the strangest party she'd ever crashed, but she was still Ace. Sooner or later the main chance would show up, she'd find the key to this puzzle, and total the bad guys. If there were any. Perhaps this was straight up, the way the afterlife was, but the librarian's words had comforted her slightly. Even if things were as they seemed, she still had a chance to save herself from, er, eternal damnation.

Ace absently spun the astronomical globe, and in the swirling masses of stars she thought she saw a picture, a flash of something. She bent closer, and spun the globe again.

'Remember home?' the stars seemed to ask.

'Yeah,' replied Ace. 'Didn't like it much.'

Well, that wasn't quite true, even if the young woman in the jacket claimed it was. All sorts of things had happened to her before the Doctor had come along, all sorts of terrible and wonderful things. And she hadn't screamed since she was twelve. Well, she allowed herself a silly grin, not in fear anyway.

She remembered Earth. She remembered her and the gang dancing in front of that big Hoover factory that looked like it should have risen up out of the ground. Some guy should have been playing a keyboard at the very top. A police car had stopped, and the coppers had even breathalyzed Manisha.

'No law against dancing,' Dorothy had sulked.

'How can you dance without music?' asked the law.

'How can you think without −' but they'd run away then, down the narrow footpaths that separated factory from factory in Perivale. And under the stars they'd panted and laughed. Like they'd never grow up. Ace disliked policemen for exactly the same reasons she disliked clowns. Still, both had their functions, she supposed.

'Remember Earth?' asked the stars.

Sometimes. Midge had once gone to Australia on holiday, and had sent Ace back a postcard whinging about how lonely he was, so far away from home. Lonely. Like twelve thousand miles was lonely. Like try a different spiral arm of the Milky Way, Midge, like try being left there to get by. Deliberately. And the Doctor acted like he was surprised when she got in the TARDIS. He'd used her from day one. Kept her like a pet.

Midge was dead, of course. Bad news to think like he was still around. Her friends had been killed by aliens, her past was a game for aliens to play with, she'd even got off with an alien. That would've made a good headline.

'Not boring,' she grinned. 'So tell me about home, eh?'

But now the stars were silent. The call was stifled. Behind the globe stood a small table, and on it lay a splayed pack of cards. Ace picked one up and smiled.

'The Hanged Man. Wicked.' Because it was the Doctor, hands fumbling with his umbrella as he hung from one leg, trying to reach upwards. She turned the card over. The picture on the other side was labelled 'The Traveller' and pictured the Doctor waving a spotted handkerchief to some tiny hut in the distance. In front of the hut stood people, or were they? No matter how hard Ace looked, they remained vague.

Another card in the pack was 'We Are Friends To The Ugly/We War With The Beautiful'. This gave Ace a moment's pause, because she was the Doctor's friend, wasn't she? Or used to be. But the card showed the Time Lord embracing a many-tentacled monster and confronting a calm humanoid, so she thought she saw the point. '*Ka Faraq Gatri* — Bringer Of Darkness/Destroyer Of Worlds' showed on one side a black and white raven hovering over a crystalline city, on the other the Doctor hanging his head in shame. She got that one, that was guilt at destroying the Dalek homeworld of Skaro. Only the Doctor could feel sad about those scumbags.

The last card that she found surprised her. It said simply 'Ace' and was the same on both sides, a mirror. Yeah. That was cool.

'Somebody's really got your number, Professor,' she murmured to the room, half expecting an answer.

Peter Hutchings had been staring out through the stained glass window when the trouble began. To him the streets of Cheldon Bonniface were red, leading to crimson marshes in the distance. A shout in the midst of the hymn disturbed him from his reverie.

He spun around, to find that his wife was lying back in the pew, holding her head in her hands. On her lap, out of nowhere it seemed, had appeared a baby.

Peter just stared. The hymn was stifled as people stood or stepped forward to offer help.

Trelaw had seen something, a movement at the back of the church, the departure of familiar coat-tails.

'Saul,' he whispered internally. 'Who was that man?'

'That,' muttered Saul, 'was the Doctor. I would have called out to him, but I did not want to alarm the congregation further. He seems to have vanished again. He, ah, delivered a baby.'

'Oh dear,' sighed Trelaw. 'I knew that something complex would happen today.'

Having searched for secret passages, ventilation ducts and hidden cameras, Ace was leafing through the pages of an atlas, her back to the celestial globe. She wanted to find something out. There. Cheldon Bonniface, on the Bure between Wroxham and Horning. It was certainly a real place.

Behind her, unseen, a silver tentacle emerged from the globe, within the constellation of Cassiopeia. Its tip was needle-sharp and shiny.

The Doctor closed his eyes and sighed, hands poised over the controls of the TARDIS, the actor waiting for his cue. One roundel of the darkened control room had been detached, revealing complex neural circuitry that had somehow been adjusted with a pair of pliers. Two fingers of the Doctor's left hand were curled into the Horns of Rassilon, the Gallifreyan protectional motif against supreme evil. Rassilon himself would have disapproved.

'It's not for me,' murmured the Doctor to his ancient compatriot. 'It's for a friend.'

The tentacle snapped out, ripping a hole in Ace's jacket. She spun round, shedding the garment with a shrug, only to find another tentacle lashing out for her throat. The globe was squirming with metallic life, and Ace found herself swatting at the sharp spines with books, grabbed from the table, the walls, the floor – she slammed against the wall, still fighting, and the things clutched her ankles, pulling her off her feet.

'No way!' she roared at them, clutching on to table legs and chairs, but the spikes stung her hands away from everything, and, flailing, she found herself dragged across the floor towards the source of the lashing tentacles.

Space was calling her again.

Ace yelled 'Professor!' as she was pulled inside the globe, and then, as her face vanished under the darkness between the stars: 'Doc –'

And then all was silence.

The door opened, and the old librarian poked his head round it. Tutting at the mess of books on the floor, he picked up Ace's jacket and hung it on a peg.

'Such a mess,' he sighed. 'I do wish he'd learn to keep it tidy, hmm.'

He closed the door and was gone.

Ace experienced the sensation of flying once more. She was getting used to it by now. The darkness parted like a veil, and before her was a wall, endless, stretching away on all sides. The wall curved, as if to protect some vast world inside.

Very seventies. Ace landed on the wall with both feet, and knew what she had to do. What she'd always done. She pulled a can of nitro-nine from her rucksack, and taped it to the brickwork. Long fuse. There was no cover in this strange dreamland. She'd just have to get as far around the curvature of the thing as possible. The sky overhead was dark, velvet black. Yet from it there came the strangest sensation, something that Ace had searched for all her life, sometimes thought she had found.

The sky loved her.

'Yeah,' thought Ace. 'Very seventies.'

She sprinted away, counting hippopotomuses in her head, and threw herself to the floor just as she reached fifty.

The wall exploded, bricks arching into the darkness and vanishing.

'Awesome!' smiled Ace.

The Doctor tensed, his mouth opening slightly, his hand hovering above an open panel in the TARDIS console. Five wires stuck out, inches from his fingers. His expression could have been pleasure or pain.

Whatever it was, it was deeply felt.

Ace slid into the hole she'd created, the bricks smooth and ickily warm. She found herself in a gleaming polygonal room. Thirteen sides, she counted. In each side, a sort of alcove, with the same live feeling about it, pulsing with life.

Seven of the cabinets contained strange, organic messes of biological circuitry, and ... oh. Six contained people.

They were half-formed male figures, white as the walls, their faces blank and their costumes basic. A kind of rot seemed to have set in, because the figures were mottled with a grey decay. The organic circuitry was growing about them, like it wanted to consume them but was being prevented. The figures were stirring, like plants searching for sunlight.

One of the figures jerked and moved, its face forming a mouth which opened and croaked:

'Is it ... time ... already?'

'No,' gasped Ace. 'Go back to sleep, it's nowhere near time yet.'

The creature began to move, to fight its way forward.

Real fear shot up Ace's spine, that old fear of mannequins and clowns. Things that weren't human, but pretended to be. *Like the Doctor was sometimes.*

'You're nearly home, girl,' a dark female voice muttered from the roofspace.

'I'm not a girl.'

'This has been a good dream, a wonderful story. Perhaps when you awake, the Doctor will laugh at it.'

Ace couldn't quite bring herself to believe it. 'You're having me on. This can't be a dream, it feels too real.'

'You're still in Cheldon Bonniface. There was something in the mead. A mushroom-derived poison. The tinkers were planning to rob you. The Doctor saved you and took you back to the TARDIS. He's attending to you now.'

'So who are you?'

'I'm your logical mind, talking to your dreaming, emotional, self.'

'Okay, I'll buy it. What do I have to do to get home?'

'Just relax,' said the voice. 'And think of Norfolk.'

So Ace thought, thought about the snow, and the inn, and the villagers, and about the Doctor, who'd obviously been running up a blind alley again. She seemed to be achieving something, because she felt as if she'd plugged into a giant, humming, power source. Was this what life felt like from a distance? She'd heard about people who nearly died and then survived. Feeling no fear, they described billowing white tunnels, and beautiful gardens.

Typical of her to try something different. Nothing that had happened to Ace had made sense, and she desperately wanted to believe this new version of events. A hand was reaching to her from the other side, as she thought of Cheldon Bonniface. Something was drawing her to it, communicating.

She wasn't dead. She was still Ace, and still alive.

And she was going to get out of this nightmare, she was going to leap the gate, break down the wall, climb the cliff.

She was going to be free.

The power flooded her nervous system, and it was all she could do to stop shouting with the joy of it. Walls of multi-coloured light closed in on her, blazing away from the surrounding chamber. The figures thrashed and faded into the glare, roaring.

The taste of blood welled in her mouth as she felt the walls of reality parting.

'Yes!' With a jerk of muscle she slammed her trainers together and wished with all her might. Wished for Earth.

The room exploded.

Inside the TARDIS, the Doctor grabbed his head and screamed. Fire burst across his vision and his ears filled with white noise. He took a staggering step forward, and reached for the bare wires, muscles jerking as if he were fighting against his own body.

His fingers touched them.

Contact.

The Doctor's body convulsed with raw energy, and blue static skittered up his arms.

Pain shrieked through him, and he stared blindly upwards and screamed.

Trelaw had run across to attend to Emily when Saul began to warn him. The sentience that inhabited the church had been initially preoccupied by his unexpected communication with Mrs Hutchings, and by the Doctor's flying visit, but the feeling of expectation he had been experiencing all morning was growing, to the point now where he could barely stand it.

Something was going to happen, and soon.

At the edge of perception it began, a distant voice calling to him, a psychic whisper that beguiled him please to help. So Saul had made contact, and had been scared to feel something lock on, visualize him, hold him in its sights.

Something was coming. A ripple of power like the bowshock of some enormous vessel, approaching Earth. Saul tried to analyze the oncoming emotion, but all he could feel was destruction and death. And hatred. Immense hatred.

He shouted to Trelaw, but the vicar seemed to have caught the feeling too, because he had picked up the baby from Emily's arms, and was trying, against Peter's protests, to get her to her feet.

'Go! Get out!' He was yelling, and the congregation were starting to obey, afraid of something ancient, some hysteria that made them feel insignificant and vulnerable.

Saul joined in, out loud, in a voice that sounded like the collected choirs of every Oxbridge college, echoing around the church like the cry of an angel.

'Great evil is coming. You must leave!'

That convinced most of them. The villagers pelted for the door. Emily stared at the ceiling and grabbed Peter's jacket, but he sat staring about him in wonder.

The last villager ran, screaming, out of the doors, and Trelaw looked down at the couple, fearfully.

'Please, you must —'

Then the storm was upon them. The doors slammed shut, and a roll of thunder echoed across the village. Trelaw glanced desperately about him.

'What's going on?' began Emily, 'what —'

The old church exploded. A vast concussive fireball burst across the village and fields. Houses were atomized, people turned in surprise and became flying ashes. The sound ripped trees and flung them like spears across grasslands that were blazing from the heat. Farm animals became calcium skeletons and liquefied. People on the edge of the explosion found themselves running against a powerful sucking of nightmare air until they were pulled off their feet and and flew screaming back into the funeral pyre to vanish as black dots in the terrible whiteness. A pillar of fire rose over the English countryside, and inside it formed the face of a woman, contorted in an ecstasy of feeding.

The face faded, and the pillar thinned, becoming a rushing column of plasma that defied gravity and logic in its upward motion, finally departing Earth with a sigh of heat eddies. A crater two miles across was all that remained. Around it, in a clear, legible hand, was scorched in letters inches high and many times repeated:

I HAVE RETURNED, HUMANS. KNOW ME.

An arch of fire rounded Earth, sending aurorae glowing to the equator. The moon was full in the reflected light of a billion-mile dragon, delighting in the fear below. Then suddenly the world was plunged into darkness, and a quiet, trembling, terror. Thunderous echoes died away.

'Know me, know me ...'

'Know me,' whispered Ace, curled into a foetus. She didn't know what it meant. What she did know was that the thing had lied. She had touched something powerful and terrible, plugged into it, and it had been like sticking your tongue into an electrical powerpoint. She was still shuddering with terror.

Ace hadn't been spirited home, and deep inside, she knew that she'd done something wrong.

Very wrong.

4: Head Dance

We are such stuff as dreams are made on.

A Midsummer Night's Dream William Shakespeare.

Hemmings trudged across the lunar plain towards where he estimated that the church had been, negotiating a crater wall that had previously been concealed as a much softer hedge. He had glanced upwards at the globe of the Earth, visible now that the camouflage field had faded, but he had failed to notice the pallor which had started to spread across Europe.

Walking on the moon. Good Lord. It was just as bleak, just as uncompromising as he'd imagined it. The perfect setting for such a strange ritual. The place was full of epic grandeur. Nothing trivial could happen here. Ariosto had it that the moon was where everything wasted on Earth was treasured. Unanswered prayers, fruitless tears and broken vows. This was the place where wasted talent was kept in vases.

The god who had engineered all this, the infinite butterfly that men had worshipped and sacrificed to throughout history, seemed to share Hemmings' sense of humour.

Still, the whole thing was tiring him. Hemmings wasn't quite like other men. He woke in the morning to a strict routine, worked like a machine, rested with his paintings in the evening.

Doubt, weakness and self-questioning played no part in his life. In their place was a vague vacuum that occasionally manifested itself as a sense of destiny. This life must be lived, and of course no scholar could deny Sartre's logic, but where was the meaning? Well, he had found meaning beyond individual concerns in the joy of National Socialism and the evolution of the species.

Happy as an ant, Hemmings had found the concept of abduction by the gods completely acceptable. Obvious, even. The only doubt he felt, even now, was in fatigue. Had the Doctor's escape from the inn meant the end of the plan? And if so, why hadn't he been spirited back to HQ?

Well, he thought, climbing over the crest of a small hill, it seems not. There lay Ace, surrealistically unprotected on the altar. But where was the child priest?

'Boo!' shouted a voice over his intercom. And there he was behind him, chuckling in that mock-adult way of his. The laughter annoyed Hemmings. If the boy was a servant of the gods, he was a most disrespectful one.

'So there you are. Have you been told what we're supposed to be —'

'Where's the Doctor?'

Hemmings sighed. He felt absurd, explaining himself to the boy.

'He managed to get away. I did my best, but ...' he shrugged. This child wasn't his superior.

Boyle was hissing, that ugly little face concealed by his helmet visor.

'What? You allowed him to escape?'

Hemmings' resignation flared into anger. 'Yes, I did. What's it to you, you nasty little brute?'

Boyle stood still, and for a moment Hemmings suspected that he had burst into tears. Then the little figure in the spacesuit gave a tiny kick, bouncing upwards to eye level. There was something strange behind his faceplate, something —

Boyle's fist shot out in a blur and connected with Hemmings. With a crack, the man's neck broke, and a blur of fluid vaporized in vacuum. The astronaut's helmet and its contents

61

bounced off across the dunes. The body, headless, fell to the ground. Boyle floated down and skipped across to where the head lay. He crouched and spoke down to it like a little boy would speak to a pet rabbit. The voice that spoke now was, however, female.

'Because of you I have had to waste precious energy. Locating the Doctor, distracting him, interfacing him and his companion's memory with the TARDIS. I am surprised, frankly, that it was possible. All because of your error.' The child/dragon hissed a sigh. 'You shall continue to serve me in my kingdom, Hemmings. Perhaps there you will prove more useful.' The creature that had been Boyle removed its helmet, revealing the stark features of the dragon. Then it pressed its forehead to the dead head in its grasp. The corpse's eyes rolled and blinked at the sudden stimulation. 'Memory drain complete,' murmured the creature, licking its lips. Then it stood and walked away.

Hemmings' corpse lay in the lunar dust, empty.

St Christopher's church flew down a butterfly corridor, through translucent purple patternings. A million shades of blue strobed around the ancient architecture. Inside, things were about as calm as could be expected.

'Where the hell are we?' Emily Hutchings shouted. The exterior scene flashed through the stained glass, making the aisle look like some infernal disco. Peter was nodding excitedly, peering out like a schoolboy in a sweetshop.

'A time-space corridor, like Edmond hypothesized last year. But the energy required — where's it coming from, that's the question. Of course, the fact of our vanishing from the material universe will have caused a vast energy discharge — conservation of energy, you see. That's why time travel would be impossible, at least it would be unless you could harness a black hole, somehow store up all the potential energy debt incurred and let it leak out of the event horizon as slow dollops of Hawking radiation ... But that's impossible too ...'

His wife touched him on the arm, and he looked up at her, a touch distracted. Then his face fell, and he hugged her to him.

'Do you know where we are, reverend?' asked Emily, slightly

comforted. Trelaw shook his head.

'I'm afraid not. Perhaps Saul can answer your questions.'

'Or perhaps only create more,' came the choral voice from on high. 'It might be a good idea to explain me first.'

'Ah,' Trelaw nodded, picking up the gurgling baby with the squeamishness of a lifelong bachelor. 'Yes. Saul has been here or rather, where we were, associated with the site, since before the first church was built. To the Celts he was a local spirit, the Saxons called him a god.'

'Pleased to meet you,' the voice boomed.

'Yes. Right.' Peter held out his hand, then withdrew it awkwardly in the absence of anything to shake.

'But ... what are you?' Emily asked.

'I'm not sure. Is anyone? I believe that I evolved as a sort of condensation of belief and worship, a focus for psychic energy. If anybody with psionic potential sets foot in here they find themselves capable of great feats.'

'Maybe that explains the size of the congregation,' muttered Trelaw. 'We've searched for other examples and believe Saul is unique.'

'Perhaps. But the Doctor said —'

'The Doctor?' Peter was getting lost in this esoteric double act.

'An old friend. He said that if you leave anything long enough it'll achieve intelligence. Apparently he had a pot of jam like that once.'

'I think that was a joke, Saul.'

'Oh.'

Trelaw looked down at his latest charge. 'What do you think he was doing, rushing in and out like that with the baby?'

Emily put a hand on her hips and raised a finger. Peter, who had retreated into lecture mode in an almost conscious effort to remain sane, was gratified to see her strength coming to the fore.

'Wait a minute now. That little Scotsman was this Doctor of yours?'

Trelaw looked up at the rafters and cleared his throat. 'Indeed, yes. That's the bit we really don't understand yet.'

'And you think he's got something to do with ...' Emily

gestured around the church, 'with what's happening?'

'Ah ... possibly. It's his sort of thing.'

'Right.' Emily sat down firmly and motioned to be given the baby. 'I'll want a word with him, then.'

'So will I,' muttered her husband, shaking his head.

The Doctor lay on the floor of the TARDIS. The column of the timecraft was rising and falling, indicating flight. If the psychic damage had been any greater, regeneration would have been in order. But that, even that, was denied him now.

This was a very dangerous game.

He sat up and examined his eyes in a mirror on the console. Bloodshot with mental strain.

After a while he stood up. The TARDIS was coming in for a landing, and he had to be ready. Time to confront the enemy.

Boylething stood beside the prostrate form of Ace. Switched off. Waiting. With a galvanized roar, the TARDIS appeared, police box shape incongruous on the lunar soil. The door opened and out stepped the Doctor, carrying only his umbrella. The creature was, for an instant, surprised.

'I extended the TARDIS's environment shields beyond the exterior,' the Doctor growled, answering the creature's unasked question.

Concern mingling with disgust at the process that had reduced to her to this vegetable state, the Doctor bent to examine Ace. Boylething had removed its helmet, exposing the dragon visage.

'Doctor. We meet in the flesh.'

The Doctor appeared unconcerned at the creature's form, glancing upwards briefly before returning his attention to Ace.

'If she's suffered any permanent damage,' he murmured, 'I'll destroy you utterly. Every last molecule.'

'You are hardly in a position to make threats, Time Lord.'

'No.' The Doctor straightened to meet the creature's gaze, his face expressionless. 'I'm not. Strange how situations get away from you, isn't it?'

'Do you know me, now? Have you grasped the smallest fraction of my plan?' The being smiled, exposing aluminium teeth.

'Tell me. Everything. You're holding the aces now.'

The creature rose a few inches off the lunar surface, spreading its arms wide. The Doctor perched on the edge of the altar, leaning on his umbrella, absently stroking his companion's hair.

'I was Qataka,' the creature began. 'I became Ishtar, transformed by technology into an incantation, a word of power ...'

'A computer virus, you mean,' scowled the Doctor. 'Spare me the rhetoric.'

'As you will. I am known to the ancients of Earth as Hel. To the Daleks I am Golyan Ak Tana, the twister of paths ...'

'An apt name. No wonder they had trouble with time travel, with you changing the possibilities all the time.'

'They sent a taskforce against me. Glorious feeding, much energy. I understand you, Doctor. I have fought your enemies. You were responsible for granting me my freedom to manipulate time.'

'I regret that. That's why I must stop you. These are not the only names you have been given. The Time Lords have long anticipated your arrival. They call you Timewyrm.'

'That is a name I approve of. I attempted to read the Green and Black Books Of Gallifrey, firstly by direct linkage, then by trying to return to the occasion of their composition. I was blocked by fierce security and powerful temporal baffles. I could have forced my way through − I have not yet calculated the limitations of my power − but it would have proved an unnecessary drain on my resources. What do they say of the Timewyrm?'

The Doctor took a step closer to the small creature, his hand open in a gesture of negotiation. 'They say that you will devour the first and last of the Time Lords. That Rassilon will be crushed in your jaws during the last moments of the Blue Shift, the final inrush of matter at the end of this universe. You will precipitate that event. You will bend and break continuity structures throughout the dimensions. The fabric of time-space will collapse. The causal nexus will shatter, and the laws of physics will cease to have any meaning.'

The Timewyrm gazed at the Doctor, its eyes burning with wonder. 'This is what will happen?'

'Perhaps. These legends come from the dark times when Gallifreyans dared to examine their own future. Nothing is certain. While you exist, though, every particle of matter in the cosmos is in danger.' The Doctor was desperately trying to persuade the creature of the truth of his words, frustrated by his inability to express what he foresaw. 'Is this what you wanted?'

'No ... but it is what I have become.' The Timewyrm paused, the lines of its artificial face softening for a moment, as if struck by an ancient memory. 'My life is strange. You must know that even this scheme is not born of malice. Much of what I am is due to the nature of the data virus that forms my infrastructure. I am not, fully, Ishtar any more, but something of destiny. Something of fate.'

'No. That is what distinguishes us from inanimate matter, Qataka. We are free.' The Doctor seemed surprised by the force of his own words. 'Fate is what we make it. We have a choice.'

'And what is my choice?' the thing that once was Ishtar almost sighed, seeming to know the answer to its own question.

'Only death,' the Doctor whispered, gazing into those scared boy/woman eyes. 'Sooner or later, with the universe or alone. Give back Ace. Cease this scheme, whatever it is. I will aid your passing.'

The Timewyrm stared at him, aghast. A small fist curled with astonishment. 'No! No! I can feed as I wish! I can control my appetites! You are interfering with my human form, stimulating things which are no longer present in my programming. I am too grand for your morality, too much of a force. If you say that I will destroy this cosmos through my feeding, then that is what I will do, if you say that I will pull on the threads of time until they break, then I will pull! I am your Timewyrm!'

The Doctor stepped back, disgusted.

'You're a coward, a selfish child.'

With a roar, the Timewyrm rushed forward, and let fly with its fist. Claws burst through the material of the glove as it slashed across the Doctor's face. He fell, clutching his cheek. When he rose once more, he was nursing three parallel scars. Quietly, he put a handkerchief to them.

'That is the very least of what you will suffer at my hand, Doctor,' rumbled the Timewyrm, visibly containing its rage. 'If you had ceased your crusade against me, I might have even done as you asked, let your companion go, found some other way of doing what I must to survive. Now I can see that indeed, I have no option. I have learnt your methods, followed your own plans, observed your actions. Now I have used them all against you. I have your companion's memory data. Her personality, her life, her self.'

The Doctor stood up, looking the Timewyrm in the eye.

'Show her mercy at least. Put her back in her body. I'll negotiate.'

'Oh, yes,' laughed the Wyrm. 'Of course you will. But only while I hold her in my power. I refuse to underestimate you, Doctor.'

'What do you want from me?'

'I'll tell you that later. First you have to follow Dorothy.'

The Doctor brought his face closer to the grinning monster, seeing his blood reflected in its cold blue brow.

'Her name,' he growled, 'is Ace.'

'At the moment,' the creature smiled back, 'that depends entirely on me. I have already tricked her into something — but no. I refuse to show too much of my hand. I will meet you here in an hour.' A vague shimmering noise was already rippling the atmosphere of the TARDIS's exterior environment bubble. 'Then you can go and visit her. In the meantime, you'd best look after your guests.'

And with that the Timewyrm hopped away, vanishing over the crest of a lunar hill. The Doctor gazed after her.

'Remember,' he said softly, 'that I offered you mercy.' He looked down at his companion once more, and removed a speck of dirt from her brow. 'Forgive me,' the Doctor whispered.

With a roar of distorting spacetime, a large object shimmered into being, its landing throwing vast clouds of lunar soil into expanding plumes. It surrounded and contained the Doctor and the TARDIS.

St Christopher's church had arrived on the moon.

To Trelaw and the Hutchingses, it seemed as if the Doctor and a police box had suddenly appeared in the aisle of the church, while a comatose woman had materialized across the altar.

Emily shrieked, then put a hand over her mouth. The Doctor simply nodded to Trelaw and sat down on a pew, thinking.

'Doctor!' blurted the reverend, amazed. 'What are you doing here?'

'Saving the world. You're on the moon. A creature called the Timewyrm's used some powerful source of psychic energy to bring you here. Don't ask why. Now let me think.'

So he sat and thought, gazing intently into the distance. Every now and then he dabbed at the wound on his cheek. Peter Hutchings looked out of the window and saw lunar craters. Then he looked at Ace. Then at the Doctor. He raised a finger to ask a question.

'Don't, love,' advised his wife. 'Let me.' She sat down beside the Time Lord and poked him in the sleeve. 'Hey, that's not good enough. We want some answers.'

'Do you really?' the Doctor looked up at her. 'You won't like them. I'm the Doctor, and this . . .' he gestured to the prone form at the other end of the aisle, 'is my friend Ace.'

'Doctor,' Saul muttered uneasily. 'You friend is registering no brain activity. She is − forgive me − dead.'

'Not yet,' muttered the Time Lord, 'not while I'm still alive.'

Hemmings wasn't Hemmings. He was a wave peak, a slight difference in an ocean of senseless chaos. He was pushed and pulled towards every strong concept, crashing against ranting emotion, scrabbling away from mongrel dogma and perverted concepts. Only a sense of what he wasn't defined him, stopped him from being absorbed into the sea of data. He wasn't a leftie or a darkie or a queer. He wasn't . . . the sea kept changing and he kept arguing himself alive. He was never asked what he actually was.

Beside him swam others, the obvious others, spiked and chattering. Devils he had once drawn in a picture and then painted over with Aryan angels. Ahead a gate was opening and he could feel the first thorns piercing his flesh as velvet hands pressed a rose to his brow.

This wasn't what he thought he believed. He thought he believed in a glorious wartime heaven, legions of bright cavalry gloriously battling and feasting. That was what his father had taught him.

But his father had silenced his mother, and she had quietly believed in something else, clutching her rosary nervously as Rupert had delighted at every German victory.

His mother had known what her son believed underneath, what woke him every time he heard a sob at night from the cells.

Hell is where torturers go to be tortured.

Ace felt leather against her cheek. She opened her eyes and looked around. Hmm. Now this ought to be the inn again, right? It wasn't. She was lying on an ornate leather settee, a cushion having slipped out from under her head. Beside the settee, a small table carried a pile of old magazines, including a couple of decaying comics. Sunlight was shining in through a bay window that led on to a small lawn. It was, according to a calendar, 20 August. Various ordinary people were sitting around in chairs, or chatting quietly. A big bronze bell sat on a desk, behind which a cheery nurse was writing in a large book.

Oh. Right. Another option. So, this was like nothing had ever happened, right? Like she'd never got picked up in that time-storm, never met the Professor, never flirted with the idea of joining Kane's mercenaries.

She sat up and stretched. Well, maybe if she got out of here, she could impress the gang, having been a loony. Hey! Midge was still alive! This got better every minute. She swung her legs experimentally, wondering just where she was supposed to be. Looked expensive for her family. Not that they'd have cared. She still had a vague sense of having done something terrible. In a moment's ecstasy she had glimpsed a blazing corpse, vanishing into the whiteout of an atomic blast. Hell of a dream. Ace hoped that the image would fade, but she had a terrible intuition that it was real, that her actions had resulted in deaths. Vast numbers of deaths. That was, perhaps, why she was in one of the last places in the universe that she wanted to be.

There's no place like home. Thank God.

The nurse looked up and smiled, closed her book and came over.

'You must be the new arrival. Sleep well?'

'Oh yeah,' Ace grinned. 'I've really got my head together now. This is Perivale, right?'

'Yes,' smiled the matron, pleased.

'And it's 1987, right?'

'Why, yes,' laughed the matron.

'Crap,' grinned Ace, standing up and ruffling her hair. 'Go on, give us the hard sell.'

'That's a bad attitude to take if you want to get well,' sighed the nurse. 'If I could have a few personal statistics ...' She picked up a clipboard and pen. 'Blood group?'

'I'm an O. Why do you want to know?'

'Oh, it's just so we can match you to the correct vampire.'

'Yeah, right,' Ace nodded. 'I could see that one coming. Hell, right?'

'Do you have any preferences — stoning, burning, or crucifixion?' The nurse smiled brightly, licking her lips. The whole waiting room turned round and looked at Ace as if she was the victim of a vast practical joke.

Ace closed her eyes for a long moment, and thought about what heaven would have been like. Heaven would have involved beautiful adventures, running with wild horses, and having her toes sucked by Ian Brown.

'How does this schedule strike you? We start at lunchtime with skinning alive, then you get the aforementioned vampire, the circus of biologically curious clowns, then tea ...' Ace did her best not to listen. She wanted to say something apt and cool, but her stomach was bulging with nausea, and sheer, animal terror was welling up inside her in waves.

No way was she going to cry. If this was Hell, then she'd take it on, fight it out, try and turn it into something good.

But she still was probably going to throw up first.

It was a good thing then, for Hell's carpeting at least, that at that moment the outer door to the waiting room flew open.

Ace spun around, ready for a fight, but the new arrival didn't even notice her. It was Hemmings, being dragged by the arms by two giggling monsters. They were heading for an inner door, and he was screaming mindless prayers and shouting to his mother. But he wasn't resisting. The nurse laughed.

'Being dissected isn't really all that bad, Mr Hemmings. It can be a very interesting experience.' The other door slammed shut behind him, leaving a vague smell of brimstone.

Ace gritted her teeth and looked up at the nurse.

'Nah,' she said. 'This can't be Hell.'

'I assure you that it is. What makes you so certain?'

'Well, if you really wanted to torture me, you'd need something else.'

'And what's that?'

'Perry Como.' The girl from Perivale reached into her pocket and slipped on her mirrorshades. 'Do your worst, I'm not scared.'

The nurse frowned. Some people were not taking eternal damnation as seriously as they might.

'She isn't frightened,' a laughing voice rang out across the room, and Ace felt the feeling of tension return to her stomach. God, that was a voice from a long time ago. It couldn't be . . .

Chad Boyle stood up from the chair he had been lounging in, throwing aside a shooting magazine. He grinned his demented grin at Ace.

'I told you that there was no way you could get away from me, Dotty! We're going to play. Don't you get it yet, stupid? Hell isn't demons and toasting forks. Hell is other people!'

Ace was almost glad to feel the tears on her cheeks.

5: Roses

But see, my companion, are you and I not equally important?
We both matter, do we not?

On The Use of Mirrors In The Game of Chess Milo Temesvar

The Doctor had an itch in the middle of his forehead. Scratching it, he stood up, and looked around at Trelaw and the Hutchingses.

'Could you answer a few questions now, Doctor?' asked Peter, driven near to distraction.

'Yes. How's the baby?' The Doctor had ceased his frantic deliberations, and now almost seemed to be at peace, a grim certainty on his features.

'She's fine.' Emily had her finger grasped by the child, who was looking up at her in silence. 'Quietest girl I've ever met, aren't you?'

'Yes.' The Doctor waved at the baby and smiled, but still there was no response. Peter Hutchings pulled out his notebook and sat down, businesslike.

'Right. Now just what is this Timewyrm?'

The Doctor glanced at Peter, and seemed to decide that it was time some of the story was made plain. He stared into the distance and bit his knuckle. If there was one talent that the little professor didn't possess in great amounts it was the ability to express himself, intellectually or emotionally.

'The Timewyrm was originally a woman named Qataka from the planet Anu —'

'An alien?' Peter looked up sharply. 'Oh, come on.'

The Doctor sighed. 'You're on the moon inside a sentient church, waiting to see if you have any part to play in the rescue of a woman's soul from the clutches of a near-omnipotent being. Broaden your mind.'

'Right.' Peter wondered for a moment whether he had fallen asleep in church, and was having some kind of postmodern Dickensian nightmare. 'So this Qataka, why has she brought us here?'

'I don't know. Yet. She's surprising me continually, and that in itself is disturbing. I feel like a fisherman who's made a net, only to find that all the knots have been untied.'

Peter shivered at the familiarity of the metaphor. Emily was shaking her head, trying to understand the situation.'

'You and she are enemies?'

'Unfortunately, yes. She's taken the memory, the soul if you will, from Ace. Hidden it in her main host.'

'And where is that?' Trelaw had joined in the conference, feeling slightly more qualified to deal with the Doctor's concepts. He was wary of equating a person's immortal soul with simple memory, but gave him the benefit of the doubt on poetic usage.

'A computer, or a mind. She's been hiding there, plotting, only hopping out into the material world to prepare her game. How do you feel, Saul?'

'I am fine, Doctor. Or rather,' the living church paused, its voice heavy with emotion, 'I was.'

'What's wrong, old friend?' Trelaw stood, gazing worriedly at the rafters. A sound was wafting through the old architecture, warmed as it was by supernormal means. The sound was like the cry of a young bird, seized by a falcon on its first flight. It peeled slowly off into a painful silence.

'Saul?' murmured the Doctor. 'I know what you've seen. Show them.'

73

All present felt their minds glow with tender new input. Colours and ghostly images spun before their eyes. Peter reached out for his wife, and was relieved to find her shoulder. It was like a kind of internal television, he thought, the pictures he was seeing of a desolate, ravaged landscape. Then, as the picture pulled back to show a newscaster, he realized that this was television. BBC news.

'. . . by an amateur cameraman. The cause of the explosion is still unknown. A nuclear detonation has been ruled out due to the lack of radiation in the area, though other characteristics, such as the blast radius and sheer scale of the devastation, initially suggested such an explanation. Experts are pondering that the Earth may have been struck by a meteor . . . A map appeared on screen. 'The blast obliterated the Norfolk village of Cheldon Bonniface, the destruction extending to certain parts of Wroxham and nearby Stockbridge. And I've just been handed this now — areas at the edge of the blast zone have been cordoned off by United Nations forces. We have in our Norwich studio Brigadier Alistair Leth —'

The image faded and Saul howled once more.

'I was listening to the electromagnetic spectrum out of Earth, trying to find out what had happened . . .'

Trelaw felt empty, unable to even grasp what had happened. 'The Toppings . . . Miss Riddler at the sweetshop . . . little Tony and Penny. They're all . . .' The Reverend found that he was starting to shake, his mind close to breaking under the strain.

'No!' the Doctor sprang to his feet, seeming uncomfortable. 'I need your help. You mustn't fail me. The lives of everyone else on your planet, everyone in the universe, depend on it.'

Emily had taken Trelaw's arm, leading him to a seat. 'We'll help you, Doctor. I don't know who you are, or where you come from,' she looked up at the Time Lord with a steady gaze, 'but somehow I know that you're on our side.'

Peter looked at her, knowing that he was white in the face. 'My God, love. You're taking this better than I am.'

'We're on the moon,' she replied. 'The Doctor's our only hope. Besides, I've always known who I can trust.'

The Doctor's face twitched slightly, as if he had been struck again, but he smiled, sadly. 'Thank you.'

Peter was holding on to the wood of the pew, as if he was on a fairground ride and afraid that he would fall off. 'How is it we're kept alive on the lunar surface?'

'The Timewyrm is empowered to draw psionic strength from its hosts and victims. It seems to have found itself a very powerful energy source, and is thus choosing to maintain us by bringing atmosphere here from Earth.'

'But that's magic!'

'No . . .' the Doctor smiled mysteriously. 'Magic is something quite different.'

'Who's this host of his, then?' asked Emily.

The Doctor put his finger to his lips, obviously pleased at the woman's perception. He wandered up to the golden eagle lectern, measured it with his umbrella, and walked four careful paces towards the wall of the church.

'Doctor, what are you doing?' boomed Saul, still sounding devastated. 'If there is anything that I can do to help . . .'

'No' murmured the Doctor. 'I'm looking for something, a little gift.'

'Who for?' Peter had replaced his notebook, despairing of learning anything useful from this mysterious little man.

'Me.' The Doctor found a certain spot in the wall, and tapped with his umbrella. Then he carefully removed a small stone. In a cavity in the wall lay a glittering medallion, which he held aloft, darkly satisfied.

'That is not possible,' cried Saul. 'I know every inch of this church, every stone. I inhabit every atom. I would have known . . .'

'Hush.' The Doctor handed the amulet to Peter, who looked at him, puzzled. The piece consisted primarily of a round blue gem, in the interior of which a distant fire pulsed. It was framed in a metal circle, inscribed with runes of some sort that Peter didn't recognize. The gem reminded the mathematician of afternoons spent in the loft of his father's house near Oxford. Mysterious crates full of knowledge, wonderful old books. The medallion was alive and ancient at the same time. He handed it to Emily.

'Oh,' she exclaimed, a frown passing over her face. 'Roses.'

'Roses?' asked Peter, noticing the Doctor's secret smile.

'Yes, the colour. It reminds me of being little, collecting petals to make perfume. I can almost smell my mother's garden.'

'Good.' The Doctor took the amulet and hid it in Peter's pocket. 'Find a use for it.'

'But —'

'No. We're just in time. It'll be back soon.'

'Doctor!' Saul cried. 'Something powerful is approaching the church!'

The Doctor nodded. 'Punctual, at least.'

The doors of the church burst open, and there stood the Timewyrm, still in Boyle's body. To the inhabitants of the church it seemed like the Devil himself had arrived. Emily gazed at the metal head and child's body, and found herself wishing that she had a deity to pray to.

The small being swept its gaze around the building.

'You should not have tried to block the doors against my arrival, Saul. I am much more powerful than you.'

'Nevertheless,' chorused the church, its voice full of disgust, 'I had to try. Your footsteps profane this place.'

The Timewyrm frowned, as if such criticism was a slight annoyance. 'Doctor.' It beckoned to the Time Lord. 'It is time for you to come with me. I have someone else for you to meet.'

Trelaw had, shudderingly, stood up, and made his way to the lectern. Now, he stepped forward, holding the big Bible before him.

'In the name of —'

With a whack of air, the Wyrm flicked its fingers and sent the reverend sprawling aside.

'Doctor, I must insist. It is time for the next round of our game.'

'Yes. It is.' The Time Lord put on his hat and turned to look at the humans in the church. 'See you soon. I hope.'

'There is little chance of that,' chuckled the Wyrm, glancing around the place as if he'd smelt something. The Doctor walked out on to the lunar surface, and the doors closed.

Trelaw had unsteadily regained his feet. 'God be with you,

Doctor,' he muttered, and, falling to his knees, he began to pray.

Peter Hutchings shook his head slowly. The Doctor seemed to have a certain confidence about him, but Peter had a nasty feeling that for all his precautions, he was as out of his depth as they were.

Death stood on the lunar surface, her robes billowing in the particle wind that lashed the dust continually. She was a classical death, a skull in a hood, and her creator had given her a spark of consciousness. In the dark sockets, a fire blazed, and behind it, she pondered her own mortality.

Life for her, thought Death, was just a function, a whim. She would complete her task and then be reduced back to the dust that had formed her. And that wouldn't be so bad. She hadn't desired consciousness in her previous state, and now she had it, she had discovered that all life brought was pain.

Her creator and her victim were approaching her where she stood, only a short distance from the church.

'Do you know Death, Doctor?' asked the Timewyrm, displaying its creation proudly.

'Yes,' the Doctor grinned as he inspected the skeletal form. 'We've met before. Very poetic. Very Jung. Does she have a scythe?'

'She has no need of one,' laughed the Timewyrm. 'I have armed her very well.'

'I can imagine,' murmured the Doctor. 'Tell me, Death, what are the hours like in your line? All go, I should think.'

'She cannot speak, nor can she act outside my will. Your words will not cheat this death, Doctor.'

'They have in the past.' The Doctor took off his hat, his face stern with what the Timewyrm took to be fear. 'Get on with it.'

The Wyrm motioned Death to stand by the Doctor. She did so, reaching out skeleton fingers. But then came a slight hesitation. Death paused, shocked by the import of her task. This man was full of concepts that she barely had the mind to think of.

The Doctor suddenly gripped her hand and her waist.

'May I have the pleasure?'

They waltzed off, the Time Lord and the icon, in great swirling steps. After four whirls in the low gravity, Death released her partner, and he fell, slowly, into a plume of lunar dust. The dancer lay still, his limbs jutting in the graceless directions of oblivion.

The Timewyrm felt almost a sense of anticlimax. Why should she bother researching all the relevant fear totems for this dimension if the Doctor was able to make fun of them so easily? She raised a finger, and the Doctor's body rose from where it lay, a puppet on invisible strings. As the Timewyrm stalked back towards the church, the corpse followed it.

Death gazed after the procession, wondering.

Ace stared at Chad Boyle's face, amazed at the fear he could still inspire in her. She quickly wiped her eyes on her sleeve. Stupid, he was just a kid. Well, no surprise that he'd ended up here, after what he'd done. At junior school, his name had been enough to scare her. He'd tormented her, spread gossip about her, called her a 'Paki-lover'.

And he'd killed her with a brick.

No! That wasn't how she'd died, she'd been asphyxiated on the moon.

God, what great options. But she remembered the bit about the brick, the weapon rising, eclipsing the sun. Nothing else. A darkness was spreading through her memory, erasing her older self. She could remember the gang, and Seniors, but what was before that? Panic was rising up her spine. This was like that time when the Doctor had erased her memory, only then it had been sudden, all bright and shiny, waking to new things. She'd even gained a memory, one of Mel's. This was a slow, relentless, oncoming nothingness. Like death, only she'd been there before and knew what the loss would be like. Help. Ace needed somebody to help her. Nobody was there.

Boyle laughed, as if aware that soon she wouldn't be Ace any more, but Dorothy, and then she'd be Dotty. And then she'd be his.

'No way.' She shook her head, advancing on the boy. 'How did you get here, you little toerag?'

'The Angel let me in to make sure you weren't lonely. I'm in charge in here, past that boring pier and stuff. I'm going to have fun with you.'

Ace wandered up to the boy and flicked his nose with her finger. 'I'm much bigger than you, now. You want to play, you go and find some toys.'

Boyle's face contorted with blind fury. His hand snatched for Ace's collar, and she found herself wrenched forward with maniacal strength.

'You what!' He was screaming and swearing, dragging her with terrifying force towards an inner door.

Ace struggled, trying to kick him, but she'd been taken off guard. The nurse and other inhabitants of the room watched, amused, as the small boy hauled the young woman through the door, slamming it closed behind him.

Trelaw and the Hutchingses huddled to each other as the doors of the church opened once more, and in walked the Doctor. His head hung unsupported at an angle, and his arms swung limp at his sides.

'Doctor?' called Trelaw, but no reply was forthcoming. From the doorway the Timewyrm watched, pleased.

The Doctor stepped up on to the altar, and lay beside the deathly form of Ace. The Timewyrm waved its fingers subtly, a tiny artistic gesture. The Doctor arranged his companion's arms in a cross over her chest, and then did the same himself before finally losing the semblance of life. If the two forms were breathing, it was only slightly.

'What have you done to them?' roared Saul.

'The Doctor and Ace are now both in my domain,' declared the Timewyrm, closing the doors. 'I think it is time for me to join them. Amuse yourselves for a while.'

Emily stared at the creature as it departed. It was obscene that such a monster should walk like a small boy, have the same pudgy fingers and gauche body language. She wondered yet again if this wasn't some fevered nightmare, something that talked of her longing for a child, and her fear of actually having one.

Saul's anger could be felt rippling through the rafters.

'Abomination!' cried the church impotently. 'Foul creature!'

Trelaw looked down upon the two figures that lay still and cold upon the altar. They were like some ancient knight and his steward, entombed here having lost the fight against the dragon.

Trelaw said prayers quietly over the comatose forms.

The Doctor strode down the corridor, a new purpose in his step. The walls were covered with pictures: the Academy, ancient Gallifreyan glyphs, the UNIT Christmas party of 1973. At the end of the corridor, in front of an imposing wooden door, the Time Lord stopped for a moment. A plaque hung on the wall.

'*This bureau is hereby licensed as a legitimate purveyor of endless suffering,*' the Doctor read. 'Very neat. Very ugly.'

He raised his umbrella and knocked it hard on the door, three times.

'Now,' he said to himself. 'All the world's a stage. Stage one . . .'

The door opened. He sauntered into the waiting room and rang the bell on the desk cheerfully.

The nurse glared up from her book.

'I'm the Doctor.' The new visitor grinned at a private joke. 'And I have reservations.'

The WyrmBoyle creature was building itself a shelter. Puffs of flame from the nostrils of the tiny dragonhead were carving out a hollow in lunar rock. Into the hollow, the child-size monster crawled, and a sheet of moondust rose up to seal the chamber off. Inside it, Boyle lay curled like a foetus in an egg, his angular new face smoothed by sleep into something that approached innocence.

The Timewyrm skittered about his neural cortex, deactivating the microcircuits that had allowed it to use the boy's form. For a moment, the electronic being considered disrupting the brain altogether, letting the instinctive breathing and heart functions cease, but then it decided that this meat might be useful again at some point.

There was no point in random malice.

The portion of the Timewyrm equation that had controlled Boyle deactivated everything but a final component, a transponder that was lodged in the boy's grey matter.

Activating it, the mathematical monster was broadcast back to join its main self in the primary host. Transmission complete, the transponder winked off. The skull was silent. Nobody, Boyle or the Timewyrm, was at home.

Outside the hide, Death stood for a while, pondering. Then, as had been planned, she found herself decaying back into dust.

Her final thought was something sad about roses.

The Timewyrm slid smoothly back to its lair, programs meshing and new knowledge being downloaded into memory stores. The different experiences of the Boyle Control fragment and the main body of the Timewyrm virus were compared, and the plan adjusted accordingly.

Here, in its natural form, the helixes of data that formed the Timewyrm would not normally have possessed anything approaching a personality. That appeared on the outside only, generally, when the Wyrm had infested a living brain. Qataka was an idea here, a precisely-logged memory that formed only part of what the creature was. Ishtar was a useful mask to communicate with flesh creatures. However, the brain that the Wyrm now inhabited did not take easily to command, and it was necessary to fully personify to keep up full identity. The matrices would have been swiftly corrupted without some unifying principle, become a mutant combination of Timewyrm objectives and host ego. That would not be allowed to happen.

So, it was the Timewyrm which returned to the host brain, but, nanoseconds later, it was Qataka who was downloaded into the holographic system, the datascape that formed the memory of a natural brain.

She still regarded herself as an artist, and was rather proud of the iconography that she had established within the brain. Much of it, like the Pier Of Seaside Nostalgia, was in areas she had only been able to spy briefly upon, and so was naturally produced. The Library was the same, a very common metaphor for the vast data store natural beings developed. Still, she had just about managed to infiltrate and control that area.

Hell, however, was hers alone.

It was located in a memory dump that specialized in the control and processing of repressed information. It was connected to the Pit of the unconscious. Dream images, powerful old icons, and thrashing, twisting nightmares were dealt with here, rationalized or thrown back from whence they came. Ishtar had simply given the place coherence, a plot. Before she had entered this land of fears and longings, this dreamland, the brain had been rebelling, actually preparing to cast her out, narrow the infestation down to the point of entrance and expel it. Once she had taken and developed the place, the subject had cooperated totally.

It was almost as if the mind wanted this torture, needed it to rid itself of some guilt. Outside control had been welcomed as a berserk psychotic welcomes the anaesthetic.

Setting foot in the mental landscape of the host's memory, the Timewyrm glanced down into the Pit, the black depths where the answers lay.

She paused only for a moment. Perhaps there were some things she did not want to learn.

Ace was thumped down into a tiny seat, and shouted.

With a thin, high voice.

Her body was eight years old again.

So, it had started now. This was the real business of pain. She had liked her body, fought hard to like it, depended on it and found comfort in it. This was distress like she had never imagined. Not actual pain, but cruelty that made you want to ask *why*. No breasts, no womanhood, no strength in her limbs. Ace's face creased into a tight ball of suffering.

No. Not yet. She was going to survive this. And the next pain. And the next.

Fighting down a tremendous physical fear, she forced herself to take note of her surroundings. It didn't matter what she looked like, she was Ace. Not Dorothy. Certainly not Dotty. Ace.

She was dressed in her old pink sweatshirt and jeans, sitting at her desk. Front of the classroom, at the left. That, she had discovered, was the only way to get the teachers to answer her questions, to be right there in front of them. Right at the back sat Shreela, whom she didn't actually know right now . . . back then.

And behind her must be . . . don't look around yet. Get used to the situation first.

The sun was shining through the dusty old windows, covered in paintings and collages. New autumn, a few weeks before her death. Brown leaves were stuck to a chart with great dollops of white glue. In front of the class sat Mr Watkins, behind his desk, his dry old bald head reflecting the sunlight dully. He was marking books while the silent classroom got on with their maths cards.

Ace looked down at the book in front of her. All done of course, in two minutes. If they'd let her, she would have finished the whole series. Miss Marshall kept saying that to her, being encouraging. Mr Watkins, on the other hand, seemed to think that she was an obstruction to his teaching. You were either a rebel or a keener. Teachers didn't understand somebody who was both, who'd be crap at some things just because she didn't like them, but could do most things quite well if she wanted to. Having a social worker didn't help. Put a label on you, just because you blew some things up and maimed some kids who really wanted maiming.

Mr Watkins' pen scratched away at the books, his glasses glittering.

The door at the back of the room opened, and Ace glanced around, noting that Chad Boyle wasn't actually at his desk behind her. That was strange. At the door was a little boy, Sanir, one of the six-year-olds.

And Ace suddenly knew why she was being put through this, remembered the everyday horror of this scene. Sanir silently approached Mr Watkins and spoke.

'Sir?'

Watkins looked up and sighed. 'What have you done this time, boy?'

'Miss Haines sent me over because I was being noisy in class.'

'Why do we have to go through this time and again, you repulsive child?' The class had taken an interest, and Watkins was playing up to them as he always did, making a sort of horrible comedy out of it all. Sanir seemed to be the only boy who ever got punished in Miss Haines' class, or at least the only one she sent to Mr Watkins, who was the Deputy Head. At least once every two weeks he would appear in the classroom to describe his latest wrongdoing. Watkins would scold the boy theatrically, then bend him over his knee and smack him, three or four times.

In the playground, they said that Watkins and Miss Haines were going out. Nobody was certain that teachers did that, though.

Watkins grabbed the back of the Asian boy's hair, and bent him over his lap. 'What will we do with you?' he asked, and raised his hand.

Dorothy had always wanted to somehow leave, or stop it, but wasn't able to even think of doing so.

Ace didn't hesitate.

'Put him down, dogbreath!' she shouted, standing up. A deathly hush fell on the room.

'What did you say?' whispered the teacher, lowering his hand. 'What did you call me?'

'I said dogbreath. That's nearly the worst insult I knew when I was eight.' Ace kicked over her desk and, to astonished noises from her classmates, sauntered up to the teacher's desk. 'I hated this place, and I hated you, because you got your kicks from doing that.' She folded her arms and stared up at the purple-faced teacher. 'Just 'cos you've made me look like a kid doesn't mean I have to act like one.'

She expected Watkins to try and punish her in the same way. Then she'd see if a kick in the gonads was any less painful with the strength of a little girl. But the door opened once more and in sauntered Chad Boyle.

'Sorry I'm late,' he muttered into the floor, and then looked up, eyes flashing with glee. 'Ah, Paki trouble eh?'

Ace glowered at him, wishing she didn't look so girly in this get-up.

'You can't help who you are. You've got your problems too. You can see that in the pain on your face. But that doesn't mean you can go around hurting other people. Don't use that word again.' The class burst out into gales of laughter.'

'What word, bossy Dotty? D'you mean Paki? Paki, is that it?'

Ace ran at him, wishing she had a catapult, or a sword or something. Thing was, how did you fight like an adult? The act itself was enough to make a kid out of anyone. At least with a weapon she could have lied to herself about it.

God, she hated this.

Boyle stood where he was, grinning. Ace hit him head on, driving her fist into his stomach, hoping that would be it, one blow and away. She was getting out of here.

But Boyle grabbed the arm that hit him, twisted it with his fearsome new strength and Ace found herself flying, landing in a crumpled heap by the door.

Watkins and Boyle stood over her. The kids laughed and jeered, even Shreela.

They got it right, then. This was Hell. The worst thing she could have imagined, being made helpless and little and girly again. It wasn't going to get any better from now on.

'You can't leave,' laughed Boyle, pulling her up by the hair. 'There's nowhere to go. We're going to do school again, with all my mates and the teachers all thinking I'm the best. We're going to show you that you're nothing special, that you're just a stupid Paki-loving girl who's a real keener and's got a slut for a Mum. Then if you're really lucky, in a few weeks' time, I'll kill you with my brick again, and you can start something else, another game. Don't worry, though, Dotty. I'll come and visit. I like it here. Who's going to save you now?'

Ace felt her head jerked from side to side by the grasp he had on her hair. She was almost ready to quit then, to let her mind snap and lose herself in a blissful dream of distant, lost, beauty.

Then there was a swish of new air from the door. The air was cool amidst Hell's damp warmth, and smelt of springtime.

'School's out,' growled the Doctor. 'Put her down.'

Boyle let go of Ace's hair and scowled at the newcomer. He

found the tip of an umbrella poking him in the chest.

'Now look here,' began Watkins, 'you can't −'

'Shut up. You're not real.' The Doctor glowered at the teacher and turned to his companion. 'Ace, are you all right?'

Ace blinked at him. She thought she was going to cry with relief, but there was something she had to do first.

'You bastard!' she shouted.

Her blow knocked the Doctor off his feet.

6: The Damage Done

Anarchy, as most people under thirty forget, lives next door to Justice. They're good friends, but sometimes Justice hears the noise from next door and decides it's time to do the shopping ... there are, of course, many ways to get what you want.

Paul Travers' review of Johnny Chess live at Moles — NME 18/7/98

The Doctor was forced back through the door, out into an infernal corridor, through another door that burst open behind him, fending off the punches and kicks that rained down on him with ferocious intensity.

'You got me killed!' Ace was shouting, 'You scumbag! I want to live! I don't want to stay here!' The assault threw the Doctor off balance, and he stumbled, landing on his back.

Ace looked down at him. The Doctor winced at the pain on her face. Her fists were clenching and unclenching, and she was gritting her teeth against the tears that were welling up inside.

'I hated that school,' she was saying, almost to herself. 'I never wanted to go back there, but you did it. You always do it.'

The Doctor looked back at her grimly. 'You wanted to come. I told you the risks. Since Fenric there aren't any secrets.'

'So how come you got me killed?' Ace desperately wanted

there to be a reasonable answer, the Doctor held at gunpoint by some enemy, forced to let Ace suffocate. The Doctor just looked up at her, his face a mask.

'I played a game. I was beaten.'

Ace looked at her feet, then up into the sky — which, she had only just realized, was a lovely shade of blue — and walked away, biting her lip.

Watching her retreat, the Doctor stood up.

'I came after you!' he called. 'I sacrificed myself . . .' He stopped. She had thrown a dismissive gesture over her shoulder. Besides, the phrase seemed to disturb the Doctor. Sacrifice. He looked around him. They were in a garden, a garden of roses. A gentle English sun shone overhead. Birds sang, bees buzzed, perfume gently infused the air.

'So, that's where we are,' the Doctor murmured, quite distracted.

Ace knew this feeling. It started in your stomach and worked its way to the tips of your toes. You got it when someone special got on a coach to go away. You got it when you could hear the rows and the blows from downstairs. You got it when you were lost, and alone, and twenty billion miles from home. She put a hand on her heart.

Oh. Back to normal. Adult, again. Thank God. She'd been so busy attacking the Doctor that she hadn't even realized that.

Normally, she'd have had some quip handy to deal with this. Something to convince the enemy that no way could they freak her. Warriors don't show fear. But this time the enemy wasn't going to go away. The Doctor had simply thrown his life away too, finally consumed by that sneaking guilt that she'd always suspected motivated him.

She was going to have to live with it. They were going to be seeing a lot of each other in between the pain.

Yeah. That was weird. If this was Hell, why was this garden so lovely? Maybe contrasts were offered to make you feel worse when it was all snatched away. Ace glanced up. At the end of a hedge of white roses, somebody was approaching.

It was the old man from the library. He was striding along,

walking stick in hand, a blue rose in his lapel. He was dressed differently now, Ace noticed, in a dark Edwardian suit and long tails. His eyes were gleaming with interest.

'Why, hello again!' he beamed down at Ace, who found herself smiling back, quite taken with the friendliness in his voice. Sweet city.

'Hi yourself. What are you in for?'

The man pondered for a moment, putting a finger to his mouth. 'The sin of pride,' he decided. 'Yes, that's it. I have far too high an opinion of myself.'

'Doesn't sound so bad,' the woman from Perivale snorted. 'You got yourself an attitude. So what?'

'Ah, child, you don't know. You don't know. Quite often I'm surprised by what I get up to. Surprised and alarmed. How are you progressing?'

'All right. Well, gonna suffer forever, can't smile, but okay.'

'Good, good!' chuckled the Librarian. 'Well, I have some things for you.' He reached behind his back. 'Presto!'

Her jacket. Her ghetto blaster. Ace dropped the garment on to the grass and sorted through the pockets. Everything was there: the signed photo of Johnny 'Guitar' Chess, the lock of Cheetah Person hair, the catapult.

She looked at the logo on the back of the jacket, just to make sure.

'Ace,' she whispered, and pulled it back around her. Then she picked up the hi-fi. 'I didn't have this with me when I got into this,' she glanced suspiciously up at the old man. 'Where did you get it?'

'Ah!' he giggled and tapped his nose. 'I can do anything I want, young lady!'

'Yeah.' Ace flexed the jacket and reached out to gently tap his nose too. 'And so can I. Thanks a lot.'

The old man moved his head back a fraction. But he was smiling.

Ace looked down once more at the fan-club card. Johnny Chess. When she was fourteen, she had been utterly in love with him. She had attended a fan club convention where he'd actually shown up, rock's greatest son, carrying his guitar. She'd known one of the committee, and he'd let her slip backstage to speak to her hero.

She'd wanted to be as cool as Johnny was, just say hi, try to act like he was some kind of normal human being, and not the crystallization of all her own ambitions and dreams.

'How're you doing?' she'd said, looking slightly aside.

'Okay,' he replied. The conversation had gone well, at first, him seemingly refreshed by her directness. But then he seemed to get scared, and started dropping big names that he'd played with, and had backed away with a kind of desperate patronization. She had become an object, something to be guarded against. A fear not to be confronted.

She'd left the convention in tears, vowing never to like anyone without knowing them again.

Thing is, that's how this strange garden made her feel. It had an awful intimacy about it, like talking to someone really distant who makes your toes curl with the thought of leaping that distance. The whole place was on the edge of some kind of awful teenage precipice, and that only enforced her own sensation of years reeling away. The old longing of fourteen, and the love and loathing of Johnny Chess, was back in a big way.

The old man looked back down the path.

'Ah! Here comes your friend!' Ace made to move away, but, frowning sternly, the Librarian caught her shoulder. 'I believe that you ought to talk to him. He has made an effort. Now so must you, eh? Hmm?'

Ace looked up at him. 'All right grandad, you talked me into it.'

The Doctor had been hesitating, watching the old man's conversation with Ace. Finally, he stepped forward warily, as if he was walking into a clearing full of Daleks.

'Hello,' he said, not being able quite to catch his companion's eye.

'Yeah.' Ace was concentrating on a bloom that formed part of the hedgerow. It should have been black, like all the other roses in that row, but it was actually mottled, full of some illness.

The Doctor, having opened his mouth to talk and then closed

it again, had turned his attention to the Librarian, who offered him his hand. The Doctor glared at it and he lowered it once more.

'What has our enemy done here?'

'She is trying to infiltrate, plant by plant, bush by bush. Arrogant pup! You know, of course, that all was not well in the garden before her infection ...'

'Yes, yes!' The Doctor waved his hand impatiently. 'What are the major effects?'

'I believe she has radically altered the biochem ... the bi ... and she's done it to the whole garden, yes! Hmm.'

The Doctor sighed. Ace got the feeling that he and the Librarian were old acquaintances. Questions didn't really seem appropriate, though. Not that she was in a mood to ask them.

'But she's not in control?'

'Never. I would not allow it. Outrageous!'

The Doctor seemed suddenly to relax. 'Good,' he murmured, and turned to Ace. 'We can talk ...'

'No. What's there to talk about?'

The Doctor leaned back on his umbrella, the expression on his face like a fox about to consume a rabbit. 'Lots. Listen −'

A thunderous explosion ripped through the air of the garden, and all three were thrown flat to the floor. By instinct, Ace found herself sheltering the old man as debris showered down on them.

A familiar laugh snickered across the garden.

'Boyle!' Ace stood up, grabbing her rucksack. 'Evil presence in the area. He's dead meat.' And she ran off in the general direction of the laugh.

'Ace!' the Doctor bellowed after her. 'Don't −'

But she was gone.

'Don't worry,' smiled the old man, brushing dirt from his silver hair. 'She might win.'

'Yes,' muttered the Doctor. 'That's what I'm afraid of.'

As Ace picked her way through the rose garden, she remembered a conversation she and the Doctor had had at Greenwich once. They had been walking in the park beneath the Old Royal Observatory. After a few pithy words about

Newton, the Doctor's mind had seemed to wander to more poetic sentiments.

'A rose by any other name,' he had mused, 'would smell as sweet. Not true. No perspective. But Will was in love. Powerful emotions change our point of view.' He seemed to be giving Ace an obscure lecture. She had tried to keep track.

'So you only know what something's like if it's in context?'

'Yes. Like Oscar and his green carnations. People loved him, but only for a while. Talent borrows, genius steals.'

'What are you on about, Professor?'

'I'm saying look for the context, and if you can't find one, establish your own. You need a sense of scale.'

'Okay.' Ace had nodded, still not sure that she understood. With distance, it seemed so fragile a thought to cling to.

That in Greenwich Park, you could get briefed for a holiday in Hell.

The old man had bid his goodbyes to the Doctor, and wandered back to his roses. He looked down at his favourite patch in sadness. They should have been rainbow-hued, a vague approximation of that memory that the Doctor so sought after. Even before this current trouble, the soil had become too acid, the earth too barren.

The Librarian bent to touch the gnarled, mutated blooms. The power of the Timewyrm had touched and transformed them.

'Oh rose, thou art sick,' he murmured.

Ace came to a maze. It was like the one that she had entered on a school visit to Longleat. Only this one was a tangled labyrinth of rosebushes, different colours following different hedges. Ace paused, tapping the toe of her trainer on the dewy grass.

'Wet surface. Not good.' Above her, something passed over the sun. She shivered, and squinted up, trying to see, but it was gone. She felt as if something was watching her. The laughter came again, from somewhere near the centre of the maze.

Right. Ace plucked a can of nitro-nine from her rucksack.

'Let's see you play with the big girls,' she muttered, and set off into the maze.

The Doctor arrived seconds later, and saw her vanish down a thorny avenue. He stared after her, like it was the last time he would ever see her.

Ace swiftly found her opponent. Chad Boyle stood in the centre of the maze, hands over his eyes. He was peeping through them, hoping to catch a movement from the gap in the hedge in front of him. Luckily, Ace was behind him. She had been speculating on just what the nature of this game was, why such an elaborate damnation had been devised. Boyle's appearance left her with few doubts. He was carrying an ugly little sub-machine-gun, and a cluster of grenades. The weapons hung clumsily about his tiny form. Ace considered just rolling her can of nitro-nine at the little psychopath and ending this here and now.

No. The Professor wouldn't like it. Why was that still a consideration? They were in Hell, Ace because of that stupid commandment about being nice to your Mum, the Doctor because of who knows what big crimes. Maybe Daleks counted as people. She ought to blow up Boyle and get some of her own back.

Nah. 'Sides, she needed a workout. Maybe this place would make her lose a few pounds. Before the answering thought, 'For what?', came, she was already moving. Boyle's count had reached eighty-five.

The Doctor was meditating, legs folded into a classical lotus, hovering a few inches above the ground. His umbrella was stuck in the earth beside him. His lips formed words, silently.

Saul found himself muttering a rhyme, something about perfect flowers and destroying planets.

Trelaw looked up in surprise. Saul had never exhibited a tendency to talk to himself before. It would have slightly worried the congregation. Peter was talking too, pacing the aisle, unaware of the whisper that Trelaw had listened to throughout his whole life.

'I just wish there was some way we could help them. I mean, we're not even sure what's going on.' His wife stood up and stopped him, laying a hand gently on his chest.

'Come on, you won't achieve anything like this. Use that brain of yours.' Her hand had encountered something. From his breast pocket, she removed the glittering amulet that the Doctor had given him. 'I wonder what this thing is,' she mused.

'Wait a moment.' Trelaw had been wandering about the pews, glancing up at the ceiling, from where the voice of Saul seemed to emanate. 'I do believe that Saul is trying to tell us something.'

They all listened. Saul was singing, distantly, fluctuating in and out of audible range. It was like a nursery rhyme, something simple and gentle. Trelaw remembered the first time that his father, the old reverend, had introduced him to Saul. It had been on an October evening, and they had been walking in Badger's Croft. As night fell Trelaw Senior had become more and more convinced of something, something about his son's replies and the maturity they signalled. With purposeful step, he had strode across the marshes towards St Christopher's, his son struggling in his wake. The grey-haired old man had unlocked the door of the church and young Ernest Trelaw had been amazed to find the place lit and merry with joyful song. It hadn't scared him, because in the song he could feel the same benign presence that he'd always connected with the place. For most of his childhood, he had assumed it was God. It had taken his adulthood to accept that God wasn't that easy to find, and in that acceptance he had taken up his ministry. Perhaps it was that process that had led to every generation of Trelaws entering the clergy. Saul and the Trelaw family were in symbiosis, each aiding the other. Trelaw glanced at the lunar plain outside. This was surely their greatest test. Saul's song was gaining strength and clarity now, and the reverend picked out a verse:

Save me from the void inside my head to the time,
The petitioner to the wise man said,
Or lay my body out and
Call me dead,
And let my mind do no more thinking to the time.

Trelaw nodded, stroking his dimpled chin. It was almost poetry.

Odd, disjointed verse. But for poetry to come floating into Saul like this was very strange. There must be a message implied.

'Bits of iambic pentameter,' Emily smiled thoughtfully. 'Though not one that Shakespeare would have been proud of. It alters quite purposefully, but not to any real poetic effect. There are feet knocked off and added all over the place.'

'Sounds painful,' Peter opined. It made a change, he thought, for him not to know what his wife was talking about.

'It is,' she agreed. 'Da de da de da de da de *da*, da da da!' In the pew where it lay, the baby was waving its arms to the rhythm. Beside it, unseen by the Hutchingses, the amulet was pulsing with a blue glow, the light dancing to the same lurching waltz.

Ace had hidden between a row of black roses and a row of red. The blooms would camouflage her most effectively. She pulled her rucksack from her back, and searched for anything that could be used as a weapon.

Ghetto blaster, copy of the NME dated 2018, tube of acne treatment. Now if she had a bunsen burner and a decent filtration system handy ... but why bother when the two cans of nitronine sat, lovingly surrounded by cotton wool, in the bottom of the bag? Ace wondered if doing harm to Boyle here would hurt him in real life. Or was this real life? She really needed to know the answers to a lot of questions before she could do anything, needed to put all this in context. Yeah.

At the start of all this, the Professor had said that small events tend to reflect big ones, that clues to the big picture could be found in the strangest of places.

She picked up the NME, and began to search its pages. This was the issue that the Professor had borrowed from her one night, claiming that there were aspects of popular culture that he ought to catch up on. At the time, she had thought that this was just a naff gesture, designed to make her think that he was interested in her life. 'The Stone Roses — Too Old To Rock?'; 'Fifi Trixabelle Geldof Interviewed'. There they were, the small ads. Personals. Right at the top of the first column, it caught her eye.

Ace – *Behind You!*

She cartwheeled forward without looking as a burst of SMG fire ripped apart the hedge behind her. Rolling behind the second hedge, she glimpsed Boyle dashing away, giggling. Ace pulled the first container from her bag. This was getting serious.

Context. Create your own, the Doctor had said. Like all these roses were making her sneeze anyway. Pity about the garden, but –

She clicked the timer on the flask on to short fuse and hurled it off into the bushes. Seconds later, it exploded, sending a mountain of soil and a hail of rosebushes into the air.

'Serious pruning,' Ace grinned as the petals spiralled down around her.

Boyle had been caught by the concussion at the edge of the explosion. He fell roughly, scraping his knee through his spacesuit. He cried out in shock and surprise. That wasn't supposed to happen here, these were only games, only pretending, for him at least. He was supposed to win, to be the boss. The Angel had said that he was to torment Dotty. She wouldn't let him come to any harm. She needed him.

Needed. That had been music to the bully's ears. Like many lost souls before him, Chad Boyle had been seduced by the concept of belonging. If things depended on him, if he had a function, he didn't much care what that function was. He was just obeying orders. If he'd run to his mother with a bloody knee, she'd just have told him that he should have been more careful, that he'd have to learn to look after himself, because she wouldn't always be there.

He and Ace had more in common than either of them would ever know. Boyle glared down at his bleeding flesh and wiped his nose across the sleeve of his spacesuit. He wasn't going to cry.

Ace had circled around the crater she'd created, hoping that Boyle had been stunned, that she could disarm him somehow. She'd made some preparations, taking advantage of the confusion which the explosion had caused. She ducked behind a hedge at a flash of movement in her peripheral vision. Another burst of gunfire cut the grass into flying shreds behind her. She sprinted along the avenue of red and orange roses and ducked into an alcove just as Boyle rounded the corner, his piggy eyes scanning the bushes.

'Come out, come out,' he crooned. 'I've already killed you once, you know, Dotty. I can do it again.'

Ace nearly asked him what he was on about, but two things prevented her. One, she wasn't going to tell him where she was, and, two, somewhere inside her she knew what he was saying was true.

That was the end of the dream. The brick had descended, blocking out the light. The light would never come on again, Dorry, Dorothy, Dotty, Ace was dead. Crouching in the rose-bushes, Ace shivered with the cold. That couldn't be true. She remembered so much about growing up, meeting the Professor, Iceworld, the gang . . .

Who was in the gang, anyway? Wasn't that a story she had read somewhere? The cold seized her again, and might have finally claimed her, but the alarm on her watch went off.

Noise blared from somewhere on Boyle's right. He swung, bringing the gun to bear, and blasted away in fright.

Ace's ghetto blaster had been working its way through what seemed to be a blank cassette until it had encountered half an album of Aztec Camera. Doing its job, it blasted them out at full volume, assuring the garden that you couldn't buy time, but you could sell your soul, and the closest thing to heaven was — Thirty liquid Teflon shells travelling at hypersonic velocity reduced it to its basic components. This happened a lot to Ace's hi-fi equipment.

Ace's foot impacted on Boyle's chest, sending him flying backwards. She had sprinted at him while he was distracted. With a desperate lunge, she seized the gun. Boyle pulled the pin from a grenade as he hit the gound. Ace gestured vaguely with the gun and then realized that he wasn't scared, he wasn't reacting at all.

Two seconds on that grenade. She sprinted away with the gun.

Boyle threw the grenade after her, but in his sitting position he clumsily bounced it into the undergrowth, erupting some more plants.

The garden was starting to look like a battlefield.

Ace flung herself into a bush, cursing at the thorns that punctured her shirt. There were times when she would have given anything for body armour. She examined the gun. Stupid little Slovak hijacking gun. She checked it out. Half a magazine left. So why not use it?

Because that wasn't the way the Professor did things.

No, it wasn't the way she did things. He destroyed planets. He kept her around as a blunt instrument.

She started to bury the gun under the bush.

Then an explosion blasted the bush apart.

Boyle was randomly throwing grenades, delighting in the noise and destruction. He knew that for every one he threw, a new one would appear in his sling. So why hadn't he been given a new gun? These rules weren't fair at all. He should have been allowed to kill Ace when she lay on the altar stone.

Kill. Yeah. He'd done that once before, with that brick in the playground. He remembered the whole series of events, Dotty looking up, him raising the brick from the new extension work over the little girl's head, looking up to see if anybody was watching . . .

Oh no. That was him. He'd seen him, standing outside the school gates. The enemy. The little man. And he was smiling.

But that meant –

Ace grabbed Boyle by the collar and connected a straight right across his jaw. The boy fell to the ground, reaching for his grenades, but the woman was on him now, pounding his chest and his face. She was covered in soil, bleeding from dozens of scratches. The left side of her face was badly bruised.

Ace grabbed a rock from the churned earth and raised it above Boyle's head, ready to deliver the killing blow.

'Stop!' The Doctor stood a few yards away, a great anger about him. He glared at Ace, and for a moment she met his gaze, ready to cave Boyle's head in.

'You're not my dad! You can't order me about, Doctor!'

'I could. But I won't. If you really want to, go ahead. End his life. Smash a little boy's skull.'

'You destroy a whole world, and then you—'

'I have to live with that!' The bellow was so loud that Ace dropped the rock. Then she was running, off into the chaotic shreds of the maze. For a moment the Doctor stood still, horrified.

'What have I done?' he whispered. The air above him rippled and guffawed.

'What I wished you to do, Time Lord.' The Timewyrm's dragon-maw twisted and furled over the garden. 'You are losing this game through your own egotism. I give you a few moments to regroup your forces!' Laughing still, it vanished once more.

The Doctor gazed around, agonized, then made a decision. He sprinted off across the burning garden.

Behind him, Boyle stirred, gingerly.

Emily gazed into the blue jewel.

'De da de da de . . . da de da de *da* . . .' she hummed. The gem pulsed back in turn. 'I think we have something here. There's a rhythm in there somewhere, though I can't make it out. I knew a training in the liberal arts must count for something.'

Peter smoothed his wife's hair and nodded. 'Point taken, love, but what does it mean?'

'Saul and I have been thinking.' Trelaw came over, carrying a plate of the biscuits that he habitually nibbled in the vestry. The Hutchingses took them gratefully. 'It seems that the song was certainly a message, if not a particularly clear one.'

'I do not dream,' chorused Saul, 'but from what the reverend has described, the sensations involved were similar. I received a strong impression of peace, a garden of some sort, and the particular mental signature that I associate with the Doctor.'

'Well, he's still alive then,' muttered Peter.

'I did not think that was in doubt,' puzzled Saul. 'The Doctor's mind has been withdrawn into some alternative dimension to our own. Ace's has been taken there, too.'

'Oh, come on.' Peter laughed. 'What does that mean? That they're asleep?'

'No,' replied Saul, sounding a little hurt. 'Their entire memory store has been emptied into another physical reality. If they are destroyed in that reality, these forms here will have nothing to inhabit them.'

'So why are the Doctor's eyes moving?' Peter had wandered over to the altar, munching his biscuit. Sure enough, the Time Lord's features were twitching like those of a fretful dreamer.

'Because ... yes, you have a point,' Saul agreed.

Peter nodded proudly, glad that he'd finally made a contribution.

The Doctor wandered into a grove full of willows, the garden starting to regain its peaceful nature. Somewhere nearby, a brook trickled.

He found her sitting against the trunk of one of the trees beside the stream, her feet trailing in the water. Ace was looking straight ahead, her face hard with the lack of tears.

The Doctor sat down beside her and took off his hat.

'Hi,' Ace said, flatly.

He put a hand on her shoulder, and she shook it away.

'Forgive me,' began the Doctor. 'I shouldn't have shouted.'

'Why not? Can't make it any worse, can it?'

The Doctor sighed, playing with the brim of his hat. 'We're in another dimension, one partially controlled by the Timewyrm. That's all I can tell you.'

'Am I dead?'

'Well, yes and no.'

'Can't you give me a straight answer for once? This place, well, parts of it, are full of stuff from my nightmares. If this isn't Hell, it's the next best thing. And why are you here?'

'I came after you because I need your help.'

'Came to reclaim your pawn, right?' Ace was so angry that she couldn't look at the Doctor.

'You're not a pawn. The Timewyrm hoped that it could separate us through you killing Boyle.'

'And what if I had? What would you have done then?' She

turned to face him, and was shocked by the pain she saw on his face.

'I don't know.'

She turned back, hugging her knees. 'I'm not like that, you know. I wouldn't have done it.'

'No. You wouldn't have. That's a lesson I ought to learn, not to interfere when it isn't needed. I couldn't take the risk.' He was explaining desperately now, as if by the force of his words he could convince her. But he hadn't explained about her own death, and that blackness she remembered from childhood, and the thing that was eating away at her past.

Somewhere in these games of the Doctor's, she had been sacrificed. An Ace thrown into the pot.

'Not this time, Doctor,' she said, standing up. Her tone of voice was the coldest it had ever been. 'Come on, let's get on with damnation, eh?'

The Doctor followed her as she left the grove, silent with a terrible anger. Ace walked three steps ahead of him, and didn't look back.

The Timewyrm squirmed and laughed with joy. The first cracks were appearing in the Doctor's armour.

The next game would rip those cracks open.

Ready for the kill.

7: Regrets

I was in many shapes before I was released:
I was a slender, enchanted sword ...
I was rain-drops in the air, I was stars' beam:
I was a word in letters, I was a book in origin;

I shall cause a field of blood, on it a hundred warriors ...
Long and white are my fingers, long have I not been a
shepherd;
I lived as a warrior before I was a man of letters;
I wandered, I encircled, I slept in a hundred islands,
I dwelt in a hundred forts.

Cad Goddeu − Attributed to Myrddin.

Ace found herself breathing hard as she trudged along. Really out of shape for a corpse. The gardens seemed to go on for ever, endless avenues of hedges, many shades of roses.

After about half a mile of this, Ace stopped.

'This can't go on for ever, can it?' she said, and looked over her shoulder. The Doctor was still following, preoccupied. He was humming to himself.

'It can. This dimension could turn out to be infinite.'

'I meant this. Me getting all moody at you.'

102

'I hope it won't. But I got you into this. I've just been considering a means of getting you out.'

Ace sat down on the grass, spreading out her jacket. 'There's a way out? Why didn't you say so? Where does it go? And what is this place, anyway? Oh, I dunno, Professor, give us some answers, eh?'

The Doctor sat beside her on the jacket, still aware of the distance between them.

'Right. The answers to your questions. Yes. Because it's something I'd never normally consider doing. To real reality. Another dimension, possibly a fictional one.'

Ace spent a few seconds working out which answers applied to which questions. Then she nodded, bunching her hands behind her neck. 'Okay, let's go to step two. Why didn't you consider it?'

The Doctor paused, apparently weighing possibilities. 'I have an awful feeling that I'm being manipulated. Somebody requires me to make this particular move. At the moment, we're still intact as personae. Taking this route might destroy even that.'

'I'll take a chance over certain death every time, Professor, you know that. So let's go for it.'

'I haven't finished exploring yet.' The words came with a kind of sulky defiance as if, absurd as they were, they hid some deeper reason, something Ace wasn't allowed to find out. She stood up and shook her head, turning away.

'Well, as soon as you're finished, give us a shout,' she murmured. A second later, her curiosity got the better of her, and she looked over her shoulder. 'What do you mean by "real reality" anyway?'

'Reality as you know it. Your dimension, as it stands without Timewyrm interference. This place is just as real in some ways. Fictions are real, too, in certain forbidden regions of space-time. There are some places even Time Lords won't venture.'

'But you've been there?'

'Yes.' The Doctor smiled ruefully. 'By accident.'

Ace was starting to feel like she used to when they'd chat late at night, respected and cared for. The familiarity of the situation was just making the reality of it worse. Now she had forgotten her chemistry teacher's name, the way Iceworld had looked, the amazing colours and sounds of the timestorm that had scooped her up. She was very scared, and something inside her, pride maybe, was stopping her from telling the Doctor about it. But then, there was something he wasn't telling her.

She edged back an inch. 'You did get me killed, didn't you? By accident.'

The Doctor took a deep breath and looked down at the jacket under him. 'Yes,' he finally muttered. 'At its most basic, that's true.'

Ace rubbed her brow. 'I ought to be able to forgive you. It should be the easiest thing. If I felt grown up any more, I could just hug you and it'd all be over.' She took a few steps away. 'But I can't. Apart from dying, I'm being eaten away inside. I just can't.'

The Doctor smiled sadly. 'I understand,' he said.

'The only person I've met in this place that I liked is the old guy. Who is he, anyway?'

'An old friend,' sighed the Doctor, 'who's being very brave. There should be other friends around, one in particular that I have to talk to. Once we've found him, we'll understand the situation more.'

Ace made a sudden decision as a black cloud swept through her mind, eating away a few more details of her past. 'Tell me about this way out, then. I want to be able to get out without your help, if you − if I need to.'

'Yes.' The Doctor flickered his fingers, and there was a map. He unrolled it, and laid it on the grass, putting a stone at each corner. 'There are seven main areas to this world ...'

'How d'you know that?'

'Mathematics. I made a quick calculation of space when I arrived. The datascape is infinite in its contours, but contained in a limited area. There are only seven main zones, though there are many smaller divisions −'

'Like the Waiting Room, and the Library.'

'Is there one?' The Doctor grinned in glee. 'I thought there might be. I'd love to get to know this place better.'

'I'm bored with it already,' Ace pointed out a place on the

map. 'So we're here, in the gardens. What's in these other areas, then?'

'That depends –'

'On who's being tormented there?'

'In a way.'

'Look.' Ace looked him in the eye. 'This is some sort of Hell, isn't it? This isn't just an alien planet? How come you've got a map?'

'The map is just an icon, a useful idea. But from little icons . . .' he shook his head.

'No! Doctor, I've had enough of this!'

'Don't trust me, then. Be angry with me. Abhor me. Either way, this isn't Hell, or rather it isn't your subjective idea of damnation. This is a private dimension, invaded by the Timewyrm, a place where good still attempts to battle evil.' He glowered at Ace. 'It's a very personal Hell. Look at this.' He tapped the map. 'At the centre, at the very heart of this darkness, there's a Pit. It leads down to all manner of horrors. That's where we have to go.'

Ace took mental note of what lay between the Gardens and the Pit. There was a river to cross, after another vast chamber. The chambers formed a kind of spiral around the central Pit, the rivers acting as dividers. The whole thing looked more like a mandala than anything else, a great wheel that wouldn't have looked out of place on some hippie album cover. She did her best to memorize it, but wondered how long she could hang on to the memory of the map. The Pit was just a black spot, almost a dent at the centre of the map. No 'here be dragons', just the quick sketch of some reckless, scared cartographer. 'Do we have to go down this pit, then?'

'If we're going to change things . . .' and the Doctor paused again, struck by another shiver of realization. 'Yes. We'll have to descend that far. Now, since we've decided to leave here, there should be – ah.'

A door had appeared in the air, a gnarled old oak affair, surrounded by twisted roses.

'If this was a computer game,' observed Ace, 'it'd sell loads.'

'Thank you,' answered the Doctor, strangely. He pushed the

door open.

The Timewyrm examined all the domain it currently held. After the initial invasion, the connection to the body store, progress had been slow. The perception centres, the pier and seashore, had fallen first, and the circus show of the pineal gland had quickly followed. The data complex of the memory, the Library, had required a major assault. The major inner chambers were shielded by a mental wall, which had only been breached on a few occasions. Ace's arrival had helped with that.

The Timewyrm had constructed her playground in the fallow uplands of memory. The Waiting Room and Boyle's schoolroom were new constructions entirely, based on the host's own experiences. Allowing Boyle creative freedom was perhaps an error, but the swiftest way to erase Ace's persona was Boyle's continual undermining of her ego. His mere presence did that. However, her rift with the Doctor was still not as extreme as it could be. Time to reveal another disturbing truth about this Time Lord, decided the Wyrm. Another crack in the shining armour.

They were back in the Waiting Room. The Matron looked up, expectantly. 'Ah, you've finished your first torment. How did it go?'

The Doctor frowned at her. 'You're a bit of a stereotype, aren't you? A very limited persona, not very frightening.'

The Matron looked down at her book once more. 'I shouldn't speak too soon, Doctor,' she muttered. The Doctor looked around the room. It was empty now.

'Professor . . .' began Ace. She had been thinking of her first kiss, a scary, sudden thing that had happened outside the youth club one freezing night when she was thirteen. She had had to lure the guy out there and nearly push him up against the wall before he'd got the idea.

But the memory had gone, as she was thinking about it. She didn't know who it was or where. Something about the Youth. What had she been thinking about?

It was gone. All there was left was the ever-growing feeling of loss. What had she wanted to ask the Doctor about? Yeah, that was it.

'Professor, last time I was here, I thought — did I do anything wrong?'

'We all do,' he muttered darkly, appearing to examine the view from the window carefully.

'No, I mean that I felt like I'd done something really huge, really terrible, like I'd killed thousands of people. Do you know anything about that?' From his reticence, Ace was getting the awful feeling that the Doctor knew all about it.

'Do you know,' he began, with a hesitation that suggested this was very important, 'when I used the Hand of Omega to destroy Skaro, I wasn't at all sure that I had done the right thing.'

'Shut up!' shouted Ace, putting her hands over her ears. Then, shuddering, she lowered them, realizing that she hadn't made that gesture since she was twelve. 'I don't need any sermons,' she said, more quietly. 'I got enough of those from my social worker. I just want to know.'

'I was trying to tell you —' the Doctor began, but from outside the room, there came the sounds of movement. Some kind of procession was approaching the place.

'Doctor,' pleaded Ace, 'please tell me. It's all I've got to hold on to, that I'm not guilty. Please!'

The Doctor seemed to be juggling a dozen options in his mind. The inner door opened. Through it strode a giant, a robed colossus in an angular metal mask. The Doctor stared at him in shock, whispering some ancient Gallifreyan curse under his breath. Behind the figure came a parade of others, Time Lords in full ceremonial costume, their faces full of hate and accusation, reptilian creatures with three eyes, a whole column of UNIT soldiers, and a baker's dozen of Daleks, their sensors searching around desperately.

The Doctor was transfixed. They filled the room, rows and rows of them, friends and foes, a potted history of his life.

One of the reptiles strode purposefully over to Ace. Seeing the Doctor silent and staring, she took a step backwards.

'Do not worry,' hissed the creature, slowly blinking its third eye. 'My people are civilized, I do not intend to harm you.'

'Makes a change,' Ace replied. 'Everything else here did.'

'I merely wish to plead with you, to ask you . . . why do you associate with that creature?' The reptile pointed to the Doctor.

Well, even though Ace had been having doubts herself, she wasn't going to take that. ''Cos I like him, three eyes. What's it to you?'

'He destroyed my people, my egg caches, my whole civilization. Then, when a few survivors had regrouped, he wiped them out also.'

'I don't believe you.'

'Consider what the Doctor has done to you. He is capable of anything once he defines what is good and evil. If you find yourself on the wrong side of that wall, he has no mercy, no compunction. Even those he loves will be thrown into the battle, used and sacrificed.'

'Doctor!' Ace called, trying to make the Time Lord pay attention. 'Tell him it isn't true!'

The Doctor was staring into the centre of the crowd. A little muscle at the corner of his mouth was twitching. He had seen something he didn't like.

Three figures were making their way forward through the masses, the crowd parting reverently around them. They stepped forward towards the Doctor, and he took a step backwards, his expression a mixture of incredulity and − yeah, Ace could see if now − fear.

One of the figures stepped forward, and bowed to the Doctor. It was a young girl in a frail classical gown. She was white with cold, veins standing out blue on her temples. Lines of frost had formed on the smooth contours of her face, emphasizing the tense muscles underneath. She shivered with every movement, her teeth chattering as she struggled to speak. But her eyes were full of martyred passion, a religious strength that made her sink to one knee before the Doctor and speak, breath rasping from her lungs. Ace was sure that she had seen her somewhere before.

'I am the first sacrifice,' the girl wheezed. 'I am Katarina, willing to die for my lord, for in death I served him and did my duty. I died blown out of an airlock, exploded in the vacuum of space. I died for a gorgeous, fantastical, beautiful lie!'

Her shivering hands reached up to receive the Doctor's blessing, but he just stared at her, shocked beyond words.

'Don't touch her, Doctor!' yelled Ace, observing how the air hissed and boiled about the woman's cold form. She would have done something to help, but the reptile restrained her.

'Don't help him,' it advised. 'For good or ill, this is something the Doctor must do.' And the third eye seemed to wink, quickly.

The second figure stepped forward, another woman. She was dressed in a smart tunic and carried a gun at her hip. A badge identified her as 'Kingdom'. In the crowd, she had appeared to be in her thirties, but as she moved forward, the years seemed to dash in and engulf her. Wrinkles skittered over her face, her hair bleached white and shrank, her spine curved and her step faltered. As she approached the Doctor, she looked about to collapse.

'I am the second sacrifice,' she croaked. 'And that's good, because in dying I served my planet, did my duty. I died for patriotism, for freedom. I died of old age in the glare of the Time Destructor, my youth blown away at a stroke. I died because of a grand error.' She knelt before the Doctor also, flakes of her skin dropping onto his shoes.

The Doctor still stared at them, unable to move. 'No,' he whispered. 'Stop this. I've seen enough.'

From the crowd rushed a young boy, howling. He had a mop of black hair, and wore a yellow smock, but as he ran towards the Doctor, his clothes burst into flame, his skin scalded, and explosions of fleshy ash burst from his form, sending him spiralling towards the Doctor's feet, a living volcano. He raised his head, blazing and wailing, his tears evaporating into steam.

'I am the third sacrifice!' he screamed. 'In death I served my own mistakes, and did my duty for him! I died in an accident! I didn't want to die! He didn't come back for me! Give me back my life!'

The last words were howled in a blaze of pain, as the boy's face disintegrated. Blindly, he reached out for the Doctor, who, for a moment, reached out with his hand, his face a picture of disgust. 'Adric,' he whispered.

The freezing girl looked up at him in icy distaste. 'No,' she wheezed. 'Don't touch him. He'd hurt you.' She reached out to touch the boiling boy's head. Fire met ice.

The blast erupted through the room, washing the walls white, searing Ace's eyes to the point where she had to look aside. The noise was deafening, shaking the room, throwing everybody off their feet.

When the blast subsided, Ace picked herself up, and looked around, her eardrums ringing.

The Doctor stood still, astonishingly, his clothes blackened and torn. About him lay a circle of ashes. His eyes still stared, but there was a hint of new strength in them, like he'd been given a glimpse of Hell and survived it. Her captor having vanished, along with the other inhabitants of the room, Ace ran to the Doctor, and waved a hand before his eyes.

'Doctor, what the hell is going on? Who were they?'

The door opened once more, and in sauntered Boyle. His hands were clasped behind his back, and he was grinning wickedly. Ace glared at him trying to fight back the slide into childish horror that he inspired.

'Leave us alone, toerag,' she shouted. 'We're having enough problems.'

The Doctor looked at Boyle coldly, seeming to recover his composure. He took one small, decisive step forward, glaring at the boy.

Boyle seemed worried. The rules were being broken again. A grown-up was getting involved. 'Don't look at me like that!' he shouted. 'Don't! I haven't done anything!'

'Big and small.' The Doctor muttered. He seemed to be debating with himself, but his words were aimed at Boyle. 'You didn't do anything big, not in cosmic terms, but to some of your victims, you were the most important thing in the world. A name that made them afraid, a word of power. Only one word in a big dictionary, but one that some of them couldn't even bring themselves to say. It's only accident that magnifies your crime, like a bloodsucking flea caught under a microscope. But the universe revolves by such accidents.' The Doctor's strength seemed to leave him, and he slumped in a chair. 'I have pity for you,' he sighed.

Boyle and Ace looked at each other. It was like their game had been suddenly disturbed. For a moment, Ace felt more kinship with the little monster before her than with the Doctor, far away in his abstract regrets.

'They were all people that the Doctor had killed, you know,' grinned Boyle. 'He's tougher than I thought he was. He's a bully.'

'He isn't. He's a good man, and don't you say he isn't. Don't, don't, don't!' Ace was glad that the Doctor had fallen into contemplation once more, because she could feel her own adulthood vanishing into the blur of speechless anger that had been hers so long ago.

'Or you'll what?'

'Or I'll — I'll scream!' The words shocked her, mainly because she meant them. Oh God, if there was a way out of this nightmare, surely it would be impossible to reach now. With the Doctor bewildered, and her own mind being sluiced away, hadn't they both fallen as far as they could go?

A dark vortex formed about the corners of the ceiling, and spun down towards Boyle, roaring until it spun about his head, crushing into his eyes and ears. Ace watched it happen, a little distantly. There was no fear any more, not even surprise. She knew what was happening as the boy shouted. The Timewyrm was reclaiming its host.

Boyle's face effortlessly contoured into that of the dragon, the curves of metal replacing those of flesh quickly in this, the Timewyrm's own dimension. Here, it was the mistress of all reality.

'Welcome to my world,' the creature spat, the soft female voice adapting instantly to its new teeth.

'You can have it,' replied Ace, hanging on to what little adulthood she had left. 'Why don't you just —'

'No, Ace,' the Doctor whispered from his chair. 'Let her talk. I'm sure she has something to tell us, don't you, Ishtar?'

'Ishtar is . . .' the Timewyrm paused, and gathered up the abstraction of a human soul. 'Here. You seem tired, Time Lord.'

Ace almost nodded. The Doctor was looking very old. If he

111

could ever be described as weak, now would be the time. Of all the things Ace had seen in this nightmare world, it was this change that scared her the most.

'I'm too clever to be tired,' the Doctor murmured. 'But I'm not too tired to plead. Let Ace go, Ishtar. Your trap worked, you forced me to come here to rescue her. Now you can let her go.'

'No. I have further use for her. Boyle insists on further amusement at her expense.'

'Do you expect me to talk? To tell you my secrets?'

'No, my dear Doctor. I expect you to die. I expect you to be consumed by the ebb and flow of this dimension, your ego splintered on some jutting rock of truth.'

'That's why you introduced me to the albatrosses, I take it? Not a very clever game, Ishtar, not really worth the energy.'

Ace guessed that she had missed out on most of the literary references. But she got the point. There wasn't much to be gained by destroying them slowly, and unless the Timewyrm was as much of a sadist as Boyle, then the creature must, eventually, have something else in mind.

'You can't understand me, Doctor. I imitate the action of the tiger.'

'Burning bright? Fearful symmetry indeed. Blake would have understood you instantly. You're trapped between your own aspirations and a base need to stay alive. You're like one of the Songs of Experience: dangerous, intelligent,' he smiled secretly, 'but not as subtle as Innocence.'

'I believe you are trying to make me show my hand. That is why you insist that I am Ishtar, because you could not play such games with my true self. I'm really here to talk to Ace.'

'Nothing to talk to you about,' Ace sulked.

The Timewyrm turned its attention to her. 'I've shown you the fate of some of the Doctor's former companions. These are just a few of those who have been sacrificed in his name.'

The Doctor raised his head slightly, using his remaining strength to deny the accusation. 'They gave their lives for their own peoples, for better futures . . .'

'Incorrect. I have been there, Doctor. I stood by as Adric

attempted to control the descending freighter. He didn't anticipate martyrdom at all. He was doing his best to avoid it. You and I know that his death was obvious, that his destiny was to aid in the extinction of the dinosaurs. Not even cause it. The arrival of the moon in Earth orbit did that. You must have known . . .'

'I didn't. Not then. I was younger.'

'And wasn't Katarina's sacrifice a little uninformed? She believed so utterly in her faith, that you were a god, that she performed a literal martyrdom. She thought that you were her ticket to paradise.'

'I regret nothing.'

'I watched as you punished your companion over the matter of Gabriel Chase, used her in the most outrageous manner to contain the manifestation of Fenric.'

'That's my business, creep' began Ace. 'You had no right —'

'You know the geography of this world,' the Timewyrm declared. 'You know there's a way out . . .' There was an evil smile in the soft voice.

'Why are you giving us hope?' growled the Doctor. 'Get it over with. Destroy us now.'

'I desire your despair, Doctor. Despair is not possible without hope. Come with me and see some despair now.'

Ace gulped back a yell as they vanished once more.

Peter was sketching the rhythm that Saul has been humming. A musician would have written it in notes, anyone else might have resorted to dots and dashes, but Peter was a mathematician, and he wanted to see the shape of what he was hearing.

The living church, made aware of the sound, had reported that it had stopped, a few minutes ago. Now it had resumed, loud and clear, and Saul had turned up the volume. Words fluctuated in and out of the beat, rising and then falling to silence.

'I've got the rhythm, and it reminds me of something . . . it's not regular. It's on the tip of my brain. Can't make out the lyric, though,' Peter sucked the tip of his pencil. 'It reminds me of epic poetry, a bit.'

Emily was sitting with an arm around her husband's shoulders. 'It has certain similarities with the books of the Mabinogi. It sounds like an oral tradition that's been written down, but it also includes, the snatches I've heard anyway, fragments of an individual imagery that are Blakian, almost revelatory. I've never heard anything like it.'

Trelaw gazed at the couple engrossed in their work. The Earthlight still blazed through the windows of St Christopher's, and hard radiation baked down on the stonework. What a predicament they were all in! And Earth, the poor village! How strong the couple must be to have witnessed such infernal miracles and yet maintain their sanity. Perhaps they were throwing themselves into the puzzle in order to avoid contemplating their surroundings.

'Indeed,' agreed Saul, silently, 'but I am also bathing the church in low-power alpha waves in the psionic range. They should soften the more jagged edges of the experience.'

'Not very ethical, is it?' answered Emily, still concentrating on the notepad. Then she looked up, brushing aside a lock of hair. 'Oh. I did it again, didn't I?'

'Yes,' Saul sighed. 'You are one of the very few humans who can hear me psychically. You are very special.'

'I've always thought so,' grinned Peter, ruffling his wife's hair. But Emily was enthralled, remembering the past.

'Peter, you know when you used to pop around to my flat in the evenings, when we'd make soft toys and drink cocoa?'

'I do indeed, amongst other things.'

'Listen, you fool. I always used to know that you were coming along the road. I was always waiting at the door.'

'I just thought I had a noisy bicycle.'

'I always knew.' Emily stood up, and shivered. 'You know, sometimes I feel that there are things watching me . . . it's like that line in *Candleford*. I'm loved by things I do not see.'

Peter stood with her, biting his lip. 'In the circumstances, maybe we should try to think more of my foolishness and less of your intuition.'

'No. No, I'm fine. I've been so blind. Do you remember that party in Bath? At Miles' flat?'

'The one where Stephen took off his tie and wore it like a headband? Yes, but I don't see —'

'That colleague of yours, Lane or whatever his name was. He was being his usual wild self, dancing like a madman. He grabbed me and whisked me off towards the balcony.' Emily was staring into space, remembering the atmosphere, all incense and autumn leaves. 'And I managed to stop us just before we stood on the thing. I told him that I wasn't going to get myself killed because I had important things to do. I looked up ... there was a big full moon rising over the city, and at that very moment the brackets gave way. Rusted through. The whole thing crashed to the ground, pot plants and all.'

'I remember a chap saying at the time that there was no such thing as coincidence.' Peter nodded and smiled. 'The big lad with the curly hair, the one who thought it was a costume party. I was just grateful that I hadn't lost you.'

'Saul,' Emily glanced up at the rafters. 'Stop singing the rhythm audibly.' The church obliged. 'Yes,' Emily murmured, moving her finger like it was a conductor's baton. 'I can still hear it. I've got it now. Such beautiful words. What a revelation they must have been. They almost transcend language. They hint that what the author saw went far beyond his ability to express it ...'

Emily began to dance with some invisible partner, perhaps the one that had looked after her throughout her life. Peter sat down again, and watched. If he hadn't been so worried, he would have confessed to being slightly jealous.

It hadn't been what he had expected. Hemmings smiled. Well, that was probably what everybody said. The demons had grabbed him, certainly, and had hauled him through that strange waiting room. But on the other side of the door, they had let him go, dusted him down, apologized.

All that, they said, was for effect, to disturb the Doctor's companion, who he had glimpsed, staring at him, in his frantic struggles.

Hemmings was, the demons suggested, the best beloved of Hell, the raw material for a minor Infernal Duke. He was to be given some power in this world, as befitted his place in the previous life.

Initially, Hemmings had rebelled at the thought. Some ridiculous part of him, something that that Jewish charlatan Freud would have doubtless pounced on, had expected, had wanted, endless suffering. That was what half of him had thought. The other half had been anticipating Valhalla, the happy hunting ground, where he would enjoy Rabelaisian pleasures with fellow warriors. To get neither was an unfortunate sort of symmetry.

The demons had indicated the vast empty whiteness before him. This was *tabula rasa*, they said, the raw material of ordered matter. The chamber was without limit. Here, Hemmings could use the mere power of naming to create his own world, his Utopia. There were foundations left behind by the previous inhabitant, who had been evicted. These should present no problems, and perhaps would even serve as useful guidelines. The previous inhabitant was vaguely akin to the Nazi.

Hemmings looked on the void and decided that it was good. The demons bowed and left.

Initially, he was suspicious. The devil, his mother had told him, was full of tricks. But she had also said that he had all the best tunes, and that had been proved wrong when the banners and loud marches of National Socialism had led her son into joining the Party. Her religion was important to her, as she had told her son many times, allowing the infant to toy with her rosary beads. Well, judging by this afterlife, she had been partially correct in her vision. She had simply made the usual mistake, that of assigning human morality to actions of cosmic significance. Hell, like genocide, was too big to be good or evil. It was only real, real as pain.

And little Rupert Hemmings was a master of pain.

He tried a line, raising his hand in a proud salute and lowering it, licking his lips. A line dutifully appeared, the rough blackness of a child's charcoal. Blinking in amazement, he waved his hand slightly, and a wave of colour washed across the whiteness.

In that sweep of colour stood a soldier, dressed in a light uniform of a kind that Hemmings didn't recognize.

116

'Corporal Blank, sir, reporting for duty.' The soldier saluted across his brow.

Hemmings frowned. 'Change your uniform, Corporal,' he paused for a moment, 'Elliot. And when you salute a superior officer, do it properly, eh?'

His uniform changing into a powerful black ensemble, Elliot's arm snapped out in a proper salute.

'Good,' Hemmings muttered, striding forward. Sweeps of his arm revealed more and more given territory, and with Elliot trotting behind, he began to explore the place. 'Who used to live here?' he asked.

'He was a bit of a hippy, sir. Kept a whole platoon of the lads around just so as he could argue with us. He had a vineyard too —'

'Ah, well, we'll keep that, of course.'

'And a racetrack, where he used to drive that car of his. That's his house over there, sir.'

The last sweep of Hemmings' arm had revealed a simple hut, adorned with hangings that the Nazi recognized as containing symbols of the Dharma-Body of the Buddha. A low hedge surrounded the structure.

'What happened to him?' asked Hemmings. 'What did those in charge here have done with him?'

'He was collaborating with the enemy, sir. He's been taken prisoner, and awaits your inspection.'

Hemmings nodded. 'Well, we'll get to him later. In the mean-time, burn that thing down. Primitive rubbish.' The soldier produced a flame-thrower and torched the structure. Hemmings influenced the fire, curling it into a raging flashpoint that reduced the structure to ash in seconds.

He smiled, considering the flares of light reflecting off the interior of his new domain.

Yes, this would suit him for Heaven. But first, some changes would have to be made.

The Timewyrm had managed the transfer of the dataspool memories of the Doctor and Ace from one chamber to the next, and had released Boyle's memory into its chosen playground.

Boyle was roaming a schoolyard again, but in this one, all the pupils loved him, and asked him to join in their games. The Timewyrm couldn't really grasp why he behaved like this alone and yet was so useful in tormenting Ace, but Ishtar had useful memories in her dataspace, and having accessed them, the Timewyrm knew humanoids a little better.

Now, the viral creature was attempting to see the datascape as the Doctor saw it, constructing the area as a two-dimensional map, a simple pattern. This Time Lord, it decided, must have a real gift for approximation. The datascape extended into time as well as space, and the wetware (a human term meaning biological computer hardware – the Wyrm had liked the sound) it was housed in was threaded with symbiotic nuclei. These had defied analysis, a fact that, considering the Timewyrm's resources, was equally astonishing. They were, as far as the being could fathom, atomic nuclei that somehow acted in an intelligent manner, coordinating the host's nervous system on a hyperspatial level.

The host, the Timewyrm was beginning to realize, was a lot more than a simple intelligence. The mere concept of memory in such a being was complex. Memories of the future, of alternate possibilities of tachyon-based fictional universes – there was the potential to access them all.

The Timewyrm wondered if the host had realized that yet. The question was left open, a winking interrogative in the Wyrm's spiral structure.

'Blimey!' Ace looked around at the great city that she and the Doctor had appeared in. Vast bridges ran between huge skyscrapers, silent monorails whizzed from place to place. It all felt rather false, though, like a superclean thirties musical. Hard edges abounded, and stirring music blared from hidden speakers. She looked back at the Doctor, who was staring around with a kind of dazed horror.

'This isn't right,' he was murmuring. 'This isn't what was on the map . . .'

Ace shrugged. 'Maybe the map's wrong. Anyway, the Timewyrm dumped us here, so it's not going to be nice, is it? Let's have a look.'

She set off, then glanced back to see that the Doctor was still rooted to the spot. 'Well, Professor, come on!'

But the Doctor had noticed something else. Across the face of one of the buildings, an enormous banner was draped. A swastika.

Ace had trotted back to see what had so concerned the Time Lord. 'Oh no,' she sighed. 'More Nazis. I hate Nazis.'

'So do I.' The Doctor glanced up at the banner. 'Especially here. This is an important place. It shouldn't be decorated like this.'

'Are you sure you've never been here before?'

'I'm sure. But I know it well. And I have friends here. One lived here. I wonder what's happened to him?'

Hemmings stood in front of his desk, putting the finishing touches to his headquarters. He had taken off his spacesuit, and replaced it with a uniform of his own creation. Those who would criticize the goals of National Socialism, he imagined, would have thought that he would have fashioned an ornate, overblown version of his guard's costume, covered in braid and unearned medals. But no. The only difference was the rank, still Lieutenant, since he had not proved that he was worthy of anything higher in the real − the mundane − world. This did mean that all his soldiers had to be lower ranks, but since they were mere instruments of his will, a higher command structure wasn't necessary as yet.

Hemmings liked uniforms, liked the way they stripped humanity of all its pretensions. A familiar face in a uniform was that individual revealed, filled with the power of mutuality. Special in conformity, free in expressing the common purpose of the whole.

That whole was absolutely realized now, also. The city was humming with life, the citizens going about their business wherever Hemmings' grand intelligence looked. He suspected sometimes that they ceased to live when his glance moved on, but that was only to be expected in these initial stages.

Perhaps soon he would give them individual consciousness,

119

give birth to a whole civilization based on the Nazi ideal without having to go through any of the trying business of political establishment. The populace would be delighted, would elect him as their leader. In such a perfect community, there would be no dissent. Or if there was, it would be swiftly stamped out.

Then, after a while, perhaps this little Dukedom of Valhalla would challenge some other region, take over some of the other territories, until the system would be established everywhere. What a cosmic contest that would be! And he hadn't even interrogated the prisoner yet! There was a lot to look forward to. He'd always wanted this chance. Complete knowledge of the world, the power to change it, the will to make it better. What he really needed now, he decided, was a companion, someone to remind him of the simpler things, someone he could nurture in his own image . . .

An orderly knocked, then dashed in with a sheaf of paper. Hemmings made a mental note to make sure that in future the proper procedures were adhered to. He shouldn't have just made the orderly enter, but should have gone through the whole business of having him knock and calling to let the man in. At least he'd had this news delivered by memo, one of thousands he was compiling on the size, growth rate and population of this anonymous city which he would leave the citizens free to name. He knew what the news was going to be. This was his kingdom, after all.

The Doctor and Ace had arrived, and were being monitored.

'Well,' smiled Hemmings, rubbing his hands together. 'Let's let them in and arrange a surprise.'

A party of guards had spotted Ace and the Doctor, and had opened fire on them.

'Come on!' yelled Ace, pulling the Doctor round the corner of a building. He seemed to be unwilling, almost wanting to be caught in the hail of gunfire that tore up the pavement.

They crouched, breathing hard. This was a house-proud city, Ace reflected. No rubbish to hide in. Bet the monorails ran on time too. She looked up. The Doctor was attempting to pick the lock on a door that was set into the wall they were hiding behind.

He succeeded, and tottered inside. Ace followed, glancing back to see that the soldiers weren't actually running towards them, but had vanished. Yeah, another trap.

Shrugging, she went inside.

The door led into a corridor, scrubbed white and smelling of antiseptic. Ace figured that this must be some kind of otherworldly hospital, maybe the place that forlorn hopes went to die. The Doctor walked ahead, still without any of his old authority. That worried Ace greatly, almost as if it were something that had been done to herself. The Doctor had made one mistake, getting her killed, and now he seemed to be without hope, without any of those schemes that were forever saving his neck. This time, all he had was a destination, and no hint now of how to get there. Even the smallest tricks of this strange place seemed to surprise him.

This time, maybe the Doctor had gone too far.

Ace was comforted by her continuing ability to think logically. As she felt herself filling up with all sorts of childish ideas and fears, she'd managed to replace the lost territory with a fierce adherence to her principles. Loyalty, trust, bacon sandwiches and high explosives. Well, at least the last two. That she guessed, was what such big ideas were for, to stop you having to think all the time. Like a modern fighter aircraft flies from moment to moment, adjusting its wings, calculating how to fly every second, right? She'd read that in some book. Well, to start flying, you need something that'll stay in the air by itself, something aerodynamic. That was what principles were, simple wings for people who had problems flying. People, at that moment, like Ace.

The thought struck her that any of the Nazi guards would have agreed with her completely about that. What with the Doctor being such a toerag, maybe all her feathers were falling out.

She sighed and joined him by a pair of double doors. He was listening to them, concentrating fiercely. 'This is where he used to live,' he whispered, 'if I remember the topography of the interior correctly.'

Cautiously, he pushed open the doors and walked inside. Ace followed.

A searchlight snapped on and the doors slammed shut behind them. Ace spun round, but they were surrounded by guards. Atop an architecturally impossible arch, Rupert Hemmings smiled grimly down at them. An Art-Deco screen shone behind him and on it images of blood and horror, glorious to its creator, continually spun and merged.

'Doctor. Welcome to the party.'

The Doctor slumped, yet another horror added to his pains. 'I'm running out of things to say in reply to such sentiments,' he sighed. 'Please get on with it. The theatrics are so repetitive.'

'Ah, but I have a surprise for you. The man upon whose foundation I built my Utopia. He's not a military man, but he enjoys associating with us. He's a man of peace who loves the ways of violence. Am I getting warm?'

'I know who it is,' the Doctor glowered up at the Lieutenant on his perch. 'Are you going to show him to us?'

Ace looked on as Hemmings clicked his fingers, and a chair rose out of the floor. In it sat a man with a shock of white hair, his arms manacled to those of the chair. He wore a simple white smock and his mouth was covered by a strip of adhesive tape.

Ace glanced between the prisoner and the Time Lord. She saw that they knew each other.

The Doctor's eyes were screaming.

8: It's A Wonderful Life

> *'You don't go into battle to die for your country,*
> *you go into battle to make the other bastard*
> *die for HIS country.'*

General George S. Patton

Emily had sat down in a pew, tired, and was playing with the baby. It seemed to respond to the rhythm that Saul was producing and was moving a hand vaguely in time.

'I'm sure it's a message from someone,' Emily mused, glancing up at the church's rafters. 'But the poetry seems so vague. If you're going to signal someone, why wouldn't you say what you wanted to say in straightforward terms?'

Peter jumped up, much to Trelaw's surprise, and slapped his forehead with quite frightening force. 'Because the medium is the message!' He started to pace excitedly, almost lecturing to the church's reluctant passengers. 'It's like the SETI programme. The Search for Extraterrestrial Intelligence, reverend. Bit redundant in the light of all this, but still. Those lads over in California aren't really looking for "take us to your leader". They're after the right style of medium, a powerful, focused transmission. What it actually says is probably incomprehensible anyway. That's what's happening here.'

'You mean that we're being signalled by aliens?' Trelaw

realized as he said it that the prospect was now one that he regarded as completely plausible. This lifestyle was getting to him.

'No, no. What I mean is, it isn't the words that are important. It's the way they're being communicated.' Peter snatched up his sketch, a wild chart of bouncing lines. 'And I can see what the pattern is too. I hadn't thought of it in these circumstances. This is a chaos equation at work.'

'Chaos equation?' asked Trelaw, not expecting to understand the answer.

'Yes. A totally irregular pattern that takes on complex cycles of regularity. Like this poetry. There's some sort of structure in there, but it's impossible to fathom totally.'

'That's why it seemd to be an excerpt from a much bigger body of work,' exclaimed Emily. 'I read that book about chaos that you lent me. A chaos equation never ceases, does it? The poem would go on for ever.'

'The words aren't very important, then,' Peter triumphantly let his notebook fall on to a pew. 'The rhythm's the thing. Saul,' the mathematician screwed up his eyes and concentrated. 'Take a look at this.'

Saul hummed in concentration. 'I can see the equation,' he rumbled. 'But I have no mathematical knowledge beyond simple counting. What am I to do with it?'

'Just feed in values at one end, and the values that come out the other — use them for the number of syllables in the line. And do it quickly, eh? This isn't my field, I'm an old-fashioned topographer, I have trouble keeping this in mind.'

'Yes,' Saul sang triumphantly. 'I see! A moment . . .'

The assembled humans looked at each other, puzzled.

'I have signalled back,' the church explained. 'I did not employ words but simply sent a carrier wave, as it were, out with the same complicated beat.'

'Any reply?' Peter was looking smug.

'Yes. More of the poem. And this is — this is different. Ah, Mrs Trelaw —'

'Please.' Emily grinned up at the rafters. 'Call me Emily.'

'I would think that you will find this even stranger than the previous verses. It seems to be −'

'Improvized!' Emily clapped her hands together. 'In other words a message!'

'Yes.' Peter lowered the finger that he'd raised to make the same point. 'My thoughts exactly.'

The Doctor had collapsed to his knees before his former self, his eyes closed. Oh God, this is it, thought Ace. It's all over. He's gonna lose it and we'll be here for ever.

Hemmings strode down the Art-Deco steps, guards following him. 'Take them both,' he commanded. 'Lock them up with their companion, here. His stories will serve as an inducement to them to tell us everything.'

'What have we got to tell you?' Ace yelled as the soldiers approached. 'This isn't real, you know.'

'This is Hell, young lady,' Hemmings smiled. 'And I feel that it is my duty to torture you both. Forgive my theatrics, they make me feel better about something I regard as my most unfortunate duty. Of course you have nothing to tell me. Neither did he.' Hemmings gestured to the bound man. 'That's why I eventually decided to gag him.'

Ace backed away from the group of advancing soldiers. Torture was something she didn't want to think about. She straightened, ready to kick the first one in the nads, but suddenly, as if a tiny instant had been taken away from the scene, they all set about her and she was seized. Had she been Ace, she would have demanded an instant replay, but since she was Dotty now, all she did was thrash and yell, panicked.

The Doctor stood up suddenly and pulled the tape from the prisoner's mouth.

'Cuckoo,' smiled the man, hardly wincing.

'To get to where I've gone ahead,' recited Saul, 'you need to find the human's head. Go out to where he lays down dead, and call me call me in the morning.'

'That's horrid,' Emily sighed. 'Really horrid.'

'You mean looking for a human head?' Her husband put an arm round her shoulder.

'No, the poetry. It must be from the Doctor, that last line is a signature in the form of a pun. Unless he really expects morning to arrive, I think he must be talking about the dead body. Mourning, rather than morning.'

'Right,' Peter nodded. 'Clever, aren't you? Well, where's this body we're supposed to be after? We've only seen these two.' He indicated the horizontal forms of the Doctor and Ace.

'Saul, make a search,' suggested Trelaw. 'As you did when little Sarah Powell was lost in the marshes.'

'Indeed,' Saul boomed, a touch of sadness in his voice. 'I was able to locate her from the faint mental activity left as a soul passes on. I shall do the same now.'

Peter was surprised that he noticed as Saul's consciousness left the church. It was like a familiar smell or taste had vanished. All that was left now was brickwork, lifeless stone. Trelaw shivered.

'I always feel so lonely when he does that,' he explained. 'It's odd not to have him here. Tell me,' he turned to the Hutchingses and smiled. 'Are you hungry?'

'Not particularly, in the circumstances,' Emily replied. 'But I'm sure that the baby must be. It should be wailing its head off.'

Trelaw looked down at the child and frowned. 'I'm glad that it isn't. All I've got is some tinned food for Oxfam.'

Saul flew across the lunar surface, his persona flitting ghostlike from rock to rock, agitating the trace elements of the moon's atmosphere in his passing. He couldn't leave the church completely, of course, but every now and then he let the major elements of his self go exploring. He had never been beyond Earth before, indeed, he doubted he could manage it under his own steam. In different circumstances, this would have been a great adventure.

There was life here. Two souls, somewhere on the lunar plain, somewhere over the low white hills, lost in the blinding Earth-light. Finding them both would be difficult. It was so lonely for them. Saul could listen to the voices of distant Earth, so far away. He could hear the planet's daily trivia, and the panic and confusion over the explosion at Cheldon Bonniface. He prayed that he and his companions would somehow be returned home. Ernest was getting old, and Saul had felt the reverend's heart flutter and strain at least twice in this desperate journey. He had no children. If he were to die, Saul didn't know what he would do, without a Trelaw to guide him.

There! In his musings, the formless being had nearly over-looked the life that blazed on the lunar surface like a star in the vacuum. Just a trace, a dead image of life as neurons fired and slowly blinked out in a dead brain. To Saul, it was like watching a little cluster of fireflies gradually fading, individual memories flickering away into nothing.

It was a head in an astronaut's helmet and it sat at a small distance from its original body. Blood would have gushed from the severed neck arteries, but the cold of lunar night had instantly cauterized and sealed the wounds.

So who had this been? Some companion of the Doctor's, or an enemy? There were traces of association, anyway. Still, how to return it to the church? It lay a good mile from the doors, not that it would have made any difference had it been only an inch away, with only the Timewyrm's power bringing new air to the interior of the building. Saul would have to move it himself. His telekinetic abilities were barely great enough to set his own bells in motion on the Sundays when the bellringers were ill. This was going to take some time.

Inch by inch, the head began to roll across the lunar surface, the helmet gathering momentum as it headed towards the distant lights of the church.

Strong hands shoved Ace, the Doctor and the prisoner into a cell, and with a thud of bolts, they were left in the darkness. Only a tiny rooflight illuminated the paving slabs they sat on.

The third Doctor looked around him, stretching his hands against each other as if unsure of his surroundings. He had not said anything else since his surreal outburst, and Ace was starting to wonder if he had been permanently affected by his experiences. He certainly was marked, a livid red brand was visible over the neckline of the smock. The Doctor seemed scarcely better. He was still shaken by his encounter with the sacrificed companions, and a darkness haunted his features. What with her own continual fight against infancy, none of them were having a good time. 'Right,' Ace said, with as much energy as she could muster. 'Let's get out of here. I don't want to be here.'

'Where shall we go?' asked the Doctor quickly, as if this was a test, and she knew the answer.

'This pit thing. The real world.'

'And how do we avoid the Timewyrm? How do we distract it, so that it doesn't know where we are?'

'Don't know.' That answer had always infuriated her teachers. She kind of hoped that it would infuriate the Professor, too.

'No, you don't.' The Doctor raised the eyelid of the prisoner and peered into his eye. 'We wait.'

Ace glared at him and wished for him to die. It was a measure of her increasing descent into childhood that it took a full minute for the irony of that old curse to strike her.

Hemmings walked around his desk, inspecting things. This business of infinite power could eventually send him insane. He could become infinitely corrupted, as somebody had said. Perhaps that was what motivated the god that had sent him here. Perhaps gods were only mortals, seduced and convinced by their own power. Or was that just a religious lie, something to convince mankind that it didn't really want to take on the heights of experience?

All speculation as yet. He would give his captives an hour or so to talk to each other, then he would have one of them, possibly the girl, connected to an electrical generator. No, not the girl. That would give the impression that he was doing this for reasons other than duty. Did it matter? There was nobody left to judge him. The man, then. The Doctor. After a decent interval, he would have them all shot. It would be interesting to see if the captives could die in this rather baroque afterlife.

The thoughts of madness had come about because Hemmings was experiencing a strange sensation of movement, as if his head were literally spinning.

He flicked his wrist, and drank from a glass of water that

appeared there. To his irritation, the liquid was slightly warm.

'Ernest,' shouted Saul, returning to the church with a rush of air that ruffled the drapes, 'I have found a head!'

'Good – oh,' murmured Emily.

'Where is it?' asked Trelaw, somewhat bemused himself.

'On its way,' flustered Saul. 'I need to ask you a few questions, Peter.'

'Fire away.' Peter had almost laughed at the church's worried tone, and the surrealistic nature of the situation. He picked up his notebook and looked to the ceiling.

'If the church doors were to open, what would happen?'

Peter gulped visibly. 'Well, in normal circumstances, we'd be dealing with explosive decompression. We'd all die in a very messy way. However, since I doubt this structure is strong enough to remain intact against the internal pressure of air, not to mention it being full of leaks, I'd say that the oxygen envelope is maintained by mag – by highly advanced science – around this building. So opening the doors shouldn't make any difference. I hope.'

'Good.'

The double doors of the church swung suddenly open, and the inhabitants were treated to an awe-inspiring glimpse of the bare lunar surface. Bouncing over the low hillocks, exciting a trail of low-hanging lunar dust, a spherical object was speeding towards them.

'Having got the momentum going, I didn't want to slow it down,' Saul explained. The object rushed towards the doors and bounced inside, leaping over the sill of the porch.

Peter jumped up like the scrum half he was and intercepted the thing in mid-air. 'Oh,' he said, looking down at his prize as the doors slid shut again. 'This is the head then, is it?' He gingerly placed the helmet on a pew.

The three prisoners sat silently in their cell. Ace looked between the men. They both had a look of quiet patience on their faces, as if they'd been in this situation many times before. At one point, the prisoner had attempted to start a conversation, but

Ace's Doctor had shushed him. He'd then adopted an expression of sulky rebellion, but had remained silent.

They were both dissing Ace. In any other circumstances, it would have been a relief to hear a key was turned in the lock, and to see Hemmings enter.

'Very well,' he smiled. 'Who's first?' Nobody spoke. His finger flicked from one prisoner to the other, choosing randomly. The finger stopped at the Doctor. 'You. Come along.'

'No!' cried the Doctor in sudden panic, looking around the cell for some escape. 'Don't take me! Take her instead!'

For a moment, Ace thought that this was some game to distract the guards, but the Doctor seemed utterly terrified. He fell to his knees and pleaded.

'She's young, she'll hold out longer. It'll be more of a challenge. Please.'

Hemmings looked aside, embarrassed. 'Yes, well, I'll take your advice, Doctor. If such betrayal adds to your mutual discomfort, I'm sure it's in my job description. Guards, take her away.'

Strong hands grasped Ace's limbs, and she was carried out, numb with shock. 'You lying bastard,' she spat at the Doctor, and began to yell at him every obscenity she could think of, which wasn't very many. As the cell door disappeared into the distance down the antiseptic corridor, she felt her mind spiralling down into the soft trap of childhood. She kicked and bit to no avail, because she'd forgotten everything she'd known about combat.

Then another door closed behind her.

The Doctor stood, his face hard. He looked down at the third Doctor who looked ruefully back up at him, rubbing his nose.

'She could be right, you know. You terrify me sometimes. I suppose you have a plan?'

'Perhaps. How did this happen?'

'I was meditating in my hut.' The white-haired Time Lord hugged his knees and became reflective. 'Trying to get through to you, as always.'

'You did.'

'Too late.'

'Perhaps.'

'And I was lured off the path. Over a period of time. It took months for me to realize, months of contemplation. Something very far in the past was troubling me. Thoughts of the past enraptured me, seduced me. My own guilt was calling me.'

'Guilt. Yes.'

'Do you remember the Inferno project? Yes, of course you do. Well, that was my first full experience of an alternate timestream. Professor Stahlman, the Brigadier, Liz — all of them were duplicated.' The third Doctor stared into the distance, remembering the whole adventure. 'Now, I'd thought that I didn't exist in that world, or hadn't been exiled to Earth at any rate. I thought that perhaps that had been the divergent factor, that somehow it was the lack of my presence that had led the world into fascism. Such pride.'

The third Doctor shook his head and looked at his hands, then he looked up at the Doctor, smiling ruefully. 'Pride hasn't left me in this afterlife of ours, much as I've tried to purge myself of it. I knew that there was something I was missing, some distant memory that eluded me.'

'Yes,' muttered the Doctor. 'I get that feeling too. My guilt is —'

'No, let me finish, old chap. This is important. I'd been exploring my memories, searching for that vital piece of information that was troubling me. The truth came to me as I sat there, tired after you called me up to deal with that pickle you were in. It occurred to me that in that fascist Earth I glimpsed, there were posters of a man, their great leader. Old chap, it took me so long to realize. That face was one of those that I had been offered at my trial.'

The Doctor's eyes narrowed in realization. Unseen by the third Doctor, he reached out a hand to him, but then withdrew it. 'Yes. I understand what you must have gone through.'

'Do you? Yes, yes, I suppose you do. At the moment I realized that, I was seized by demons, fearful creatures of the mind, as the Buddha describes them. Anywhere else, they'd be metaphorical, illustrations of guilt or hubris. Here, they can be all too real. They dragged me off —'

'And you let them, because they were your own demons, your own nightmare. You didn't resist.'

'No. Indeed not. I should have realized, tried to control them, but I was in such torment. They imprisoned me, or perhaps I did it myself. They left me bound and erased my little acre. Before I could tell you about the cuckoo —' The third Doctor looked up, as if expecting an accusation, but his future self was planning, staring into space.

'Inferno indeed. Very neat. I wonder how much say the Time-wyrm had in structuring that alternate reality? It certainly left us vulnerable. In your meditations over the years, have you discovered any more of the machine code?'

'Yes.' The elder Doctor smiled at the choice of words. 'A considerable amount. Have you met any of the others?'

'Yes. The original me.'

'Is he still looking for the daisy?'

'Yes. But he insists it's a rose.'

'He understands more about manipulation than any of us do,' sighed the dashing Time Lord. 'After all, he's been here the longest. Perhaps you should listen to him.'

'Flowers. Only useful at funerals. No.'

'Very well. What do we do now?'

'What any rational being would do,' muttered the Doctor. 'We sing.'

Emily nervously pulled up the visor of the helmet. Hemmings' dead face stared back at her, eyes frozen in shock. The pallor of the skin was the only indication that the face wouldn't move at any moment.

'Perhaps I should deal with this,' murmured Trelaw. 'I have had some experience with death.'

'No,' Emily shook her head grimly. 'If the Doctor wants us to make use of this head in some way, well, I think that's my job somehow.'

Ace stared up in fear at Hemmings as he busied himself around the chair she was strapped into, connecting crocodile clips to her fingers and ears. She was in a cellar, a brick dungeon with dark patches of dry blood on the walls. Instruments of torture stood on all sides, from the historical atrocity of the iron maiden to the horror of electrically heated hot irons. Incredibly, in the midst of all this, a painting was framed on the wall. A muscular Aryan gazing proudly into the sunset, clutching a sub-machine-gun.

'It's one of mine,' Hemmings nodded at the picture. 'Do you like it?'

'No,' Ace muttered, her mouth dry with fear.

'Normally I'd get somebody else to do this.' The Nazi smiled. 'But here, the difference would be purely perceptual.'

'Why are you doing this?' pleaded Ace, a horrid squall creeping into her voice. 'Why do people want to bully other people?'

Hemmings considered the question. 'Because they have to,' he replied. 'Because they enjoy it. In the end, because they can.'

The two Doctors were concentrating, foreheads together, arms linked above them. They were singing at cross purposes, the seventh Doctor improvising his chaotically metered verse, the third Doctor providing an incantation of his own that added counterpoint and tonal depth.

'What does "aroon" mean?' asked Emily. Peter shrugged. The rhythm was once more pounding out from Saul's rafters, and she could hear the words even more clearly this time. Ignoring the nonsense that seemed to underpin the poetry, this time there were deliberate instructions contained in the words. Emily turned to the Reverend Trelaw. 'I get the feeling that you're not going to like this bit,' she muttered.

Saul had been inspecting the head. 'I think,' he declared, 'that this dead brain contains a clue. All electrical activity has not ceased. Tiny memories will still be intact. And, as you can see,' Trelaw visibly jumped as the head's eyes began to blink, unsteadily, in time to the beat that Saul was rebroadcasting, 'there is a connection to wherever the Doctor has gone.'

Emily sighed and sat down. 'Saul, can we talk to it?'

Trelaw stared at her in horror. 'No! This man is dead, his

soul has passed on.'

'Ernest.' Saul's voice was comforting. 'His soul has gone, but not as we believe it should. It is still within human grasp. Thus, in a way, you could say that he is not dead at all.'

Trelaw paused, considering. So far, this adventure had been almost morally stimulating. It was but rarely that the eternal conflict between good and evil could be seen in such direct terms. The shadow of the Timewyrm did not contain many shades of grey. This however — he refused to think of it in terms of utility. Just because this offered a chance to get the Doctor back . . .

'Please, reverend,' pleaded Emily. 'This is Ace's only chance too, and I'm not prepared to let it slip by over a — a point of theology!'

Trelaw stared at her as if he had been slapped across the face. 'Very well.' He turned away and leant on the golden eagle lectern. 'Do as you will, Saul.' His voice was full of troubles.

Saul sighed. 'We shall talk about this later. Emily, this may be a little unpleasant —'

'No, it's okay. There isn't time for distaste.'

'Then put your forehead close to the head in the helmet. Your power and mine will suffice.'

Without hesitation, Emily did so, and Saul began to beat out the by now familiar rhythm. Peter looked on proudly. This was what he loved about his wife: her practicality, her refusal to get in the way.

The eyes of the head began to roll and twitch.

Ace wanted to scream, to plead with Hemmings as he wandered over to the big red switch. All the fight against childishness had deserted her. She was Dotty, through and through and through, the victim, the one who bore all the guilt and evil in the world and the playground.

Hemmings reached up to the switch with a weary resignation. This was, after all, the dullest of tasks. Nothing to be gained here, no information to be extracted. Indeed, he wondered at what point he would cease the torture. Perhaps not at all.

Pain shot through his head, and his hand wavered above the

switch. To Ace, tensed and shivering in the metal chair, this seemed to be pure malevolence. 'Get on with it!' she shouted. 'Go on! Stupid man! Kill me! Go on, kill me! See if I care!'

But Hemmings bucked backwards, his body jerking uncontrollably. It felt as if his mind was being pulled out of his brain. Some animal urge straightened him and, every nerve in his ectoplasmic virtual body misfiring, he reached for the switch in final anger.

He slammed it down.

The Doctors concentrated, singing high, complex melodies. The sounds seemed to warp space around them, the corners of their cell buckling and inverting, twisting into multidimensional impossibilities.

The Timewyrm sensed something powerful and odd happening, as if the map was reinventing itself into its true strangeness. The topography was folding, stretching, curling around itself. The rest situation at any given place was now uncertain. The virus quickly sent out probes into the datascape to neutralize the more obvious disruptions, but for each it changed back, a dozen more twirled into the possibility-space.

This must be the Doctor's doing. What error had Hemmings made? Letting the Doctors talk to each other should only have increased their mutual despair. The Timewyrm slammed portions of its helix-form into the datascape itself, seeking to bring the memory store once more under its direct control, but there it saw the nature of the problem.

The very nature of the host had changed. In computer terms, in which the Timewyrm still thought in surprising situations, the machine code, the program responsible for the actual functioning of the wetware, had been altered. The Wyrm was no longer in absolute control. It could regain it, adjusting to the new world it was finding itself in, but it would take a while.

The Time Lord had gained himself some time.

Trelaw heard a cry from the recumbent form of the Doctor, and, wanting to distract himself from that awful business with the head, went over to the altar to investigate.

The Doctor's eyes were open, and for a moment the reverend thought that he had somehow returned to the land of the living. But it was not so. The body lay rigid, its muscles clenched into an uncomfortable arch. Trelaw peered into the Doctor's eyes, hoping to see some sign of life.

As he watched, the Time Lord's pupils shrank to dots. The irises seemed to sparkle for a second, and then, to the vicar's astonishment, changed colour. The eyes that had been a beautiful blue now shone a vibrant green. The pupils rushed back to fullness, and the eyes closed with a flutter.

For a moment, Trelaw had been convinced that the Doctor had winked at him.

Hemmings was sucked out of the datascape like a bat out of hell. He glimpsed the chaos that whirled around his passing, saw that the gardens were blossoming at high speed, that his beloved architecture was twisting and swirling into liquid bursts of energy, that his troopers were dancing and singing and tripping over.

'Linford, Pound!' he screamed. 'Don't dance!' But they ignored his shade as it ripped through the city and was catapulted out into the void.

The void, past the intercepting claws of the Timewyrm, out into greyspace, through the wall, over the beach, blustered by the sweet gales of nostalgia, his senses full of roses and regrets.

Further, further, to a point where space boiled, a raging singularity where colour and sound and motion were stripped of all meaning and reduced to a terrifying, horrifying nameless *now*. Concepts were ripped asunder, names died on the bite of reality, and Hemmings, that meaningless word, fell, to the destructive point, and was −

Awake. The musty smell of a church. A beautiful woman was looking into his eyes.

He tried to move his arms.

And found that he couldn't.

* * *

136

In the cell, Hemmings' body exploded into an expanding ball of pixels, a burst of glittering stardust.

Ace shouted out in expectation, and for a moment thought that the pain had arrived. Then she relaxed and found that it hadn't. Power was bursting around her and the room dissolved into light and sound. It almost like a firework display, like a wonderful bonfire, only little Dorry was the Guy. The cell was sparkling and exploding into bursts of firework glitter. In the midst of it all, a vortex formed, swirling the colours and shapes of the place into a roaring mess.

The chair flew into nowhere, and Ace gulped back a shout as her senses tried to cope with the blasting nothingness around her.

She shouted as the world became a roller coaster of colour. Her lips shuddered with a desperate intake of breath and the universe changed on the exhalation.

Hemmings fought down a sickening feeling of panic.

'This can't last long,' a choral voice was exclaiming. 'Ask him where the Doctor is.'

'Listen.' The woman desperately touched his cheek. 'We've saved you from wherever you were. There's no hope left for you. Please, tell us where the Doctor is.'

'Doc-tor,' Hemmings croaked, feeling his throat amazingly filled with air to speak with. 'In Hell — my Hell. My name — my name is Rupert Hemmings. Lieutenant —' His eyes fastened on the image of the woman, and he thought for the last time of his childhood, of the destiny that had been promised him. '*Heil*,' he gasped, trying to repeat his creed one last time.

And then, pushed farther than flesh would stand, his head died. The muscles slackened and the eyes lolled, a last breath sighing from the mouth. Rupert Hemmings was gone.

Emily let go of the head and burst into tears, hitting a fist impotently against Peter's chest. 'Stupid — stupid,' she blurted. Trelaw stepped forward, shaking his head, and began to administer the last rites — not, he chided himself, without an accusatory tone in his voice.

* * *

The Timewyrm saw Hemmings' memory depart, distantly, flashing across the night, and sent a tendril to investigate it.

'What happened?' the virus asked the jumbled personality as it tumbled into the void.

'I failed. The Doctor . . . did something. Changed the world.'

'I know that. Go in peace.'

As the Hemmings data flew into the night, the Timewyrm's claw reached out and plucked a tiny memory. The boy so long ago on his mother's lap. The darkness closed in as the Wyrm consumed the memory, ate it, understood it, and somehow, perhaps, became saddened at the closeness and necessity of death.

This conversation might have happened, it might not. It was something that the Doctor imagined, at least, as he raised his head from communion with his former self.

It was a good dream.

'Well,' smiled the third Doctor, 'I do believe we've done it.' He clapped his future self on the back and stood up. Looking down, he discovered that his white smock had been replaced by a velvet smoking jacket and ruffled shirt. 'Oh yes, what a nice thought,' he grinned. 'Could have made the cuffs a bit longer, but nobody's perfect, eh?'

The seventh Doctor didn't seem too pleased at this metamorphosis. 'Come on. This zone is changing. We must be gone before she wakes.'

'Where are you going, old fella?'

'To the Pit.'

'Oh dear. I was hoping that you wouldn't say that.'

'So was I.' The Doctor knelt on the floor and lifted a paving slab, tossing it aside as if it was made of plastic. 'Beneath the pavements, there's a beach,' he muttered. 'Let's go for a stroll.' The Doctor's face was still haunted by the memory of his dead companions, but his eyes were as hard as any warrior's. 'Time to pay the ghosts.'

9: Schoolgirl Chums

> *'If you can keep your head while all about*
> *you are losing theirs ...'*

If Rudyard Kipling.

Dorry woke up.

Everything was fine. She was in her bedroom, with the row of soft toys looking down at her and the pink bedspread tucked neatly up to her chin.

Of course, the first thing she thought of was chocolate. Horrible stuff, she insisted to herself. Gives you spots, makes you fat. She was proud of her slim figure, worried that her thighs were getting a bit too porky. Pete, the nice one behind the bar at Spiffy's, had said that he thought she looked fine, but then he was a boy, he didn't have to see her in the mornings.

She reached under the bed and pulled out a Mars bar. It had been hidden there in her secret horde, along with a tattered Jackie Collins novel and a white suspender belt that Tricia had dared her into buying at Chelsea Girl. As she peeled the wrapper from the chocolate, Dorry shook her head slightly. She must have been dreaming, because she remembered all sorts of strange things. She'd been in Germany, and a soldier had been there. Something about a man with his mouth all taped up. Wonder what that meant? Alison had a book with all kinds of dreams in it, and what they meant. It'd be in there. Dorry didn't often dream, probably because she was so happy with everything. People with problems dreamt about those and she was fine.

'Dorry!' her Mum shouted up the stairs. 'Tricia's here to see you. Time to get up, love, even if it is Saturday.'

Dorry yawned and swung her legs over the end of the bed, pulling off her Care Bear nightshirt. 'Okay, Mum,' she called. 'She can come up in a minute.' Dorry hit the button on her tape player and stared at herself in the mirror.

Strange feeling. No words for it, really. As if the girl with the long, plaited hair who stared back out of the mirror was somehow a surprise. The sensation was somehow familiar. That spot was still battling away on her chin. She set to with the old cleansing lotion, wondering if she was going round the bend. Maybe she'd buy a new dress today, something to go clubbing in. She wanted to buy a single, though she had no idea what. Whatever Tricia bought, probably.

Just as she'd finished pulling on her jeans, tucking in the brightly coloured blouse, Tricia popped her head around the door. 'Hiya, Dorry. I've just been talking to your Mum. She made me a cup of coffee. She's really ace, isn't she?'

'Really what?' Dorry frowned a bit as she looked at her best friend. Tricia was prettier than she was, maybe because she knew how to do make-up better. Her cheeks were a soft rose, and her eyelids were flecked with gold.

'Really sweet. She was talking about how your Dad was working hard to get you three a nice holiday in Tenerife this year.'

'Great, yeah, I'm looking forward to it.'

'Maybe you'll find yourself a fit Greek waiter.' Tricia dropped onto the bed and wiggled her feet in the air. 'New trainers!'

'Great.' Dorry tried to smile at the shining white and pink shoes, but a headache was pinching at her brow, and she didn't know — well, Tricia was her friend, right? So why couldn't she remember that much about her? Oh yeah, she sat next to her in school, went out (sort of) with Martin Day, the football captain, and had taught Dorry to kiss, up against the mirror. Right. Still all fogged up from the dream. 'Wait a minute. Tenerife isn't in Greece, is it?'

'I don't know, isn't it? I never really listened to what Mr Freeman said in Geography. He's far too sexy for me to pay attention to the maps and things.'

'All you think about is boys.' Dorry moved Paddington aside and sat down next to Tricia.

'So do you. I saw you looking at Simon when they were playing "Unchained Melody" the other night.'

'I wanted to dance. He was with that Elaine, though. And she's older than he is. A lot. He's twenty and she's twenty-three.'

Tricia shook her head. 'That won't last, then. You coming out?'

'Sure. I look a bit of a mess, though.'

'You look fine. You look like that girl in that film.'

'What film?'

'You know the one. The one with that record by that guy.'

'You'll remember,' giggled Dorry, standing up and reaching for her pink anorak. 'Eventually.'

They wandered down the street towards the shopping centre. Dorry was getting a bit scared now, because she couldn't remember what the name of the city she lived in was. Her mum had kissed her on the cheek and told her to be back for tea, since Dad was bringing a surprise home that evening. Dorry pretended to wonder what it was, but guessed it was that kitten she'd been going on about. Who would she name it after? Mum had waved from the step, her apron covering the slight plumpness which marked the imminent arrival of Dorry's little sister. Maybe this was one of the last times Dorry would be able to go out so easily. Soon she'd have to help out. She didn't mind. Now, what about this city?

'Oh, no,' Tricia muttered, glancing along the pavement ahead of them. A dirty youth in a dark coat, his hair tarred into a cluster of mangy dreadlocks, was approaching people as they walked by.

'Please give us some change, love,' he asked them pathetically. 'Got nowhere to sleep tonight.'

Tricia looked up at him with her best bitchy stare, the kind that made boys blush and look at their feet. 'Can't you get a job, then?' she asked.

'No.' The lad managed a grin in return. 'You need an address to do that, and I —'

'Yeah, well, you ought to get one then, oughtn't you?' Tricia stalked off and took Dorry by the arm. 'Look at him. He can afford to tattoo that "A" thing on to the back of his hand, but he's asking us to give him money. My Mum says they're all child molesters, those. Did you see he had a big penta — thing on the back of his coat? No, don't look back, he might come after us!'

Giggling, the two girls ran the rest of the way to the shopping centre.

The Reverend Trelaw was still upset, Emily knew. He had emptied a box of biscuits put aside for the church poor appeal, and had carefully placed the head in the box, replacing the lid with scarcely a gimace.

'I don't want to add to the indignity of all this,' he had muttered, 'But I have no other container.'

Emily hardly knew what to do. She knew that the attempt to talk to the head had failed, but felt quite powerfully that she had done exactly the right thing. She had a sense, somehow, of a powerful process of change being set in motion.

'Well, what do we do now?' asked Peter. He had been attempting to play with the baby, but the infant didn't respond to any of his tricks. It wasn't even interested in his efforts to hide behind a pillar and then reappear again. Wasn't that supposed to be one of those basic things that babies caught on to?

'I don't know,' Emily said, pacing the aisle, her hands clasped before her. 'I feel as if Ace and the Doctor are a bit better off because of what we did, but I don't know why.'

'Something has changed,' confirmed Saul. 'Something about the nature of the transmission.'

'You're still getting it?' Emily was surprised.

'Indeed. In its old version, without the extra power or lyrics, but it seems clearer than it originally did, as if some interference had been removed.

'Well, that's good then.' Peter gazed out across the lunar landscape from the window. 'Isn't it?'

The Timewyrm was trying to reassess its territory. The area of the datascape it had given to Hemmings was in a chaotic state, changing by the moment, rolling like a thunderhead, denying interface to any monitor it attempted to plant. This was random space from the outside, impossible for the Timewyrm to view. An unmonitored internal datum had been given control of the place, creating a self-referential loop of information. What was going on inside was, by nature, a mystery. Was the Doctor in that area? If not, where had he gone? The map was metaphorically flexing, changing its layout and its nature.

The Doctor was not to be found anywhere. His personal data signature might have been somewhere out there, but the Timewyrm was still trying to get used to the changed nature of the datascape, never mind the billowing chaos that had erupted in the one where the Doctor had been.

Ishtar provided an apt metaphor: the Doctor was like an Azukoi, a creature from Anu, a household pest which could slip in and out of cracks and survive despite everybody's best efforts to kill it.

Mouse, the Timewyrm accessed, cheese, bait. Traps. Cat.

The virus accessed Boyle's playground, glad that it still had control over one sector at least, and found its pawn surrrounded by an adoring crowd of younger children as he told a story. If it had waited a moment more, the Wyrm would have discovered that Boyle was telling his own story in legendary terms. A hero had been captured by a fierce dragon, and had fought it until it had to leave him alone and went away. The Wyrm hadn't time to listen.

The chaotic explosion of data had given the Doctor a breathing space. He would make use of it to escape, would head for the Pit at the centre of the map. He'd told his companion that he was planning to descend into it, probably thinking that that way

lay escape. Fool. Blind, random fool. That was the last place
he could find sanctuary.

He would expect the Wyrm to try to attack him on his journey
there.

The Wyrm shunted Boyle's data from his little playground
Heaven towards the map. Maybe it had lost Hemmings, but it
still had the boy, and one agent would be enough. Enough to
crush the Doctor's most distant hopes.

Dorry and Tricia were trying on clothes, taking turns to swish
out of the changing rooms in some amazing party dress.

'What do you think?' giggled Tricia as she smoothed down
a lilac and cream number.

'It's not you,' Dorry smiled. 'It needs some more tassles,
or a floral design. It's too, too −'

'Yeah, too classy.' Tricia pretended to be hurt. 'Know what
you mean, dear. Still, can't live all your life in jeans, can you?'

They wandered past posters covering a dead shop. It was a
beautiful day, and the sun was shining. The posters fought with
each other, competing for limited space, limited pockets.

'How many of these have you heard of?' Tricia ran a red nail
along the hoarding.

'Happy Mondays, yeah.'

Tricia squidged up her face. 'Yeah. Dunno how come they're
so successful. Look like they're a bit, well, dodgy. Not nice.'

'Voivod . . . no. Jason Donovan . . .' She smiled. 'Well, I
used to know who he was.'

Tricia laughed. 'He's a prat.'

'You used to like him too.'

'I never did. I only said I liked him, 'cos Tracey Dodds liked
him.'

'Me too. Tracey Dodds went away, didn't she?'

'Yeah. Went to university. Always was a bit stuck up. Too
good for us, Dorry. I saw her after she came back, end of term,
like. And she'd gone all political. She told me she was a feminist
now. She even asked if I was! So I told her that I liked boys,
actually. Something funny there.'

'She probably still likes Jason Donovan. If she likes anybody.'

Dorry and Tricia laughed their heads off and hugged. Dorry's headache was getting worse, but it was good to have Tricia there. They'd been best friends ever since they'd shared a desk in the third form. Tricia had a good sense of humour and always had time to listen to her. She also knew how to snap Dorry out of her moods. 'It isn't good to think too much,' she'd say. 'Thinking only gets you depressed.'

Dorry flapped the ragged end of a poster with her finger. 'New Model Army. They're a bit political aren't they?'

'Yeah.' Tricia wrinkled her nose in distaste. 'They don't think that anybody should have any money. My Dad says people like that usually have loads themselves. I mean, I think politics are boring, they're all the same, aren't they? But I liked Mrs Thatcher. She's a woman, like, so she must have known what she was doing.'

'Right.' Dorry nodded, frowning. Was that true? She didn't know, but something in her had kicked at the idea. They'd come to the end of the posters and she had a moment of panic over what they could possibly do now. It was like she was running away from something, something that was following her through the streets, waiting for her to stop moving. 'Look, can we go to the record shop later? I want to go to the library first.'

'The library?' Tricia frowned, puzzled. 'All right. Lovely.'

As they walked away, a red line appeared across one of the posters, cutting bloodily across Jason Donovan's hairdo with a fuzzy crimson dash. Three lines crisscrossed into a rough 'A'.

The library was a dull place, full of dull books like they got you to read in school. The only books that Dorry and Tricia liked were pop annuals. Adult novels were too big and took you ages to read, and were usually boring. Fact books made you aware of things that you didn't want to be aware of. Kids' books were stupid.

'So, whatcha looking for?' Tricia glanced along the racks and immediately hid behind one. 'Look out, it's Takeaway!'

Dorry didn't remember who this was supposed to be, so she poked her head around the corner of the bookcase, and found herself being smiled at by a young Asian girl who was talking

145

to some of her friends in the record section. Dorry quickly smiled back, and ducked round the rack again. Didn't she recognize the girl from somewhere?

'Oh God, she saw me!' she whispered.

'Well, I just hope she doesn't come over,' muttered Tricia, adjusting her hairband. 'I mean, I'm not prejudiced, but — well, she smells, doesn't she? And, like my Dad says, they're not like us, are they? She's always going on about that music of theirs that all sounds the same.' Tricia said some more things, not all of which Dorry really agreed with, but she supposed that Tricia's Dad knew what he was talking about. She didn't want to argue with her friend about something as stupid as politics, anyway. Besides, she had spotted a book on the shelf in front of her. This, somehow, was what she had been after. It was elegantly bound in black, with a complex spiral pattern on the outside. Dorry pulled it out, no longer listening to her friend, and opened it.

I was twenty-one years when I wrote this place, it said on the inside cover. *I don't feel my age, I don't feel like Ace.*

Ace. That word again. Like whoever wrote this book knew about her, knew about this comforting world where you had to swallow cotton wool to stay alive, only to discover that it was really fibreglass. Itchy, hard in your throat, poison in your guts. A sick set of words, ready to spill out and burn everything down. Burn it all down.

'I mean, I don't go to church or anything, but I suppose I believe in God, and what that lot do — gods with elephants' heads and all that — well, it's wrong, isn't it?'

Suffering, Dorry turned the first page of the book. It was headed *Chapter One: Little Dorrit*, and it began with a big illuminated 'T'. In the swirling letter stood two tiny clowns, just like the ones Dorry enjoyed watching at the circus. They were throwing bread buns at each other. Dorry put a finger on the page and read, her lips moving slightly.

This is what she read:

> The ferryman slid his pole into the brackish water and pushed. The punt moved forward. 'Are you going to pay

me?' he asked, his voice cultured and full. 'It's traditional. And I think in this situation, we should respect tradition.'

Against the bleakness of the dark river, the ferryman's bohemian costume stood out a mile. His scarf looped around his two passengers in a multicoloured spiral, and his greatcoat flapped in the stiff breeze that lapped the water into little waves. A distant landscape behind him flickered with arcade neons, blue flaring buildings outlined in a rabid city of night.

'Do get a move on, there's a good fellow,' the third Doctor muttered, annoyed. 'We haven't much time.'

'Time?' the ferryman's voice grew a trifle louder, as if he was talking to an undergraduate. 'If we had world enough and time – well, I'd show you my lodgings. My study's full of information, but that's what studies are for, isn't it?'

'That's why I asked you to meet us,' murmured the seventh Doctor. 'You were investigating the Matrix. While Ace has this place in chaos, you can get me to where I want to go.'

'He knows just about as much as I do,' sulked the third Doctor. 'He could have found a boat with an engine, at least!'

'An engine?' cried the ferryman. 'An engine which would disturb the water, interesting not only what's in the water – do you know what's in the water?'

'My dear chap,' began the third Doctor. 'I seldom venture on to the rivers between the zones.'

'Well, perhaps you should. In these rivers live things that I wouldn't joke about. They form a basic barrier between zones, a security system to prevent the occupants meeting.'

'I daresay that might be a very good idea.'

'You kept the Timewyrm out of your sector,' the seventh Doctor murmured to the ferryman, not bothering to suppress a slight smile. 'How?'

'Oh, well, you know, I just keep on my toes,' the ferryman blustered. Then his voice hardened. 'How are

147

you going to defeat it, Doctor?'

'I don't know. Not yet.'

'Well, if you ask me, and, I mean, I'm not the greatest expert about this sort of thing but I've been around a bit —'

'Stop prevaricating and get on with it, man!' snapped the third Doctor. 'I've explained the nature of the problem to him.'

'I'd say,' the ferryman gazed into the distance, 'that you need to fight the Timewyrm on its own ground, so to speak. It's a fundamental principle, after all. The universe has adapted to it, perhaps even used it to bring the Blue Shift closer. You might as well put on full armour and attack a banana split or a doughnut.'

'Useless,' sighed the third Doctor.

'Exactly,' murmured the ferryman. 'We're here.'

And, surprisingly, they were. The punt slid to a halt on a darkling shore, shiny black pebbles rustling aside as the craft landed.

'The central zone,' murmured the Doctor. 'Here be dragons.' He stepped onto the shore, and gazed out across the forbidding landscape ahead. Barren moorland stretched as far as the eye could see, lashed by the first gusts of the oncoming storm. 'Good.' He turned, looking determined, and addressed his two fellow travellers. 'You had better get back, you to your zone, and you,' he looked keenly at the third Doctor, 'what are you going to do?'

'What I should have done a long time ago.' The third Doctor looked back steadily, with only a hint of injured pride. 'Fight the Timewyrm when I have to. I'd like to assist that young lady of yours —'

'She's not mine,' the seventh Doctor muttered darkly. 'She may not be rescued. I forbid it. She's facing the same situation that you did. That we all did.'

'Yes, yes,' the white-haired Doctor sighed. 'I was just — just wishing, old fella. Perhaps I was wishing that somebody had helped me to face my demons sooner. Then we wouldn't be in this mess.'

'I doubt it.' The Doctor frowned, his face contoured

in worry. 'We all have our crosses to bear. I have the feeling sometimes that I'm being taught a hard lesson.'

He turned and without a word of farewell strode forward into the Central Zone. The two occupants of the barge watched him depart.

'I'd better be going,' said the ferryman. 'Shall I take you back?'

'Yes,' replied the third Doctor pensively. 'Tell me, when you give such good advice, why do you act like such a fool?'

'Oh,' smiled the ferryman secretly. 'When a wise man gives thee better counsel, give me mine again. I would have none but knaves follow it since a Fool gives it . . .'

'I have taken too little care, haven't I?' mused the third Doctor quietly, catching the allusion.

'Yes.' The ferryman let his answer hang in the chill air for a time as he paddled away. After a while he added, more gently: 'Perhaps we all have.'

Dorry looked up from the book, and it was evening. Tricia was sitting on a chair, reading *Brides* magazine. There was nobody else in the library, they were getting ready to lock up for the night.

Tricia looked up and grinned. 'I thought you'd never finish!' she exclaimed, taking the book out of Dorry's hands and shoving it back on the shelf. 'Come on, we're going out tonight, remember?'

'But I'm not,' Dorry began to say, and looked down to discover that she was in her black frock. Her face was made up, too.

'Don't touch your mascara,' Tricia scolded her and hustled her off into the waiting streets.

Peter Hutchings closed the ragged old children's book that he had been leafing through. It was one of the presents that was to be sent out to the poor of the parish of Cheldon Bonniface. It made him think of the children that he wanted and now would probably never have, the life that he would probably soon lose too. 'I don't think that children's stories have much to offer us now,' he sighed. 'We're such a long way from home.'

'I don't know,' said the Reverend Trelaw. These were the first words he had spoken in half an hour. He had been praying by himself, clearly disturbed by the business of the head. Now he stood up and stretched. 'Most parables are children's stories, you know.' He looked at Emily carefully, weighing up how he felt. 'Forgive me,' he said finally. 'You were only doing what you thought was necessary.'

'That's not a good excuse,' said Emily, looking down at the floor. 'It never has been. We should be asking you to forgive us.' The reverend smiled and put a hand on her shoulder.'

'We'll regard it as mutual then,' he said gently. Saul sang a little scale that was his equivalent of laughter.

Peter smiled too. It was heartwarming. Perhaps in this situation, he could take that to be literal, because his heart certainly felt warm. In fact —

He leapt up and pulled the medallion that the Doctor had given him from the breast pocket of his jacket. The others looked up, startled, as he dropped it, sucking his fingers. It lay, shining red-hot, on the church floor.

'Oh dear,' murmured Saul. 'Strange things are happening again.'

The Doctor stalked across the empty landscape, the winds howling around him. The sky was darkening with the approaching storm, and the Doctor was leaning heavily on his umbrella as he walked. He shivered occasionally, and his face sometimes contorted in pain as if a particularly unpleasant memory had come to mind.

'Old friend,' he muttered. 'I see what you meant. I see what your words meant. Protect me now, for I go into the dark.'

And walking beside him, or so it seemed, was the one-eyed old man in the cape, his frail form impervious to the blast of the winds and their terrible howling. 'My child,' rumbled the ghostly Hermit. 'My elder, and my contemporary. How fare you?'

'Badly.' The Doctor didn't look at the phantom of the storm, but kept his eyes on the hummocky ground. 'I've left her. Deliberately. She may stay there. I don't know what her situation is, I can't control it.'

'There are always things that you cannot control, Doctor,' the ghost murmured, its voice wavering with the storm. 'You chose your way, and now she must choose hers. She is good?'

'Yes.'

'And the Timewyrm is evil?'

'Yes. Evil beyond anything I imagined. It may be immortal, beyond my ability to destroy it.' The Doctor stopped, his face contorting with a sudden, inexplicable fear. 'I might lose this time. I might lose the battle, lose her.'

'*C'est la vie*,' rumbled the shade. 'One life for billions? Isn't that a reasonable cost?'

'*C'est la guerre*,' spat the Doctor.

'It's the same thing,' the dark form sighed. 'I wish I could offer you advice, Doctor, but this is the realm of dreams, the place of dread conflict. I have no power here.'

'And you aren't real, either.' Shuddering, the Doctor began his march once more. 'You're just a fiction of my invention.'

'True, true,' laughed the Hermit as he faded on a sharp breeze. 'But just because people aren't real doesn't mean that you can't talk to them.'

Lightning split the sky with a roar, and a chill downpour of icy rain began to spatter the earth into mud.

Dorry had been dancing to Kylie, but the DJ had put on a tune that none of the girls who were gathered in the corner liked. Tricia had lit up a cigarette, which she smoked because they kept her slim, and they were looking around the disco, sizing up the talent.

Or Sylvie, Jane, Sharon and Tricia were. Dorry was drinking spirits (not sniffing them, quickly, like Sylvie did) and listening to the tune she couldn't dance to. It was called 'Inbetween Days,' Dave the DJ had said, and it carried with it a kind of longing, a distant ache.

'He's nice.' Tricia was glancing quickly over her shoulder at a boy who was leaning on the bar, a blond crew cut and sharply-cut chinos. He had a mouth full of shining teeth, and looked rich but normal, the way Tricia liked them. 'He's well lovely.'

'Don't say "well" anything,' Sharon scolded. 'It's not good English.' Her Dad was an English teacher, and she was always joking about it, having them on.

'Sorry, I'm too stupid to use good English,' smiled Tricia in a sweet voice. The others giggled, but something inside Dorry made her frown.

'Doesn't matter,' she muttered under her breath. 'No such thing as good English. Language changes, right? Changes all the time, like it's alive. You're not stupid for that, you're stupid 'cos you think you should be . . .'

'What?' Tricia asked above the music. 'Don't you think he's cute?'

'He's okay,' grinned Dorry, trying to enjoy herself. 'If you like them like that.'

'Well, what do you like?' asked Sharon.

Dorry rubbed the bridge of her nose distractedly. 'I like to dance,' she murmured. 'I want to be free, to do what I want to do . . .'

'What are you saying?' asked Tricia, more loudly. 'You want to dance to this crap? God, you must be pissed.'

'I'm saying — I don't know what I'm saying. I think I want to go!' She stood up and walked around the dancefloor to the door.

'Oh, what a time to throw a wobbly,' sighed Tricia. 'Come on then, we'd better follow her, girls.'

The Doctor had his arms up in front of his face, shielding himself from the blast of the storm. Voices seemed to yell and scream around him as he approached the mountain that loomed in the distance.

'Traitor!' they screamed. 'User! Hypocrite!'

'I am not . . .' the Doctor tried to shout back, but his words were sucked away by the wind. Water was blasting down on him now, and he was soaked, mud cloying at his coat and trousers. His face was bleeding and scarred from bulleting hail, and the scratch the Timewyrm had given him was livid with fever.

He stumbled, and nearly fell, staring at the question-mark handle of his umbrella as if it were all he had to support him.

Through the red circle of the handle, he saw a figure.

The Timewyrm had planted Boyle here a while ago, not bothering to discover the Doctor's escape route. He had told his companion, after all, that he would be heading for the Pit. The boy had been kicking divots out of the ground since then, bored and increasingly angry.

Chad was carrying a sword, laughing in the storm now that he had sighted his prey. The boy was screaming his mirth at the sky, and wore a suit of gleaming armour. His teeth came together in a biting smile as he saw the Doctor tottering towards him.

'Big Professor!' he called, his voice wheezing with the laughter in it. 'Dangerous man! Great hero! Aren't you strong! Only a little way to go now, eh?'

The Doctor desperately looked over his shoulder, looking for cover. 'You found me,' he gasped. 'How? I thought —'

'You thought we wouldn't know where you were going?' Chad strode forward through the flattened and whipping grass. 'We know everything, me and my Angel.'

'Listen to me.' The Doctor glared at the armoured figure. 'You're being used. The Timewyrm is using us all, playing us against each other.'

'I don't care, I don't care!' shouted Boyle, tired with the Doctor's words. 'She gave me what I wanted! Now it's home time! Time for you to die!'

The boy raised his sword and stepped forward like a butcher.

Dorry flung herself flat against the corner of the building and felt the drizzle on her face. Please let it wake her up. Please, she wanted to know where reality began and dreams ended. She wanted to know why her friends and her life were making her so sick.

The girls hustled out of the doors of the nightclub and began to fuss around her, putting arms around her shoulders, helping her along. Here was all the help she wanted. They'd get her home, they'd make sure that her lovely Mum, her Mum and lovely Dad in their lovely house would make everything lovely. Nice, nice, nice. All nice. Warmth of bodies and friendship supported her, let her totter along on her white stilettos. Her feet didn't hurt because of fashion, and her passon didn't hurt because of common sense. You didn't argue with the world, with normal life. If you wanted to be different, you did it somewhere else, not in the city. You went off to be weird.

The scream came from nearby, and the girls all stopped, and quickly turned to walk the other way. They walked Dorry with them. She twisted her head desperately, trying to see.

Four boys were standing over someone, backed against the same wall she had been leaning on. It was the girl she'd seen in the library, desperately trying to get away from her attackers.

'Come on, best not to get involved,' muttered Tricia. 'She was asking for it, anyway, they're probably all friends of hers —'

Dorry felt that sharp pain against her forehead again. Christ, all she'd wanted was a home, a few mates, a place where she didn't have to fight.

She didn't have to fight. No, she could just walk away and it would all be fine. All it required was silence, acceptance, a bit of common sense.

Oh, damn common sense.

Dorry broke away and dived towards the fight. The girls shrieked and panicked, running in all directions. The boys at the wall looked up from their prey and laughed to see this girlie, in her frock and party shoes, weeping as she sprinted in their direction.

'What's up, darling, you want to join in?' shouted one of them, a jokey smile from above his expensive sportswear.

'Yeah,' grinned Dorry, as she flew past, and hacked him aside with the blunt end of one stiletto, plucked from her foot into her hand. He went down clutching his forehead.

Pure chance that. Should have been the heel. Before the other three could react, one of them had a bunched fist in his stomach, smashed in with the weight of Dorry's run, and the other was flying towards the ground, a foot having caught him in the groin. When the injured assailants got up, they ran away.

The last man didn't know where to turn. He retreated up against the wall, grinning hopelessly. 'Look, it was just a bit of fun, wasn't it, eh?' The Asian girl was looking up at Dorry, and there was a kind of recognition in her eyes, as if her rescuer was an old friend.

That was impossible, wasn't it? It wasn't like Dorry knew her name beyond 'Takeaway'. It would be something confusing and hard to say.

There were words you couldn't say. There were films you couldn't see, there were people you couldn't know, there were ideas you couldn't think. Not if you wanted to fit in, not if you wanted to be part of the world.

Dorry slammed the man up against the wall, her hands on his collar.

'What's her name?' she screamed. 'What's her name?'

'I don't know!' the man shouted.

'My name,' the woman looked up at Dorry with trusting, anciently powerful eyes, 'Is Manisha.'

Dorry stared down at her. A shiver convulsed her face. 'My God, forgive me. I forgot.' She released her grip, and the man sprinted away, sobbing into the night. 'Manisha . . .'

'I am not the one who has to forgive you.' The smiling young woman rose, and opened her palms. In them was cupped a pure red fire, impervious to the little drops of rain that were blowing down on this cold and dirty alley.

'You were injured in the fire,' Dorry muttered. 'Was that a story? Or was that −?'

'Your memories are a story,' Manisha smiled. 'A good story, too.'

At a distance, the girls had regrouped, gazing at the scene, not knowing quite what to say.

'Dorry,' Tricia called. 'Come on love, let's get you home.' And then, a second later, as if she couldn't resist it: 'Say goodnight to the Paki.'

The young woman stared at the fire that magically fluttered in front of her. She could feel it now, the pain that she had wanted to rid herself of, welling up inside. She turned and glared at the girls, shivering in their skirts, tapping their tiny feet on this tiny planet, ignoring the storm and awaiting their homes.

'Her name,' she shouted, wincing at the difficulty of swimming against the tide, 'is Manisha Purkayastha. And my name isn't Dorry.' She looked up at the sky above and yelled it as loudly as she'd ever yelled anything in her life.

'*My name is Ace!*'

And she hit her fist into the wall, the pain jolting up her arm. She hit again, and again, until the blood flowed on to her fingers. Manisha vanished into a haze of pain, letting the fire free like a child releasing a butterfly. The fire consumed Ace's vision, and the streets and dirty towers and shopping centres began to explode with it in great gouts of flame. In front of Ace, on the wall, a scarlet 'A' was forming, splashed out of her own blood. As she smashed at the wall, the blood spilled into the brickwork, steaming with fury. 'C' and 'E' splashed up against the wall.

Light burnt from around the brickwork, an outline of a door, an idea of a door. And maybe that was one of the things you weren't allowed to think, that in this world was a door, a way to change things, a painful fight for difference.

The light defined a door marked 'Ace'. And Ace rammed her way through it, and the world collapsed behind her.

Somewhere amongst the falling buildings stood a dashing white-haired figure. He had been a busker on these mean streets, playing a whistle and watching as the crowds wandered by regardless, not a penny on his cape. Having returned from the river, he had bided his time, a storybook figure in a world which, to him, was just as much a story.

Now he stood to his full height and took control of the world as Ace departed. As the winds and burning buildings warped to his raised hands, he spared a grin for the running companion.

'Well done,' he said, simply. 'Now go and win the war.'

Ace blasted down a corridor of doors, each one showing a different symbol. The pentagram, the pink triangle, the black flag and the raised fist. She ran through every door, and with every step things got better, her stride became firmer, her clothes became her own. Her rucksack and jacket grew back on her arms and back, and her mind filled with proud knowledge.

Ahead of her a final door was glowing, etched with three runes: a square spiral, a bent 'S' and a horizontal bowl.

Behind the door, a voice was shouting for her. Needed her.

'Professor! Ace shouted, rushing for the door.

The Doctor had gone down on the first blow, the grip of the sword smashing across his forehead. The boy had thrust the Time Lord's face into the mud, nearly drowning him, and then had pulled him to his feet by the collar, nearly choking him, before throwing him once more to the ground. Blinded, struggling to regain his feet, slipping in the mud, the Doctor called vainly to Chad Boyle.

'Stop! Stop! It mustn't end like this! This isn't the way!'

All Boyle could do was laugh. 'Isn't it? You've lost it, old man! You've lost Dotty, you've lost your mind, you've lost everything!'

'You're a small boy. You don't want to harm me. Not really.' The Doctor growled, stumbling to his feet. He felt a hard, small hand on his arm, and leant against it, trying to stand straight. He put a hand to the face of his attacker. 'Look me in the eye. Use your sword. Take my life.'

'Well,' snarled Chad Boyle, 'you said it!'

The sword thrust straight through the Doctor's side and blood boiled out of the wound, splattering onto the muddy ground. The Doctor doubled up around Boyle's firmly-held blade, and bellowed in agony.

'You're finished!' laughed the child. 'Who's gonna save you now?'

10: Chaos Song

Who shall decide when doctors disagree?

Alexander Pope.

A groan, a sort of choked howl, came from the prostrate form of the Doctor and the Reverend Trelaw dashed over to the altar.

'What's happening, reverend?' asked Peter, following, the glowing medallion momentarily forgotten. 'Is he coming round?'

'Quite the opposite.' Trelaw put his hand on the Doctor's chest, feeling the heart inside beating irregularly. Then, feeling a strange sort of echo, he felt on the other side and found another heart, just as chaotically faltering. 'I think he's dying. Oh my God!' The exclamation was heartfelt. The Reverend Trelaw looked up at the inhabitants of the church. 'His hearts! They've stopped beating!'

Chad Boyle was about to finish it, about to twist the sword and pull it out. 'Bye, Doctor!' he smiled. 'It's all over, now I can go back home.'

His grip tightened on the hilt of the sword.

Nine and a half stone of flying ex-schoolmate struck Chad Boyle in the upper back. He fell, letting go of the sword. When he looked up, there stood Ace, glaring down at him.

'Leave him alone, you bastard!' she yelled.

The Doctor was still on his knees, clutching his side. He held up a hand to Ace. Watching to see if Chad tried to stand, she took it.

'We must get to the Pit . . .' The Doctor winced.

'But, Doctor, what about —'

'Ignore him. We haven't much time. Trust me.' And with that, the Time Lord started to hobble off, looking as if he was about to drop any second, towards the mountain in the distance. Ace glanced back after Chad, who was scrambling for his sword, then dashed after the Doctor.

'Say thank you!' she blurted out as she caught up with him, more directly than she would have liked.

'Thank you,' replied the Doctor, his voice a whisper. He was parchment white, blood slopping down his waistcoat.

Oh God, he was going to die. Ace took his arm, and added her strength to his.

'You're angry.' The Doctor gritted his teeth. 'With yourself? With me? Come on, talk to me!'

Ace realized that without the distraction of her speech, he would pitch over there and then. 'I was angry with you,' she replied, letting her words trip over each other as she spilled out all the emotion that she had stored up. 'But I'm angry at myself too, 'cos I got a world where everything could have been great, a really soft place, but I couldn't make it work. I made it full of things that I hate in the real world, 'cos some bit of me still wants to go out there and fight. For Manisha, for me . . .' She bit her lip as the tears started to fall. 'For you!'

'Yes.' The Doctor glanced across at her, his eyes dark and half-closed. 'You live in paradise, you start to wonder who empties the bins. I made the same move long ago. Do you still hate me for getting you killed?'

'I got myself killed when I got on board your bloody TARDIS!' cried Ace. 'That's the deal, right? You can fight the world, or you can be safe. If you're safe, you don't get hurt. If you fight, then you do. No choice, Doctor. No choice at all!' They fought on up the hill, the wind whipping around them, and Ace had to shout even louder to make herself heard. 'But you always seemed to be so good at this! You always seemed to be in control!'

A dot of blood was running from the Doctor's nose, and Ace, somewhere in her jumbled thoughts, realized that he was concentrating on something else, something far away. 'If there's a smile on my face,' he whispered, 'it's only there trying to fool the public. When it comes down to fooling you ...' He left the sentence unanswered.

Ace grinned, quickly, feeling that her tears were only the edge of a vast lump of grief that was fighting its way up out of her stomach. She glanced back, and saw that Chad Boyle had stood up and was clutching his head, reeling. 'Doctor! What's up with him?'

'The Timewyrm's having trouble keeping control. Its communications were breaking down anyway. They'll be worse now it's killed me.'

'Killed you?'

'Yes. Come on ...' The lumbering couple made their way towards the lower slopes of the mountain and began the slow climb up its rocky heights.

'I can't save him.' Trelaw was administering artificial respiration. 'Saul, do something!' he shouted.

'I cannot!' Saul was as distraught as the reverend. 'I am attempting to shock a heart into action, but with only minor response. Ernest —' the church's voice broke with grief. 'The Doctor is dead!'

The Timewyrm had felt the datascape convulse with pain, the map spasm suddenly. Territory began to swiftly erode. Several books in the library burst into flame, the knowledge on their pages dying moment by moment.

'It is time!' the virus had cried out, checking to see that its perception of the scene was not at fault. 'My freedom is at hand!'

Chad had wanted to end all this, here and now. He had a feeling that if he slew the villain, came to the last chapter in the story, then he'd be whisked back home.

The pain in his head was telling him the opposite.

Excited by the approach of victory, the Timewyrm had taken him in its fist and possessed him. Boyle's face calmed, and the dragon mask of the Timewyrm blended with his features.

'Now,' hissed Wyrmboyle. 'Battle is at hand!'

The Doctor and Ace had nearly reached the summit, clambering painfully over escarpments and large boulders. The Doctor was leaving a trail of blood behind him.

'What'll we find down this pit, then, Professor?' Ace was trying to be cavalier, treat this as another exciting adventure.

'Terrible things,' the Doctor muttered. 'Terrible. What's the time?' He fumbled for his fob watch.

Ace frowned. 'Does time mean anything here?'

'My own time. Internal time. Wait.' He paused, closed his eyes, and a gout of blood burst from his nose, trickling down his face as he concentrated frantically. Ace twitched as she saw it, wondering how much the Doctor had to lose. Whatever this place was, it looked as if the Doctor wasn't long for it. 'Good,' he muttered, opening his eyes once more. 'Come on.'

They resumed their ascent.

'Doctor.' Ace decided that it was time for some answers. 'Why don't I feel like a little girl any more?'

'That's a good sign. It means we might win. The probabilities are balancing. If the Timewyrm wins, you'll never get into secondary school. If I win, you've got a future.'

'Win?'

'Get out alive,' the Doctor quickly corrected himself, with a suspicious look around. As if talking to an audience, he added, 'I think that's as much as we can hope for.'

Saul was panicking, little gusts of air running this way and that across the church. 'What can we do?' he cried. 'What can I do?'

'Saul?' shouted Emily. 'Don't worry, I can feel it ... they're in terrible danger, but I know it's not over yet!'

'But he's dead!' Trelaw held up his hands in futility. 'What else is there to say? Who can save us now?'

A grinding roar filled the church, together with a hum of

building power. Saul's senses buzzed with the pulse of energy.

'Look!' cried Peter. Where it had been left, on the floor of the church, the medallion was doing something astonishing. Before the startled eyes of the congregation, it was growing, getting bigger and bigger, the gem at its heart pulsing with an inner light.

Emily and Peter hugged each other in fear as the ornament reached the size of a doorway — which was what it resembled — and then stopped. A vast gem stood in an enormous setting, upright and facing them.

'What is it, Saul?' asked Trelaw, his voice full of wonder. 'Is it a miracle?'

'That depends on your definition,' the church replied. 'It is a very powerful object, giving off low-level radiation — quite safe for the moment — and capable of containing vast power.'

'The runes on the setting,' Peter walked over and cautiously reached out for the medallion, 'look at them now!'

In the ornament's smaller state, the runes had been just that: indecipherable symbols, products of an alien culture. Now, they formed recognizable English words.

'Good lord,' Emily muttered. 'They're in French.' Her husband looked at her, puzzled. 'No,' she squinted at the letters, 'they're in English, aren't they? For a moment, I thought that —'

'The letters do have a certain malleable quality,' chimed Saul. 'I am able to perceive them in Latin, also.'

'Well, now that's a novelty.' Peter took a step back and read out the letters. 'Thank you for your faith. Fly down the corridor. Saul must create a power link. Time running out. The Doctor.'

'Quite hopeful for an epitaph,' Emily murmured.

The Doctor and Ace stood before a gaping abyss. They had arrived at the top of the mountain and had found it to be hollow, like a volcano. The Pit descended into darkness, and there was a horrible echoing doom about the place.

Far below, a tiny bridge stretched from one side of the crater to the other. A circular path led down to it. Carefully, the Doctor started down the path.

'What is this place?' asked Ace.

'It's the doorway between one thing and another,' murmured the Doctor, his voice getting steadily weaker. 'And the bridge is a connection, a pathway between two worlds also.'

'Cheers, Professor. Nice to get a straight answer.' Ace's tone was flippant, but the Doctor stopped and looked at her seriously.

'I haven't been able to tell you anything. You never know when the Timewyrm might be listening. You're a good actress. But not that good.' And then he continued down the path. Ace wondered if she'd been insulted or not.

'A power link ...' Saul was pondering. 'How do I do that?'

'Well, it sounds like you should know.' Peter was running his hands over the smooth surface of the gem.

With a shout, he stepped backwards. 'Dad!' he exclaimed. 'Dad! But you're dead!'

Emily ran to him and pulled him back from reaching out again. 'That's what I felt,' she exclaimed. 'It takes you back to the past. It's full of memories.'

'I saw my father ...' Peter rubbed his brow. 'He was opening an old box of books in the loft, cutting the string with a pair of scissors. I saw it so clearly, like I was there.' The mathematician looked up at the rafters. 'Is this what this thing is, Saul, a time machine?'

'No. No, I see it now.' Saul became excited. 'I felt its power when you touched the gem. It is a doorway into the mind, a tunnel into the depths of memory.'

'A tunnel?' Emily stared at the gem, and, before her eyes, it dissolved into an endless kaleidoscope of vanishing purples and blues. The colours formed a tunnel that blazed away to a vanishing point. 'I see what you mean.'

'That's the same effect that I saw outside the church when we were travelling.' Peter raised a finger and tapped his nose. 'So this is a time vortex too.'

'Which will lead to where the Doctor is!' Trelaw concluded triumphantly. The Hutchings looked at him. 'Well, I'm not a complete philistine, you know,' he smiled.

Wyrmboyle sprinted up the mountainside, regretting his host

form's short legs. The storm was buffeting harder and harder, the winds nearly plucking the small boy off his feet. The Wyrm was shouting powerful codes into the breeze, hoping to control some aspects of the rapidly disintegrating datascape. Nothing worked. The world was falling into chaos.

In moments, it would all be over.

The Doctor had reached the bottom of the spiral path, and stood at the end of the bridge which, as Ace saw, was a thin span of organic-looking rock, like something formed by sediment in a cave. The lower surface was hung with stalactites. The whole scene felt wet, horribly biological. The pit below echoed with a distant sound that felt like breathing. Sharp gusts of hot air were buffeting up from below.

'How do we get down there?' she shouted, seeing no handholds on the smooth, vertical walls.

'We fall,' the Doctor muttered. His gaze was sweeping the edge of the crater above him. 'Come on. I'm not going to die because you're late. Not again.'

'Professor, what's down there?' Ace had thought she'd seen a movement in the depths below, a stirring of liquid darkness.

'I don't know.' The Doctor glanced at her and smiled, sadly. 'How long is the coast of Britain?'

'What? No idea.' Ace was staring down into the pit, wondering if this was really important at the moment. Shakily, the Doctor reached out a hand and raised her head to listen to him.

'Don't gaze into the void,' he advised. 'Nietzsche said something similar, also interesting things about fighting monsters. Pity about the rest of it. No. This is important. You could measure the coastline, couldn't you?'

'Yeah, 'spose so.'

'But how carefully do you measure?' The Doctor was deadly serious. 'With a metre ruler? With a tape measure? Do you map every pebble, every tiny rockpool, even if they remained after the tide?'

'Well —'

'You could go down to atomic level, making finer and finer

164

measurements. You find more and more length, more little details. The length of the coast is infinite, the measurement depends on your distance from it.'

'That's stupid.' Ace checked herself. For a moment she had sounded like her citydream self. She was a citizen of the universe, so she was gonna listen, right?

'Perhaps. Like the edge of a snowflake or like this place. The dimensions are fractional, the length of information is infinite . . .'

Above them, night was falling. The Doctor talked faster as the darkness of the sky above became of the same texture as that of the pit below. 'You can express shapes like that as equations. The Timewyrm virus is an equation like that.'

'You mean it's infinite?'

'Yes. Fractal. Its appearance depends only on the scale you view it from. Like that bully, Boyle. He's not important, he's very important, he's the whole world. Are you following me?'

'Yeah.' Ace quickly nodded. She had a horrible feeling that this was the last lesson, that this wisdom was an epitaph, something to take with her.

'Using the equations you can write poetry, verse that corresponds to the dimensions of the Wyrm itself. I learnt a poem like that, a long time ago. I found it deep in my own dreams, instructed by a great teacher, before I found out all of what I am. The Timewyrm doesn't know its own potential, either. It can't hear the equations that make it, and it can't hear the message I sent, either.'

Ace was lost. 'I don't know what you mean, Professor,' she sighed. The darkness was closing in. A low twilight was winding its way through the surroundings, and seemed to be infesting her thoughts as well.

'Life is a fractal thing, Ace,' said the Doctor, his face hidden in shadow, his voice very far away. 'From a distance, a distance like Hemmings saw it from, it's very simple, a question of cause and effect. You push, it moves.' Ace could barely glimpse him now, fading as he was into the dark. Far away, she could hear songs like ancient memories, female voices calling the Doctor home. 'Life isn't like that. The smallest things have the biggest consequences. The beat of a butterfly's wing may topple a civilization. Life is chaos, and chaos never dies.'

'No, Doctor!' called Ace. 'Don't die!' She looked around, trying to see through the gathering darkness. 'People need you! I need you! Don't go!'

'Death awaits . . .' the voice roared from the rim of the crater, a blast of flame illuminating the darkness. The Timewyrm dropped onto the bridge, its arms held wide, its nostrils belching gouts of fire into the night. It was majestic and triumphant. 'It is time! Come to me, Doctor!'

In the glare of fire, Ace glimpsed that the Doctor had fallen and was lying at the edge of the crater, his body still. The Timewyrm strode forward. Ace stepped into its way.

'Move aside, girl!' the virus snarled. 'He must die that I shall live! And I will live!'

'So go ahead.' Ace bit her lip and summoned all her courage. 'Try it.'

The two enemies stared at each other as the darkness closed in.

'If I were to use the rhythm that I was receiving earlier,' Saul muttered, 'I could power up this gate, and somebody could go and visit the Doctor.'

'Let's do it.' Peter pulled off his jacket and threw it on to a pew. 'Ready when you are.'

'But –' began Emily.

'It will require more than mere power,' Saul continued quickly. 'I will be able to open a – this is all merely instinctive to me, what did you call it?'

'A time vortex.' Peter frowned.

'I will be able to open a time vortex corridor into the Doctor's location, but it will be necessary for somebody else to compute a path down the corridor. Somebody who can picture mathematical topography as we work.'

'Very well,' Trelaw nodded, stepping forward. 'Peter will do that work, and I shall go. If the corridor does lead into memory, as you call it. Well, perhaps I am to be allowed a glimpse through the veil.'

'It would kill you,' Saul blurted, trying to be matter of fact.

'Your heart has been pushed too far — we have no idea of what is on the other side of the gate.'

'Wait a minute!' Emily shouted, waving her hands to quieten the debate. 'I'll go. I'm young, I'm strong, and I don't have to do any maths.'

'No.' Peter shook his head. 'Absolutely not.'

'Listen. That's why I'm here. Don't you see that we've been put here for a reason? A whole bundle of tiny circumstances brought us here, tiny chances. We can't see the whole picture yet, why I was given that baby, for instance. But there's a plan at work. And God, I want to go.' Emily reached out to touch the edge of the spiralling vortex field. 'I want to see what's down that tunnel.'

'I cannot help but agree,' chorused Saul. 'Emily must go.'

Peter looked at his wife, hurt. 'How can I persuade you not to?' he whispered.

'You can't.' She kissed his forehead tenderly. 'You can just make sure I get to where I'm going. Listen, if you didn't want adventures, you shouldn't have married me.'

'Maybe I didn't have a choice,' muttered Peter.

The Timewyrm was roaring as the darkness closed in, little bursts of blue flame puffing from its nostrils.

'Don't be a fool,' it rumbled. 'I can destroy you now without compunction! You are no longer of use.'

'Yippie ay-ai, toerag,' Ace grinned, wiping tears on to her sleeve. 'It's a good day to die.'

'You will die anyway.' The Timewyrm grinned steel. 'You do not understand —'

'Too right. So tell me.'

Emily had an urge to hold her nose as she stood on the edge of the medallion's gateway, preparing to jump. She felt like a little girl, ready to hop into the pool for the first time.

'Are you absolutely sure?' Peter was saying. 'I'm quite prepared to go if you don't want to.'

'That would be impossible,' Saul chimed in. 'It would be impossible to link with your brain as you moved down the hyperspace tunnel.'

'Shut up, Saul,' muttered Peter, holding his wife.

'No,' murmured Emily. 'I want to do this. To save their lives — and I think it's time that somebody saved that girl — but also because it's going to be interesting. That would be motive enough for you, dear, wouldn't it?'

Peter grinned and kissed her. 'I won't let anything happen to you,' he promised. He had taken a deep breath, and was trying not to cry. She, as always, was keeping a stiff upper lip.

'Don't worry.' Emily gave Peter a final kiss and stepped towards the medallion gate. 'Ready, Saul?'

Peter felt a gentle mental tendril settle amongst his beloved equations. It seemed to delight in them as much as he did, if in a more instinctive, unlearned, way, and he found himself experiencing the fond feeling of brotherhood that he associated with talking to fellow mathematicians.

'Ready,' the church chorused. Peter found himself saying it at the same time.

'God bless you, my child.' Trelaw touched Emily's head and looked into her eyes. 'May His power keep you safe, wherever you go.'

'I appreciate that, reverend.' Emily took a deep breath. 'I really do. Okay, here we go.' With a quick grin over her shoulder, the woman stepped forward, flinging herself into the purple-blue vortex. She spun away, getting smaller and smaller until she was a dot vanishing into the distance.

'Contact maintained,' sang Saul. 'We have locked on to the Doctor's harmonic pattern, and are calculating a link ...'

Peter found himself visualizing multi-dimensional topography with fierce speed, aware that Emily's life depended on the precision of his work. A couple of times he panicked, and nearly missed a contour, but Saul had the wit to see trends at least and was able to correct him. It was like being connected to a powerful computer, their collective resources being used to fly a distant kite through a thunderstorm.

A living kite. A kite that Peter Hutchings loved more than ever before.

* * *

The Doctor's thoughts were a flock of birds, flapping up in the path of the ferryman's barge. The ferryman caught the glint in one bird's eye and frowned, his worry spurring him to reach the dreaming spires of architecture that were his home.

'So close,' said the sound of the birds' wings. 'So daring.'

The third Doctor was standing on the battlements of a proud fortress, simple designs covering its walls. He stood alone, his hands on his hips, staring out for the first sign of attack. He had no need of soldiers. The Doctor's thoughts came to him as the crying of a wolf in the far distance. He frowned, but his gaze did not falter.

The Librarian was running through the library, shunting aside books from the blaze that was consuming the place. He was holding up his hands in worry, scuttling between the blazing racks as fast as he could go.

The Doctor's thoughts came to him in the form of blackened shards, blowing into his path like a fall of leaves. Some of them were still alight with decaying ideas.

'Am I on my way?' said the shards. 'To the zone that is prepared for me?'

'No!' shouted the Librarian angrily. 'You are destroying the Library! There is no life for any of us now!'

'Too late,' sighed the burning scraps, crackling. 'It didn't work.'

'Then get back and make it work!' The Librarian threw down a volume on the floor. 'There will be no peace for you, no peace for any of us, until you win!'

The shards fluttered away, the flames having left them.

The Librarian raised his nose and nodded, proudly. Perhaps the youngster was finally paying attention to him.

Emily spun down a corridor of voices, flashes of experience bursting all around her.

Darkness, war, too much to remember, too much to die fully. Something ancient and powerful crying its defiance as it was destroyed, its blood bursting over Emily in a burst of scarlet.

But it lived on, in centuries that dashed past like translucent ghosts. Change, change, change . . . the wheel sped round, the cosmos expanded, whole worlds rose and fell.

In all this time, there was only Emily . . . and the Other.

A squeal of forgetful pain, like brakes being applied, and Emily found herself shrieking too as she fought to clear her lungs of liquid and to gulp air. Things she remembered were forgotten. Birth thoughts blossomed around her, and Emily's tears streamed at the closeness of a mother's breast. Rough surroundings, someone watching from the door, a grand power that washed away into . . .

Bitter fights, little wars, a dark child that seethed with jealousy, smashed glass, time running wild, and teachers roaring their rage. Robed figures shunting this way and that through endless corridors, endless plots, dark whispers, and young eyes that saw it all and understood nothing.

One-eye in his hood, smiling and nodding, seeming to see Emily's flight and welcome her. Before him stood a bloom, a . . . my God! It was beautiful, it shimmered with an internal rainbow . . . and it was gone, flashed by, never to return, off on a burst of roses. Sadness eclipsed her, and she smelt gunfire and death, a figure stalking purposefully through the buildings, pulling a hood over his stark features.

Time to run. Time to get away from this old place. Time to change the world.

The memories swept past her, speeding up into a babble of voices, one voice, every voice. They dashed over her, as she whisked down the time vortex, their personalities washing over her like the tides.

Such impertinence these humans had, bursting in like this! And at such a crucial time! Why, their presence could mean so much. Yes, perhaps it was for the best — after all, my goodness, there were some horrible things in this universe, things that wouldn't ever be nice to anybody, my word! Humans did get in a pickle sometimes and it was dashed uncomfortable being stuck on one planet with them. It was really quite intolerable, and here was the Minister, on the phone again! It was like some ridiculous cocktail party . . . well, I always did like a party, but if I was holding one I'm sure I wouldn't be invited. Silly sort of things, humans, you know, short life spans, far too few limbs, but still, still! There's something rather charming about them, I think. Absolutely. They're very good company in difficult circumstances and I wouldn't have it any other way. Trying sometimes, but in general, I think they're absolutely splendid! Splendid? Splendid? I have always found them to be trivial, annoying, and unfortunately ubiquitous! I can take them or leave them, preferably the latter. Yes, take them, look after them, use them in games of skill or chance. That's what they'd say, isn't it? Doctor, heal thyself!'

'Doctor ...' Emily found herself saying, 'you've lived one hell of a life ...'

The Timewyrm regarded Ace with its stolen eyes. They were glinting with a humour it might have inherited from the body it occupied. Around them the world had grown dark, and things in the Pit below were baying and calling. With every second, the darkness and confusion increased. This seemed to delight the dragon.

'You think that this world is the afterlife?'

'No.' Ace frowned. 'Not really. Dunno what it is.'

'It is my natural habitat. I am a computer virus.'

'We're in a computer?'

'Let me finish. I am a computer virus that can live in any sophisticated data processing system. I can take over brains like Boyle's by implanting mechanisms within them, or I can inhabit them totally. A normal human can only fight my control for a short time. This brain has been fighting me for months.'

'This is a mind.' Ace looked around with a new realization. 'This is a person's memory, their dreams.'

'Exactly.' The Timewyrm took a step forward and bared its teeth, hissing. 'I brought you, Boyle and Hemmings here as pure data, pure memory. You stand on the bridge between the brain's twin lobes, above the pit of the unconscious. Can't you guess where you are?'

'Oh my God.' A horrible suspicion was dawning on Ace. She looked down at the fallen form of the Doctor, the blood that was spreading across the rock around him. 'No!'

'Yes! This isn't just a mind, a vessel for my intelligence. This is a powerful entity, a lord of space and time. Do you not see, human?'

The Timewyrm's claws burst from their sockets and the creature bellowed its secret until it echoed from the depths of the Pit below.

'This is the mind of the Doctor!'

11: Sympathy For The Doctor

'How may I live without my name?
I have given you my soul; leave me my name!'

The Crucible Arthur Miller.

Ace stared at the creature that stood, exulting, in the middle of the synaptic bridge. 'So this is all the Professor's mind?'

'Indeed. Five of his previous selves are here. When a Time Lord regenerates, a copy of the old personality is held in the memory space, prior to transfer into the Gallifreyan Matrix data bank. Most of his species hold their ghosts sleeping. The Doctor is, as always, individual and thus vulnerable. When he released the personality of the third Doctor to aid him, I took advantage of his mental confusion and planted a tiny seed of myself in his memory space, a bolthole in case the chase for me ever became too dangerous. I hid, as humans say, under his nose.'

'Five?' was all Ace could say.

The Timewyrm was too busy orating to pay attention. 'When the second Doctor visited the Doctor in dreams, I was there, gaining ground. Now I am ready to take over the whole data-scape, and the body with it. When the Doctor's mind is dead, the Timewyrm shall be truly unfettered!' The creature strode forward, its claws springing from their sheaths.

'Oh yeah?' Ace was trying to be cool about this, but it really did look like this was the end.

'Once I had brought you into my kingdom here, I tricked you into interfacing with the Doctor and his TARDIS. You focused their psionic power on the church and brought it to the moon. Do you know why?'

'No.' To be honest, Ace didn't know what the hell the Timewyrm was on about, but if the beast was talking, it wasn't attacking the Doctor.

'Because the death of a Time Lord mind releases a vast amount of mental energy, energy I shall use the being known as Saul to focus into a huge explosive pulse. The moon's orbit will be disturbed, it will fall closer and closer to Earth. Before it destroys the planet, there will be one long night, one vast total eclipse in its final orbit. Billions of timestreams will be altered or destroyed. Billions of choices, of alternate possibilities, will be wiped out in the face of that terrible certainty.' The Timewyrm continued its slow pace forward, laughing at its words. 'Is my scheme not glorious? Is it not perfect? I gain a permanent physical form, the powers of a Time Lord and his craft, and a vast new feeding ground. My power will be infinite.'

'Yeah, so what have you done to me?' Ace remembered the brick, shadow against the sun, the crack of stone on bone.

'When I have the Doctor's form, I will alter your timestream. You will be killed by Chad Boyle in that playground incident. Chad has told me that he saw the Doctor outside the school gates, and he made no attempt to stop your death. That is me, girl, watching as you die.'

'Why? Why do you want to do that?'

'Because that is part of what undermines the Doctor's mind here, your instability. I am the Timewyrm, I have no more malice than a volcano or a waterfall. Now,' it stroked a claw on the opposing palm. 'Time to die.'

Ace stepped carefully back. There was no hope left now. Darkness surrounded them, the Doctor was on the verge of dying from his wounds anyway. What would he do, facing this creature with no reason left for hope at all?

Yeah. He'd fight. She had some nitro-nine left, but she

couldn't use it on this thin bridge without collapsing it. Falling into the Pit was, despite the Professor's plans, not something she wanted to do. 'Sides, the Timewyrm could fly.

What other weapons did she have? Well — it was worth a try.

'Professor? Doctor? Can you hear me?' she thought to herself. From the Pit below, there came a faint cry, the noise, she guessed, of the Professor's unconscious mind answering her.

The Timewyrm was grinning deadly metal at her retreat.

'I need to fight it. I need to defend you.' Ace concentrated. 'Give me a sword.'

She didn't expect it to happen so quickly. From the depths of the Pit, a streak of brilliant light flashed upwards, illuminating the whole landscape for a split second.

And in her hand there was a sword. Exactly the one she had visualized.

Ace dived at the Timewyrm and slashed the weapon across the creature's abdomen. The beast screamed in rage and a sword flickered into its own gleaming fist.

The beast hacked straight for Ace's head, the blade missing by an inch. Ace sidestepped and stabbed for the creature's legs, but it parried. Up, across, down, the combatants attacked and matched each other, blow for blow.

A knot of swords brought them face to face, the Timewyrm's strength gradually overcoming Ace's determination.

'I'm not going to let you kill the Doctor!' Ace shouted into the Timewyrm's face. 'I'll die first!'

'Where did you learn to fight like this, human?' spat the Wyrm.

'On the playing fields of Perivale, scumbag!' Ace saw the glint in the metallic nostrils, and kicked the beast in the chest, swishing her sword aside. The jet of flame blasted over her head.

The Timewyrm slashed forward, taking advantage of Ace's lack of balance, and pushed her backwards along the narrow bridge, the young woman desperately blocking the flurry of savage blows.

'Your precious Doctor will soon be mine!' roared the Timewyrm, enjoying the combat. 'You are just prolonging his agony! He is only an idea in his own head now ...' Ace found her sword knocked aside, on to the bridge, just out of reach. The Timewyrm raised its sword for the killing stroke. 'Like you, he is only a dream!'

'A dream to some,' the voice growled from behind the Timewyrm. The Doctor was standing there, his face in shadow, his eyes shining. 'A nightmare to others!'

He grabbed the Timewyrm's small frame, and with a cry of effort threw it over the side of the bridge. With a gout of flame and a horrible roar, the monster plunged into the abyss.

'Saul!' the Doctor shouted to the sky, blood running down his face in streams. *'Now!'*

The chamber exploded with white light.

Emily burst out of the time vortex above a fantastical landscape, a wheel of green fields, great libraries, fortresses and shining towers. Perhaps it had been dark a moment before her entrance, but now the place was echoing green, illuminated by a glorious dawn.

She was falling through clouds, through blue skies, and for a moment she thought she glimpsed the whole of this world, a whole person, with a tremendous burden and a great sadness . . . and then the clouds closed in again. When she emerged once more, she could only see the details of the ground coming up to meet her. A Pit was opening up before her, and only a slender bridge lay across it.

This wasn't right! She was going to die! How –

The world changed, reached out and helped her.

Laughing with joy, Emily slid at tremendous speed down the banisters of a vast spiral staircase. The staircase was pure white, and the medallion gate shimmered at the top. The staircase was organic, made of gleaming bone, and down the steps beside her cascaded a stream of pure water. The end of the banister was approaching.

Emily flew off it, and found herself sitting in the Doctor's arms.

'Hello,' he said. 'Welcome to my brain. Sorry the place is such a mess. This is my friend Ace.'

He put her down gently and Ace realized that he had been

saving his strength for this last effort. Pale and shivering, he staggered forward, and dropped to his knees in the water that cascaded down the steps, over the bridge and into the void below.

He reached forward, took two handfuls of water and splashed his face with them. The claw wound vanished. 'Saul's power,' he muttered as Ace looked on amazed. He quickly took some more of the water to drink. 'Mending my data structures. We haven't much time.'

'Isn't the Timewyrm dead?' Ace had been staring at Emily and had found her gaze met by something the woman from Perivale wasn't very comfortable with. A kind of maternal love. Both would have said something, but the Doctor's expression was urgent. His wounds were sealing and vanishing as he stood up.

'No. Only distracted. We've got to get up that stairway to the time vortex. The Timewyrm will have realized that Saul's breached its security. They'll be coming.'

'Who?' asked Emily. She was looking around, amazed, full of questions. But she could see the answer for herself. Out of the material of the stormy plain, creatures were forming. Daleks and UNIT soldiers, Time Lords and the horrific dead companions that Ace had witnessed earlier. They started to shamble towards the edge of the pit, calling and crying for the Doctor to stay. Their expressions ranged from imploring to threatening.

'All my doubts and fears,' the Doctor whispered grimly. 'And the occasional famished aspiration. They will not give me up easily.'

They ran up the stairs. It was hard going, Ace quickly realized, against the tide of water that was flooding down. She hauled herself along, step by step, but she still had questions.

'Professor, who's she and what's she doing here?'

'She's Emily Hutchings, an old friend.'

'But I don't know you,' panted Emily. 'That is to say —'

'You feel like you've always known me. Yes. You will.' The Doctor smiled a secret smile. 'She and an intelligent church known as Saul have helped me to trick the Timewyrm. It was

177

expecting me to go down the Pit, not up out of it. It didn't know I had help. It thought it had brought the church to the moon for its own ends ...'

'But I thought it knew all you did!' Ace exclaimed. 'I thought — but that means —' a grin began to spread over her face. 'My God! This is part of the game, isn't it? You're playing a game!'

The Doctor stared at her for a moment as if surprised. An old smile spread over his features. 'Yes, and I'm winning. As always.'

'You really are a bastard!' Ace laughed.

'I don't know,' the Doctor muttered, reaching out to touch her hair. 'Perhaps we'll find out.' Ace grabbed the hand and clutched it, grinning. Then she grabbed Emily's. The three of them pushed upwards against the current, seeing the top of the stairway looming closer.

The creatures had started swarming up the stairs after them. Emily glanced back over her shoulder as she ran. Lord, the creatures were faster than they were. They were catching up. If she didn't still feel the pull of Peter and Saul, the invitation home, and if she didn't have such a desire to help this pair of adventurers, this place would have driven her crazy. As it was, it felt like a dream, a glorious adventure, and she was treating it as such. She had a feeling that this was something the Doctor did, involve people whose lives were bleak and show them how terrible an exciting life could be.

How terrible and how wonderful. Good God. She looked at Ace beside her. The girl's cheeks were red with exertion, and her face was somehow full of joy, the kind of joy you get from facing your greatest fear and conquering it. Oh, why aren't you my daughter?

She looked at the Doctor, and was shocked. It was that same thought, about facing your fear.

The Doctor hadn't. And so, he was still terribly vulnerable. Emily had a bad feeling about this.

They sprinted up the vast staircase, the shimmering form of the medallion gate getting ever closer. Behind them, the Doctor's demons were getting closer too, their steps polluting the gushing water, turning it a brackish brown. Their howls rang across the Time Lord's internal landscape.

With the gate a bare two hundred metres away, Ace felt herself falling behind. Her strength as she ran up the staircase was declining, more than it should have. Of course, she was tired, but it was more than that, it was like . . .

She tried to remember Iceworld, and couldn't.

But that meant − no. That would mean that the Professor wasn't going to win, that she was still going to die in that playground.

He seemed confident. But then, he always did.

The demons were close behind, led by the blazing boy Adric, little puffs of blue flame coming from his mouth as his insides boiled. A metal star on his breast was slowly melting across his form, contorting into a strange swirl of colour.

Emily reached the gate, and looked back. The Doctor was staggering up the last few steps, battered, bruised, but with a strange compulsion on his face. He turned back.

'Come on then, Ace. The final −' But she wasn't able to come on. She'd tripped on a lower step, and the demon horde was surging against the tide up towards her. The Doctor started to hop back down the steps after her but Emily grabbed him by the collar.

'No you don't. I'm not going back without you. Let me.'

'No, that's not right, that's not the way it should work . . .' The Doctor looked around desperately. Ace had stood up, elbowed the burning boy in the face, and was splashing her way fiercely up towards them. The Doctor reached out with his umbrella and his companion grabbed the end, using it to haul herself up against the flow of the waterfall. Dark hands flailed and grabbed the air behind her.

She was almost on the same step as the Doctor when one claw clasped and held. The gnarled hand of the ageing woman, Kingdom, bit through Ace's jacket and clasped her arm. Others followed it, despite the young woman's kicking and desperate shouting. The Doctor hauled harder on his umbrella.

Realizing that they were about to be overrun, Emily made a decision. Clasping the Doctor's hand firmly, she jumped into the vortex once more.

'Come on Doctor, we're going home!'

The tidal force of time wrenched her away into the void, whirling off along the corridor, held to the gate only by the Doctor. He was hauled after her, pulled off his feet until the only thing keeping him back was the hold he kept on his umbrella. Ace hung on to the thin end grimly, more and more hands grasping her and pulling her back.

The Doctor felt his muscles tearing, caught as he was between the rush of the vortex and the strength of his inner demons. He roared in agony, his hand turning white with the effort of holding on.

Ace looked at his face, contorted with pain. His eyes met hers, full of human failing, human courage and sadness. But there was something else there as well. Heroes have feet of clay, sure, but the Doctor was more than a hero. He was a principle, something that applied universally, almost a definition in the face of meaningless horror. The good that triumphed over evil.

Ace knew then that she hadn't a hope. There were just too many of the demons. If they kept on pulling, they'd get the Doctor and this woman Emily as well.

Ace felt the tears burning her cheeks, but managed a grim smile. God, she had done more, gone farther, than she'd ever dreamed. She'd danced the best dance in the whole damn universe. All because of him. All because he'd seen something in her that mirrored himself. The will to win against insurmountable odds, the courage to stand up and be different, the attitude needed to kick arse.

Well, Doctor, she thought. See it now.

'Bye, Professor,' Ace yelled against her tears. 'Remember me!'

And she let go of the umbrella.

The Doctor shot off down the butterfly tunnel of the time vortex. His voice echoed in a single shout.

'Ace!'

And the horror on his face was terrible to see.

12: Cruciform Blues

When I am dead, I hope it may be said:
his sins were scarlet, but his books were read.

Hilaire Belloc.

Trelaw looked down at the sleeping figure of the Doctor on the altar, wondering who should concern him more, this man or Saul and Peter, both lost in trancelike mutterings.

The medallion gate was humming with power. And as Trelaw glanced into it he was amazed to see two tiny figures spin into view, growing bigger with each second amongst the maelstrom.

Emily leaped out, laughing, and grabbed the vicar's arms. 'It was wonderful, it's all so strange, I never imagined ...' She turned to look over her shoulder. 'Wait a minute, I had the Doctor with me.'

'I have returned him to his proper body,' Saul chimed, and Peter woke, realizing that his mathematical dreams had been real. He clutched Emily to him and groaned with relief.

'We did it, love,' she told him proudly, 'we rescued them.'

The Doctor was stirring. Trelaw looked down at him, concerned.

'Ace, I've had the strangest dream,' the Time Lord muttered, blinking. He raised a hand to his face. 'I dreamt that I woke up, and it's all true!'

He sat up suddenly, and looked at his hands, as if searching for blood.

'No! No!' he yelled wildly. 'That isn't right! Ace! *Ace!*'

Trelaw put a calming hand on his shoulder. 'Doctor, you're back in the land of the living. What happened?'

The Doctor shrugged off the reverend's hand and sprang up, ignoring his rescuers completely. He looked round the church, still seemingly dumbstruck. 'That was the game. I isolate the Timewyrm in my head using Ace as bait, then pull her out and use my mental power to crush it out of existence . . . and I got it wrong . . . I sacrificed her just as Ishtar said I would. *I got it wrong!*' He slammed his fist into the wall, and when he looked at it, there was blood on his knuckles.

'Doctor!' shouted Saul, and the Time Lord spun to see the dark form of the Timewyrm speeding towards the mouth of the medallion gate.

'No!' muttered the Doctor. 'You're not getting out that way. Close!' With a roar that diminished as its size did, the medallion shrunk down to its proper size and the Doctor pocketed it.

'Please, Doctor,' asked Emily sadly, on the verge of tears. 'Tell me what went wrong. I thought I'd rescued her.'

'You did your best.' The Doctor collapsed into a pew and glanced back at Ace's comatose form. 'The fault is mine alone. I thought we would all get out on Saul's carrier beam. I've had this escape prepared for a long time. I was aware that I was being controlled in my sleep. One of my other selves had warned me. A lot of them cropped up in dreams, telling me various things . . . and I recognized the inner landscape instantly.' The Doctor stared down at his hands, flexing them, as if horrified at their lack of strength. 'I had hoped that the Timewyrm would concentrate all its resources on taking me over internally, and it did. In the meantime, I concentrated on building up my mental defences. Now, I have it trapped inside my mind. The only being or thing containing the Timewyrm virus is me. It can't get out, but it has Ace's soul inside with it.'

'Hardly stalemate, then.' A deep voice echoed across the church. In the corner stood an ancient, bearded figure, one eye blazing out from under a dark hood. The being had appeared without a sound.

'What?' shouted Saul. Then, more softly, 'Forgive me, you took me somewhat by surprise.'

Peter sat down heavily. 'I've had enough of this,' he sighed.

The Doctor bowed to the Hermit. 'I was expecting you.'

'Indeed. You employed the rhyme I taught you, the one you learned from the heart of your own being. You rescued yourself. What else is there to consider? I have watched you, Doctor. I know that you do not hesitate to risk innocents in your war with the dark powers of the universe. This human chose to journey with you. She knew the risk. For the good of the whole universe, end this now. Make the final move.'

'I . . .' The Doctor walked to the corner of the church, shaking his head.

'If you keep the Timewyrm inside you, it will gradually erode your inner defences. It will torment you with guilt and grief. Then it will consume you, and you will have given it your form, the TARDIS, all it needs to feed without end. It is a cuckoo in your nest. Destroy it now.'

The Doctor paused, and then nodded. 'Yes,' he said simply.

Once more without sound, the figure was gone.

'And who,' Trelaw blinked, amazed, 'was that?'

'An old teacher,' muttered the Doctor. 'An old friend. And he's right. Even now I can feel the Timewyrm wandering through the Library, distorting my memories, altering my ethical perspectives. Soon the damage will become permanent. I must end this.'

Emily stepped forward. 'Listen, I don't understand very much of this, but I won't let you kill the girl, even if it does mean stopping the Timewyrm.'

'Won't *let*?' the Doctor rounded on her, his voice a roar, his teeth bared. Then fear flickered across his face. With a grimace of mental effort, he reached out to touch Emily's shoulder gently. 'Forgive me. It's happening already.'

Trelaw looked carefully at the Doctor's face. It seemed as if a shadow was playing across his brow, creeping about every line.

* * *

Ace expected sudden death, was ready for the claws to tear her apart, the flame or the ice to kill her. Instead, the phantoms of the Doctor's psyche simply gathered round her, a hushed awe on their faces.

The water ceased to flow down the steps once the gate had vanished. Ace sat down on a step and glanced up at the army of monstrosities, the fatally wounded UNIT soldiers, the monsters and the martyrs.

'Well?' she demanded. 'What're you waiting for? Get it over with!'

The blazing boy stepped forward and bowed to her, his face erupting in little explosions of flesh. 'We salute you. You are one of us now.'

'Listen, mate, I did what I did deliberately. I'm no sacrifice.'

'But that's the whole point!' the ageing woman croaked, laying a wrinkling hand on Ace's head. 'We gave our lives freely also. The Doctor still regrets it, still keeps us in mind, still maintains us through his guilt.'

'Is that it then? You're here because he feels guilty?'

'Indeed.' The shivering woman, Katarina, kissed Ace's boot. 'I heard priests say while I was alive that we are but the imaginings of the gods. This proves it.'

Ace withdrew her boot. 'Where do you lot, well, live?'

The blazing boy pointed downwards. 'In the Pit. We live deep within the lowermost reaches of the Doctor's mind. There his conscience is still alive, forever suffering, enchained.'

'What happens if I free it?' The monsters looked at each other, murmuring.

'We would cease to exist,' rumbled the giant in the angular mask.

'Ah,' murmured Ace. 'That's definitely something I'm not planning to do then.'

'But you must!' the blazing boy pleaded before her, his hands melting as he did so. 'Do you not think we crave death? Why, this is Hell, nor are we out of it!'

'But what would it do to the Doctor?'

The reptile to whom Ace had spoken earlier emerged from the crowd. 'We are creatures of repression. The Doctor believes that he has silenced the voice of his conscience, believes that since declaring himself to be at war, he can reconcile himself to the deaths he has caused. That is not true. If he can face his conscience, allow it once more into the light, into its proper place within the ecology of this mind, then he will have the strength to see that there is another solution to his dilemma. He must not kill again.'

'If you lot know this, why doesn't he?'

'We try to tell him,' sighed the ageing woman, 'but he doesn't listen.'

That made sense, thought Ace. She'd been quite keen on her conscience, used her inner impulses as a guide when there was nobody else to talk to. Somebody like the Doctor, who'd got this vast universal hype to live up to, he'd put a pillow over his head at night and try not to dream. She briefly wondered what Johnny Chess's internal landscape looked like, or hers for that matter.

'Right,' Ace stood up. 'Let's make him listen.' She put a hand to her brow to shield her eyes from the light that now infused the datascape, and spied her sword, still embedded in the synapse bridge.

'Come on, let's go and have a look at that Pit.'

After a short walk down the stairway, which was crumbling now that the medallion at the top had vanished, they came to the edge of the Pit. Ace contemplated the crater of grey matter that surrounded the entrance to the abyss. She was standing on a gusty precipice, grass on top, brain below.

'If this is all an illusion, why does this bit look so like a real brain?' she asked the group of strange figures around her in general.

Corporal Higgins, a UNIT trooper who cradled his head under the crook of his arm, raised a hand. 'Well, miss, I think it's probably the Doctor's way of dealing with something he doesn't fully understand. He treats it in the most basic way possible. Down there are powerful archetypal forces, gods as Jung would have it. The Doctor prefers to indicate the reality of the situation around there.'

'Bit like you, right? You all talk like the Doctor, not like your real selves.'

'He can't be expected to keep us fully in mind all of the time,' muttered the ageing woman, now back to being quite young. 'We're like the characters in a book he's continually rewriting. If he were anything less than honest, he'd have rewritten us so much that our deaths would have been our fault.'

'But they're not exactly his fault, are they?'

'That's a sore point,' began Kingdom.

'And the subject of some debate amongst the lads,' finished Higgins.

'Well,' said Ace, fixing a piton from her rucksack into the cliff and tying the end of a nylon rope to it. 'If this is a book, it's a severely strange one.' She put on a pair of leather half-gloves and began her descent. 'Don't try this at home, kids,' she muttered to herself.

'Be careful,' Kingdom called after her. 'The Timewyrm must still be down there, as well as all the archetypal gods. The company will be pretty dangerous.'

'That's okay,' Ace shouted back. 'I used to go for the drinks at the Brixton Academy.'

The climb wasn't the hardest that Ace had ever attempted, but it was certainly the weirdest. The material she climbed throbbed with life, and it was all she could do not to wince every time she put in a new piton. A lot of the descent involved free climbing, and glancing at the landscape of the abyss didn't exactly inspire her to continue. Darkness seemed to go on forever beneath her, and strange echoes and lights blossomed occasionally in the murk. Once, she hailed something that seemed to assume a flying shape, but all that came back was a strange, laughing echo.

Lightning jumped across the pit, setting her backpack ablaze with a minor strike. She thumped it out against the wall. A strange heat was rising from whatever was below, and a powerful musk came with it on the upward-flowing air. The scent spoke of untold longing, agonies of despair.

Ace bit her lip and concentrated on climbing.

Eventually, a landscape started to reveal itself. The bottom of the Pit was covered in golden sand, and small tunnels ran off in all directions.

Ace climbed thankfully off of the Pit wall, pulling out the final peg, and looked around. Choose a tunnel, any tunnel.

The one she chose led, after a short walk, to the outside world. Sort of.

An oppressive, stormy sky swirled crimson above a stark, angular landscape, full of sharp-edged rocks. The whole effect was alien, like this was a nightmare version of some territory from the Doctor's youth.

Some of the rocks looked like gravestones.

In the distance, and distance in this wasteland was a hard concept to get your head around, Ace thought she saw a group of figures. They were standing there, on the horizon, apparently watching her.

Well, nothing else to do. She set off in that general direction. She was determined not to think until she'd found this conscience, whatever it looked like, and restored it to its proper place, up out of the Pit. It was like her, when she'd had the chance to sneak that expensive book about explosives out of that bookshop in London. She'd turned back, and put it back on the shelves, but instead of feeling all righteous, she'd spent the rest of the day dissing herself for being a coward. Well screwed up.

If the Professor could defeat the Timewyrm, but she couldn't be brought back to life, then maybe she could live the same sort of afterlife as his old incarnations, a bit of Berlin in the 1930s, fighting the fascists, or Paris in the 1880s, flirting and plotting with everyone she'd ever fancied.

Getting closer to her destination, Ace counted three figures, gathered around a cauldron. A certain suspicion, drawn from English Lit. and a dozen comedy sketches, made her know what to expect.

Three women stood over the cauldron. A young girl with blonde tresses, slightly younger than Ace, a Rubenesque woman with dark eyes and darker red hair, and an old crone with snowy white hair. They looked up as Ace approached.

'Hi, anybody seen a conscience around here?'

'She has come,' whispered the crone.

Ace knew this was going to be difficult.

'Come here, child,' murmured the mature woman, her voice full of vaguely North Country experience. 'There is something we must show you.'

Strangely, Ace felt quite at home with these three, as if they were old friends she couldn't place. She wandered over to the cauldron. 'Okay, just for a minute.'

'Look into the cauldron,' giggled the girl.

Ace looked. At first she saw only her face, mirrored in the waters. Then something else appeared, something far distant. A tree. A vast tree, that stretched up higher than the cauldron's whole view.

'What is it?' she whispered, but got the feeling that she already knew.

'It is the omphalos, child, the world tree,' muttered the crone. 'It is the very centre of the Doctor's group mind, the focus of everthing he is, was, and will be.'

'Pretty special, then,' said Ace. 'How do I get there?'

'Follow the road,' sighed the mature woman. 'And don't let yourself be distracted, sister. There are many ways to lose your way. The Doctor has discovered that.'

Ace looked up to see that a stout, well-constructed brick road was now visible, leading off into the distance. She wandered towards it, and then turned back.

'Look, I have to ask. Who are you lot?'

'We are the Doctor's female self, the principles of maiden, mother and crone,' whispered the Mother. 'He has long lost sight of us. In many ways, you fulfil our function to him. That is why you are here, to perform a task that the Doctor should do himself.'

'No change there, then.' Ace stepped on to the road and began her journey.

The landscape was pretty bleak all round, Ace thought, after about half a mile. The path stretched straight on into the distance, the sinister angular rocks all around, and Ace was once more reminded of a computer game. Well, that made sense, after all.

Both were representations of a reality that would otherwise be incomprehensible in human terms.

'Dorry!' the shout came from behind one of the rocks beside the path. Yeah, of course, that was the obvious one, wasn't it? Ace stayed where she was.

Into view stepped Audrey, Dorry's, no, Ace's Mum. She stumbled forward, holding out a hand towards her daughter. 'Dorry, I've been missing you for so long. You've been so far away.'

She was just the same as she'd always been, voice trembling with emotion she couldn't show, full of explanations that her daughter would never hear. Her slippered feet were sinking, Ace realized. The ground between her and the path was boggy. Step after step, she was sinking into quicksand.

'Look, I know you're just an illusion, but go back, eh? You don't want to see me.'

Audrey was sinking, up to her neck, a short distance from the edge of the path.

'Dorry, please,' she was crying. 'Please . . .' she sobbed in anguish.

'Audrey.' Ace spoke carefully, shuddering. 'If you were real, I'd help you. I really would. But you're not. People that live in your memory aren't real. You spend enough time worrying about the ones that are. I know that now, even if the Doctor doesn't.'

Her mother's head went under the sand, yelling and gurgling in terror. Ace forced herself to watch. 'Ashes to ashes,' she muttered. 'Dust to dust.'

And she walked on, her burden feeling a little heavier.

The path presented her with many illusions. Ian Brown beckoning her to a curtained four-poster ('Come on, naff or what?'); the Cheetah People calling her to come and join the wild hunt ('Not today, thanks.') and Johnny Chess offering friendship and a place on percussion ('You know what you can do with those maracas, don't you?').

She had seen it from a long distance, the Tree. A gigantic ash. Its shape filled the sky. It grew upwards as far as the eye could see, its branches seeming to meld into the darkness.

Overhead, a storm was brewing.

This was the root of the Doctor's self. Everything else, all he was or wanted to be, was built on the upper branches of this tree.

And there was somebody tied to the thing.

Ace ran closer, feeling a knot of fear form in her gut. She stared up at the captive in disbelief.

It was a young man. He had hair that might once have been fair, had it not been smeared with blood and dirt. His white clothes were in tatters. His eyes were closed.

A wound had been inflicted on him, a great incision in his side, and round his throat were the burn marks of savage strangulation. His mouth was white with lack of blood, and he wheezed as if every intake of breath was an effort.

Above the man, the three runes that Ace had recognized as the Doctor's signature were carved on the tree, brought together as one sign.

She got the awful feeling that this was his handiwork.

The man's arms were tied back around the trunk, and his feet dangled inches from the ground. His whole expression was one of pain. He blinked as Ace approached.

'Don't . . . come any closer. Save yourself,' he whispered through clenched teeth. His voice high-pitched with agony.

'No,' replied Ace, shocked. 'I'm Ace, I'm here to rescue you.'

Then she noticed something else.

In front of the tree grew a flower. It was a tiny thing, but quite astonishing. It was some way between a rose and a daisy, and, well, everything else you could think of. A mixture of grand design and simplicity, its petals shone with multicoloured life. Their edges were intricate, and Ace couldn't quite see where their tiny folds ended. Fractal. Right.

Ace knew, in that moment, that this was the whole torment of the Doctor's conscience, to be aware of this perfect flower, to remember it from a single glimpse, long ago, but to be unable to touch it.

She drew her sword, intending to cut the dirty cords that held the man in place.

A rasping hiss came from the branches of the tree.

Sliding down the trunk came the thick trunk of a gleaming metal snake, it eyes flashing with dark intelligence. The Timewyrm.

'Yes,' the Wyrm whispered. 'I am here. I fell here from the bridge. I am consuming the Doctor faster than ever, playing on his every doubt and fear. Do you know the meaning of the storm forming overhead, Ace?'

'No.' Ace didn't really want to play games, here, but information was always useful. Her younger self would have attacked the snake instantly, but she knew now that a real warrior doesn't just leap in and bash away. There really weren't, now she searched for them, as many memories in her mind as there should be, but a sense of self remained, a comforting strength. She looked the snake in the eye. 'So tell me.'

'That storm is the Doctor gathering his mental energy. He intends to crush us all out of existence, to erase the Timewyrm data and everything else alien in his brain. That includes you.'

'Yeah?' Ace felt a tremble inside, but her sword didn't flinch. 'Go ahead, Professor.'

'But it won't work,' the Wyrm laughed, hissing over its new teeth. 'I am not simply a foreign datum, to be wiped from the Doctor's memory. I am part of his mind now. I am integral with his experiences. I have read all his memories, and become part of them, also. He has fought me and will fight me wherever he goes. Even if the actual Timewyrm virus is extinguished, here, in the deepest pits of the Doctor's mind, his guilt will construct me once more from his awful memories. He will use me to punish himself for your death. Ah, I planned deeply and right!'

'God, Doctor,' muttered Ace to the sky, 'why did you have to get so screwed up?' This nightmare just went on and on.

Death might be quite welcome, compared to the endless coils of this creature. She turned to it once more. 'What if I free this bloke?'

'You will not,' smiled the Timewyrm. 'Boyle —'

Chad Boyle stepped from behind the Tree.

Oh yeah, thought Ace. He'd fallen too, hadn't he? Carrying the Timewyrm in his head. Great.

The little boy was grinning as always. He was covered in spiked armour, shiny and pristine, almost a humanoid approximation of the Timewyrm's snakeform. He carried a vast axe, its edge razor sharp. 'Hello again, Dotty,' he laughed. 'Isn't this a great game? Won't it ever stop?' There was a strange edge of hysteria to his voice, as if that was a question he'd been asking himself.

Ace raised her sword. In doing so, she felt that awful draining of age and experience again, her future flooding away. With every year that flew off her, she wanted to lunge at Boyle more, to spill his blood.

'Go on!' the bully chided. 'Use your sword! Try and take my life!'

The years were flying away, and Ace knew that this must be the wrong thing to do, that killing Boyle here would mean the Timewyrm would win, and wipe her from history. But it was so hard. It was what the Cheetah People would do, what a soldier would do, what the Doctor —

No. She lowered the sword, and felt the power and grace of experience return to her.

'You're a little boy,' she said to Boyle. 'And you don't know better. But I do.'

Ace lifted the sword and broke it over her knee, throwing aside the pieces. Then she advanced on Boyle.

The child backed away, stammering. 'That's not what you're supposed to do. You're not playing the game! You're not obeying the rules!'

Ace quietly took the axe from the scared boy, and pulled the helmet from his shoulders. 'No. I'm not. Life isn't about games.' She reached the tree, and glared at the snake.

The Timewyrm was looking around, as if trying to marshal

non-existent forces. Ace raised her axe to cut down the Tree's prisoner.

'Please don't,' cried the Timewyrm desperately. 'I want to live, too. Ishtar doesn't want to die. Please!'

Perhaps only a year ago, Ace would have said something pithy and grinned at the destruction of an enemy that had put her through so much torment. Now she only nodded. 'That's something else that the Doctor got wrong. Something you'll have to take up with him.'

She carefully undid the binding that held the blond man to the Tree. He fell into her arms, his eyes wet with tears of relief.

'Hello,' he whispered up at Ace. 'I'm the Doctor, or rather I was, a long time ago.' He attempted to stand, but found that he couldn't. Ace supported him. 'I wanted a place to play cricket, you see, a sunny glade and a pot of tea, but he wouldn't let me. We were at war, he said.' The old Doctor's voice was full of injured innocence. 'And we were all needed. The other Doctors all co-operated to some extent, but I − I objected.' He stared at the landscape all around, as if seeing it for the first time.

'That's what I call being brave,' muttered Ace.

'Perhaps. It wasn't his fault he imprisoned me . . . he couldn't help it. Now,' the fifth Doctor's voice hardened, 'there's something that I have to do. Help me to the flower.'

The Timewyrm and Boyle looked on in terror as Ace put the young Doctor's arm over her shoulder, and stumbled with him towards the bloom.

Above, the storm was gathering strength.

The Doctor was looking at his hands as they clenched and unclenched.

'I must do it', he muttered. 'I must take her life. Win the game.'

'No, Doctor!' Saul was shouting. 'This is not you, this is the Timewyrm!'

Trelaw and the Hutchingses gazed at the Doctor in panic. Emily had picked up the baby, and was holding it to her, almost afraid of what the maddened Time Lord would do next. It was as if he was fighting a mental battle, and losing. His face was contorted with the effort of the struggle. 'There is another option, of course,' he whispered. 'I can take the TARDIS into the centre of a star. Order it to self-destruct. The Timewyrm will perish with me. The universe will be saved . . . even if Ace isn't.'

Wincing with pain, a pain which seemed to encompass his every movement, the Doctor stumbled over to the altar where Ace lay. His hand shaking, he moved a hair from where it had fallen on her brow. 'And maybe somewhere there is an afterlife, more genuine than the Matrix or the dimensions of an old Time Lord's mind.' He looked down at his companion with infinite sadness, his voice cracking. 'It is a dream I have.'

Supported by Ace, the fifth Doctor reached out, his hand closing on the stem of the flower. 'I remembered what it was that you had lost, Doctor,' he sighed. Then his voice became harder, more determined. 'Now I return it to you.'

The Doctor gazed out across the lunar surface through the stained glass windows of the church. His face was still creased with inner pain. He was talking to the comatose Ace as the rest of the humans looked on, or perhaps he was talking to himself.

'War,' he muttered. 'Not good for anybody. Nobody wins. Nobody ever wins. You have such a hard time looking after the tactics that little details, individual lives, escape you. Sometimes I wonder if I'm just a pawn in some vaster game.'

The fifth Doctor picked the flower, and smiled a triumphant smile. Somewhere, a vast sigh was heard and a group of tormented figures faded into the dear country of nostalgia and fond memory.

The exploding boy and his friends were no more, and they rejoiced in it as they departed.

The Doctor's head snapped round, eyes suddenly narrowing on the baby. 'What's that baby doing here? And why hasn't it cried yet?'

194

Emily, fearing that this was another onset of evil temperament, pulled the child away from him. 'Listen, Doctor, you handed me this baby. You don't want to hurt it, do you?'

'What? Did I?' the Doctor sprang up, vaulted over the seat in which he sat, and whistled a dawn chorus of sounds at the child, clicked his fingers, jumped up and down.

'Doctor,' began Saul.

'Hush!' The Time Lord walked from one end of the church to the other, tapped his forehead, smelt his fingers and threw himself to the floor, plucking a piece of chalk from his pocket. There he swiftly sketched a complex pattern on the stonework, an intricate maze labelled 'if' and 'then' at intervals. Finally he jumped to his feet and looked up at the assembled company, grinning an infectious grin.

'Got her!' he said, and took off his hat to Mrs Hutchings. 'Sorry if I frightened you, or will frighten you. You'll get used to it.'

'Will I?'

The Doctor stared at her for a moment. 'Yes. You will.' He gazed at his hands once more. He had stopped shaking. 'Do you know, I think that this may be the first day of the rest of my life.'

Emily was amazed at his grin. In the circumstances, the reversal was nothing short of miraculous.

The blond Doctor stood straight, his wounds healing, and looked about him with a new vigour, stuffing his hands in his pockets.

'I'd better take this to where it can do most good,' he muttered, glancing at the flower that he had placed in his buttonhole. 'I'd say brave heart –' he glanced at Ace and smiled a lovely, honest smile, which faded into a strange sort of puzzled frown. 'But I think you have one anyway.'

And with that he was gone, a vision fading on the warm breeze that was gathering across the wasteland. Ace found herself smiling also. On the distant horizon of the Pit, dawn was coming.

'*No!*' shouted the Timewyrm. 'I will not be stopped now!'

The snake slithered quickly into the higher branches of the

tree, shouting as it went.

'All you dark archetypes, all you inner demons and deadly gods! Come to me now!'

Distant roars rose from across the plain, and Ace leaned against the tree, glancing up at the Timewyrm. She had a feeling that company was coming.

Peter Hutchings watched the strange little man as he made final preparations for ... well, for whatever he was going to do. All this seemed so far away from his world, the comfy jacket of academia. This was so far beyond his understanding that he might as well have been one of the ants that infested the canteen at Jodrell Bank. Still, he had made a contribution, and in doing so, gone on a mathematical adventure.

The strange figure in the paisley scarf seemed to bridge the gap between infinity and humanity, between the Holy Grail and the cup of tea. Peter supposed that he really should be taking the opportunity to observe the lunar surface, but what was going on inside the church was far more interesting.

Finally, the Doctor seemed ready, having checked the contents of his pockets. He fished out a key.

'Doctor.' Peter thought it was time to ask. 'What exactly was that medallion thing?'

'A portable temporal link which I stole from the black collection in the Prydonian Academy on Gallifrey while I was president of the Time Lords. I knew it would come in handy.'

'So you hid it in here?'

'While I was brass rubbing last summer, before the Timewyrm had first manifested itself in your continuum. There was no way it could have known of the device.'

'But you had planned all that?' Peter was astonished.

'It's not as surprising as all that.' For a moment, it seemed as if the Doctor was going to leave it at that. Then he seemed to make a decision. 'Let me tell you a story.'

He sat down on a pew, and Emily, Peter and Trelaw gathered round. Even the vicar was aware of a certain reverence in the act.

'Long ago,' began the Doctor, 'when even far Gallifrey was

young, the peoples of that planet fought amongst themselves. They used what they knew of time travel to gain advantage on their enemies. In doing so, they saw many strange and awful things. One mad prophet martyr journeyed too far and saw the Timewyrm.' Peter realized that the Doctor was reciting, remembering some ancient text. Or was he describing his own memories? It was hard to tell. 'He saw it in a timeline that he could not be sure of, devouring Rassilon or his shade, during the Blue Shift, that time of final conflict, when Fenric shall slip its chains and all the evil of the worlds shall rebound back on them in war. For the Timewyrm is the Addanc, the wyrm that circles the cosmos, it is sleeping and it wakes, it is good and evil, choice made carnate.'

The Doctor paused, slipping back into his own explanation. 'The Timewyrm is something that the Time Lords have always expected. Some of us were sufficiently convinced by the legends to prepare. Long ago. Its appearance now means that the end cannot be very far away.'

'The end of the universe?' queried Saul. 'The day of judgement?'

'A conflict, a time of darkness. Don't worry. The Gallifreyan concept of a near time is much vaster than yours.'

'Well, that's all right then,' muttered Emily.

Trelaw's head was swimming. He sighed and stared into the Doctor's eyes. 'Is there no hope then? Is the end so pre-ordained?'

The Doctor seemed to consider his reply carefully. 'There's always hope,' he whispered, finally.

Trelaw nodded, thankful for this small consolation.

'Ishtar must glimpse only a small part of this,' the Doctor sighed. 'She's just a pawn too, fulfilling her part in a game that may be part of the physical laws of destruction and rebirth. That's her dihenydd, as the Welsh would say. I've fought her more often than she knows, already defeated her, already lost to her, chased her round the walls of Troy, been chased by her through the caverns of Nessanhudd. And as far as she knows this is our fourth meeting. May it be our last.'

'Doctor, I've taken a lot, but that really doesn't make sense,'

Peter began. 'How can —'

'No more words. Time for action.' The Doctor stood up, and opened the door of the TARDIS. 'Thank you for your help.'

'Where are you going?' asked Trelaw.

'Inside. If I don't return, there's something you must do.' He touched Emily gently on the nose. 'Ace will have ceased to exist. The body here will continue to function. Put an end to it.'

'Doctor!' cried the woman, 'that's a terrible thing to ask.'

'Yes. I ask terrible things of people. That must end too. If I don't return, somebody will aid you, get you back to Earth. The Time Lords are very thorough about things like that.'

And without another word he stepped inside the TARDIS and closed the door.

'Where's he going, Saul?' asked Trelaw as the TARDIS faded away.

'A long way,' replied the church. 'Further than he has ever been.'

Ace had grabbed Boyle's hand and ran, off across the storm-racked plain of the Doctor's mind. All around, dark forms were rising, things more ancient and terrible than the Doctor's own inner doubts. These were gods, as near as the term meant anything here, powerful racial symbols and principles, from both Gallifrey and Earth. Amongst them Ace glimpsed things that she might have seen in old nightmares.

'Close your eyes!' she gasped out to the little boy as she ran. 'It'll all be all right.'

'You sure, Dotty?'

'Yeah. The Doctor'll save us. And it's Ace, or Dorothy if you really want. All we have to do is keep —'

The creature sprang out of the ground in front of them, a vast sheet of emptiness. Before Ace could even glimpse what it was, it had covered them both, smothering them in darkness.

The Doctor was walking widdershins around the TARDIS console, talking to his oldest companion, the timecraft itself. He wasn't expecting an answer. Every now and then he tapped a dial or flicked a switch. They were in the vortex, hovering.

'Dorothy wanted to go home. The Scarecrow needed a brain. The Tin Man needed a heart. And the Cowardly Lion, he needed courage. Each found that the quest wasn't in the adventure, but in themselves. They discovered that what they seeked to find was meaningless, that the only thing worth having was inside. Yes, I ought to play the Hermit at chess again. But he wouldn't play to win ...'

The Doctor suddenly stopped, and reversed the direction of his walk, hitting switches quickly and diving at the coordinate board. He was about to enter the new directions when his left hand, which had been jerking and flexing, thrust itself into the still bare wires of the exposed section.

There was a flash. With a yelp and a cry the Doctor fell backwards. When he sat up once more, he looked darkly determined. 'But it's difficult to play for the game's own sake when your opponent is playing to win. Ah well, *alea jacta est*!'

The Doctor assumed a perfect lotus on the floor of the console room, his hands forming a tantric meditation posture. After a while, the pitch of the TARDIS's motors changed. The coordinate keyboard bustled into life, and all over the console, emergency cutouts shorted, restraining switches exploded, warning bells were silenced.

The cloister bell, the most awesome and urgent sign of impending danger, rang three times ... and then was silent.

The TARDIS swerved off its path in the vortex, whirling towards the rushing, kaleidoscopic walls of the gravity well that punched a hole through reality. It struck the corridor and distorted, wrapping itself around spacetime, vanishing instantly as a swirl of royal blue in the susurating colours of infinity.

The Doctor flew his craft by instinct, diving it into the interface between his mind and his craft, seeking the still point of singularity. The TARDIS spun into the dreamtime, into the Doctor's memories, carrying him into his own unconscious.

Carrying him into the darkness.

* * *

The arena was dark and hushed, the audience expectant with waiting. Amongst their number could be found all the ancient things of Gallifrey, the dark gods of Earth, every fundamental horror and woe. They were not comfortable in these uplands of the mind, but the Timewyrm had forced them by biology, changed the chemical balance of the Doctor's brain until they had to come here or perish, into the arena that Ace had encountered on her journey into this mind, the circus of the pineal gland.

The spotlight sprang into life.

In its bright gaze, a solid blue form flexed and groaned its way into reality. The TARDIS had arrived inside the Doctor's mind.

The crowd cheered and yelled.

The door of the craft opened, and the Doctor strode forth, his gaze sweeping the arena. 'Where's Ace?' he growled.

'Professor? I'm here . . .'

A figure stumbled forward, into the glare of the light. Ace was clutching her face, her breath coming in rasps.

His expression a picture of dismay, the Doctor gently took her hands in his. He pulled them away from her face.

Ace opened her mouth, there was a glint there, a glint of —

The blast of fire caught the Doctor full in his face.

13: Total Eclipse

A seeker of silences am I,
and what treasure have I found in silences
that I may dispense with confidence?

The Prophet Kahlil Gibran.

The Doctor reeled aside, clutching his face in agony.

The Timewyrm guffawed. 'When you might have destroyed me, Time Lord, you chose to return. You revealed your weakness. Your weakness is the girl. I know you better than you know yourself.'

'No.' The Doctor removed his hands from his face with a flourish, and stood up once more. He was unharmed. 'You don't.'

The last words were a whisper, but the ancient strength they conveyed hushed the demonic audience. Every one of them had heard that sound, banishing them from turbulent dreams, horrific visions. It was the word of the wise man, the force of rationality.

'How?' exclaimed the Timewyrm, clearly shocked. Its form swirled back into the metallic snake. 'In my kingdom I can harm your data structure, I can destroy your memory!'

'Oh you could when I allowed you to.' The Doctor affected nonchalance, his hands behind his back as he looked around the arena. 'I've never been here before. The pineal gland.

Fascinating. Where's Ace?'

The Timewyrm waved a finger, somewhat perturbed. Two clowns marched the Doctor's companion out into the arena.

Ace could hardly believe it. The Timewyrm had reclaimed Boyle, and kept her shut up in a dark little cell. A for/next loop as she rationalized it, a bit of the datascape she couldn't escape from. She had hoped, had thought, that the Doctor would somehow get her out, but she didn't expect this.

She stared at the Doctor in amazement. The idiot had come back for her! She couldn't help but feel glad though. The expression of casual control on his face was a joy to see.

The Doctor was back.

She wanted to dash up and hug him, but instead she just sauntered over, not letting the clowns rush her. Strange that they didn't bother her now. It was just a silly childhood thing, one of those fears that leave you with experience, and God, had she got experience.

'Yo, Professor,' she called. 'I thought you were out of here.'

'I changed my mind,' the Doctor smiled. He looked up at the assembled dark masses of the crowd. 'All the world's a stage. I'm going through.'

'Yeah, well, that's not what I call a good audience.' Ace nodded up at the ranks of ancient demons that surrounded them.

'No, they probably wouldn't appreciate a quick burst on the spoons . . .'

Glancing over her shoulder, Ace noticed that the Timewyrm had vanished. The crowd was roaring with anticipation. It was like the few seconds before kick-off, Ace realized, the spectators waiting for the big moment. A hum of power was building in the amphitheatre, and the air was crackling with tension. The smell of brimstone was getting stronger all the time.

'Ace,' the Doctor murmured. 'It's time. Get in the TARDIS.'

'Not yet,' Ace replied, and put a finger up to the Time Lord's lips as he was about to order her more strongly. 'I've got to find Chad Boyle. It's kind of my fault that he's here.'

The Doctor might have been about to argue, but at the moment the spotlight blazed into life again, picking out a figure that stood in the archway that led into the amphitheatre.

A squat figure, eyes blazing. The Timewyrm had possessed her favourite host one last time. BoyleWyrm stepped forward, lifting claws of burnished steel. The Doctor turned carefully to face the creature. The audience roared its appreciation, stamping feet and hooves, thrashing tails.

'So,' the Timewyrm whispered. 'It comes to this, as it always had to. The Doctor and the Virus. Why didn't you kill me, Time Lord?'

'Because my friend did me a great service.' The Doctor met the being's gaze calmly. 'She showed me that there was another option. If I destroyed you, you would only have returned in time. Like my guilt, my remorse, you're part of a terrible cycle. I can't take your life. I refuse to. But I can give you peace. Come with me, Ishtar. Let me help you.'

'Why should I trust you?'

'I asked the same question.' Ace stepped forward, a little surprised at her own confidence. 'You trust him because you have to trust somebody. Okay, so he's made a few mistakes, but he's on the case now.' Ace paused, and looked the Doctor in the eye. 'I trust you, Doctor.'

A strange look passed over the Doctor's face and for a moment Ace thought that the Time Lord was going to cry. But just as quickly the look vanished and was replaced by an utter conviction. 'I swear to you, Ishtar, if you're still in control of that organism, I mean you no harm.'

'You lie!' screamed the tiny figure, puffs of fire flaring from its metal nostrils. 'This is another game! I have beaten you once, I will do so again! I will kill your conscious mind here and now, take over your form, and pillage the universe! I will feed on your precious Earth!'

'If you're gonna be so stupid,' Ace shouted, 'then give back Chad Boyle. He doesn't deserve all this.'

'Chad Boyle?' cried the Timewyrm. 'A tiny life form? I feast on whole worlds!'

The little body that the Timewyrm inhabited stared to jerk and contort, the muscles spasming under some inner tension. The legs gave way, and it fell to the floor, thrashing.

With a sickening splintering of bone, the body of Chad Boyle split open.

Gouts of blood poured from the tearing flesh as huge coils of gleaming metal burst from it. The dragon maw swept upwards from the neck, its expression triumphant.

The shreds of Chad Boyle's human form were swept away under the gleaming bulk of the vast metal lami, its claws brushing aside scraps of frail humanity, until there was nothing left to mark the child's passing.

The Timewyrm had assumed its true form.

Ace found herself weeping, angry at anything that could sweep aside a human life like that. It took her a moment before she realized who she was weeping for.

Chad Boyle. Her tormentor.

She hoped there was a heaven for him somewhere.

The Doctor watched, his face dark with ancient power. The Timewyrm thrashed about the arena, drawing energy from the assembled demons of the unconscious. They screeched and squealed and faded away, dissolving into a boiling ocean of dark steam which rolled around the seating as it itself dissolved, sucked into the growing form of the Timewyrm. The arms grew, huge scimitar claws bursting from the fingers. Legs and torso were blended into a gigantic, lashing tail of shining chrome. The angles of the dragonhead crushed in upon themselves, smoothing into the features of a young woman. The pupils of the Timewyrm's eyes, the last vestige of Boyle's soul, vanished inwards to reappear a moment later in a shade of red, glowing with angry intelligence. The new form cried out in pain and triumph.

'Get in the TARDIS,' the Doctor shouted to Ace. '*Now!*'

Ace dived for the door of the timecraft, dizzy as the surroundings spun faster and faster, their colours and shapes blurring into a void of pure white. All there was left was the reassuring blue shape of the police box and the two adversaries, Time Lord and Timewyrm, facing each other. Qataka's transformed self towered over the tiny figure of the Doctor. As Ace watched, peering out of the door, the creature raised its head, bellowing.

'Don't be a fool!' the Doctor was yelling. 'There's no reason

204

to fight, nothing left for you to gain!'

'Your death, Doctor!' bellowed the monster. '*Your death!*'
It blew a jet of blue flame straight at the tiny form below it,
and the Doctor screamed, his clothes catching fire and his flesh
withering beneath the assault. Whatever power he had
summoned to heal his form, it was not infinite. He stumbled
forward, raising a hand to protect himself, and the Timewyrm
leaned forward, opening her mouth to consume this arrogant
insect.

The Doctor glanced backwards at Ace, and in that second,
the woman from Perivale saw a kind of pride in his face. It
was as if he was saying goodbye.

The Doctor turned back and glared up into the jaws that were
descending on him. 'Too much death. Too many conflicts!' he
shouted at the Timewyrm. 'This must end now! *Begone!*'

He reached out and touched the creature.

The universe exploded with light.

In a rose garden, the first Doctor gazed down at the perfect
bloom that the fifth Doctor had brought him. The Sarlain. It
had taken well to the garden, and the old Doctor smiled and
nodded. This was the bloom that he had been trying to cultivate
for so long.

The younger Doctor smiled, stuffed his hands in his pockets,
and stood up from where he had been squatting, admiring the
flower.

'Well, I must get on,' he smiled. 'There's the ground to
prepare, and I have to get my old bat out of storage. It's good
to be out and about again. Will you be there for the match?'

'Of course,' giggled the old man, clutching the lapel of his
scarlet Prydonian robes. 'I have always been there for the game.'

The Doctor floated in nothingness, his form encompassing a
billion pinprick galaxies, a slow burst of nuclear life. The rough
sphere of the cosmos blossomed within him, growing as he
watched, life pushing forward against the shade of night. As
he gazed, cosmic civilizations rose and fell, concepts of order
and chaos waxed and waned, and languages flared into life and

died with their cultures, each reaching to describe what the Doctor carried inside him. All failing.

The moment went on forever, the Doctor contemplating the inner progression as a passage of endless music, an infinite remix as one theme arose to counterpoint another, life and death and resurrection. In the surging galaxies, haloed by blazing quasars, stars bloomed and collapsed, clusters broke against each other like waves under the rule of gravity. Laws were formed from the way matter played matter, laws that were broken at the surface and centre of the sphere.

And in another moment, there was the Timewyrm.

As the poets of many cultures had glimpsed it, it encircled the globe of the universe, and hence the Doctor. It swallowed its own tail, endlessly feeding on its own selfhood. It was everything there was and would be. Fighting it would be like battling a pattern, or shouting against the storm. Its scales reflected the light of the cosmos and all its tiny battles.

Yet, inside this conception, this grand poem of encirclement, a single life still blazed. Obviously. The Timewyrm was as much a part of life as breathing or blood. It was what cats howled at on August nights, what the Kurylie traced across the skies of their dreamtime, what babies were thinking of at the instant of their birth. The Doctor reached out and touched the life.

It was a short life, and an infinite one. Qataka had known love, and pity, and laughter. The Doctor simply presented himself to her, and she saw in him what her mechanical form could not. She said yes.

She wanted to go home.

The Timewyrm felt its essence dissolving, computed the approaching fact of its dissolution. The head reared up from its own tail, roared towards the Doctor, impacted in a ripple that disturbed the evolution of whole clusters of galaxies.

They fought in the biology, poetry and astronomy of a thousand races, the stellar man battling the snake.

The snake was about to seize the man's neck, the storytellers said.

And then the man smiled.

* * *

Saul laughed.

'What is it, Saul?' The Reverend Trelaw looked up in alarm. The laughter had startled Peter and Emily too. They had been watching Ace's form nervously, waiting for something, anything to happen.

'I do not know,' laughed Saul. 'It just strikes me that the universe is a very humorous place!'

Peter made a twirl with his finger against his skull, and then was amazed to discover that his wife was laughing too.

'Yes,' she giggled. 'I know exactly what you mean. It's wonderful, it's like the whole world has just gone on holiday.'

Trelaw couldn't resist a smile himself. The baby that he was holding began to wave a hand around, the first real movement that it had made. One finger wavered into a vague pointing gesture. 'And what are you trying to tell us?' the vicar asked.

There was a sudden blast of colour, a sound beyond sound. Emily had time to open her mouth, Peter to grasp the baby to his chest. The church shuddered with some tremendous power. Trelaw, though he would not later confess it, swore he heard a voice, a voice old and terrible, echoing down the corridors from a time before time itself.

'*Go home!*' said the voice.

With a roar like the tide receding, sunlight burst into the church. Real winter sunlight, suffused with snowy air and distant clouds. A chorus of rooks flapped up from nearby trees in a blast of sound, and Saul shouted with all his might.

'Home! We have come home!'

Peter and Emily hugged each other, and Trelaw fell to his knees, giving heartfelt thanks to his Lord. Under Saul's power, the doors burst open, and a burst of freezing air rushed into the church.

It was late afternoon and the village of Cheldon Bonniface was alive in the little hollow below the hill where St Christopher's stood. Smoke rose from chimneys and distant sounds of children playing and dogs barking floated on the chill breeze.

'But how?' cried Saul. 'I saw this place destroyed! I saw it!'

'Look,' cried Emily, dashing over to where Ace lay. The

young woman was stirring, her hands rising to her face. She sat up quite suddenly, and looked around.

'Doctor?' she asked.

Emily hugged her suddenly and Ace found herself clutching the woman in return. 'You came to rescue me,' Ace gasped. 'He did it, the stupid old man. He sacrificed himself to get me home!'

The two women parted for a second, and looked at each other. Then they both began to sob, and embraced again. In amongst their sobs came choking laughter.

Peter would have made a wry comment but, putting his hand to his cheek, he found that he too was sobbing uncontrollably. He sat down beside the two of them and encompassed them all in his arms.

Trelaw stood back a little, holding Saul in that special mental space they shared. A few moments went by in which nothing but grateful weeping could be heard. 'Fear makes companions of us all,' he whispered after a little while.

The whole universe. Calm, seen from this far off.

Inside that globe were battles, conflicts, fierce adventure. Here, in the space outside the stars, there was only peace and reconciliation now.

If he went back, he would have to fight again.

He could stay here, at one with the cosmos without ever encountering it on an individual basis. He could keep his distant sense of scale, enjoy real peace.

Oneness and calm, or conflict and pain.

The Doctor looked down on the stars and sighed.

Ah well, pain it was.

'He's gone.' Ace wiped her face on her sleeve. 'But that's okay, that's really okay. He finished off the Timewyrm . . . I think.'

'We owe him much,' chorused Saul. 'I have examined broadcasts from the outside world, and it seems as if the blast which destroyed the village never happened.'

'What blast?' asked Ace.

'Exactly,' concluded Saul.

'I must write a paper for the Royal Society,' Peter muttered. 'This whole experience, the whole —' he waved his arms vaguely.

'No, love,' murmured Emily, who still had an arm looped through Ace's. 'They'd have you certified. I'll write a novel instead.'

'There's no place like home,' Ace sighed, patting Emily's arm and disengaging from her to move towards the doors. She looked out over the countryside.

Her past was back, complete and lovely, a gorgeous catalogue of fond memories, people and places, alive with the recollection. 'That's what they say, anyway. They're right, too. Maybe there are some places better, but there's nothing that smells the same, feels the same ...'

'I didn't really get to know him very well,' Emily moved to stand beside her. 'But the Doctor seemed to be a very good man.'

'Yeah, and he didn't get that, either.' Ace watched a dove alight on a gravestone in the churchyard. 'He knew all about the good bit, about what was expected of him, but he never caught on to being a man. I dunno why I feel so happy about all this. Maybe in a few days I'll start grieving, eh?'

'Perhaps so,' Emily smiled.

'I just get the feeling that he's still out there somewhere.' Ace stared out over the encroaching mist, blinking against the low winter sun. 'Somewhere ...'

She caught a familiar sound, distant, like something heard on the edge of a dream. Maybe it was only a memory, but it meant so much. It meant freedom, a love that embraced the alien, the outsider, and the oppressed. This sound couldn't tolerate hatred and violence, but found itself unable to be silent in the face of evil. That's why it rended, tore its way across time. To Ace, the wheezing, groaning sound seemed to be blown from the distance on some Christmas breeze, a legend as silly and as powerful as Santa Claus in the gathering twilight.

But the sound was real. It grew in strength every second.

Ace spun round, grinning her head off. 'Never,' she smiled, sniffing. 'It can't be.'

The TARDIS roared into life in the aisle, the light on its roof blazing, and settled, with a clump of halting machinery. A second later, the door burst open.

'Doctor!' shouted Ace.

The Doctor stumbled out, clutching his head and shouting incoherently.

'So let me grasp the rose that grows inside under the surface,' he yelled. 'Allow me strength and not to hide, Or give me a friend who seeks the lie . . .' With a great effort he grasped the baby in Trelaw's arms and pressed his forehead to its. 'And let my mind do no more fighting!'

There was a blaze of blue static between the foreheads. The Doctor rocked back on his heels and gazed down at the baby.

The child seemed suddenly possessed. Its hands clenched into fists, and it looked around itself, an intelligence seeming to fill it for the first time.

'You've put the Timewyrm in the baby!' Ace realized, running to the Doctor's side and supporting him. 'But isn't that – ?'

'Hush . . .' the Doctor murmured, unsteadily. 'Watch.'

The baby seemed about to lift itself up out of Trelaw's grasp. It raised its fists over its head and glared at the world angrily.

Then it let out a mighty howl and started to cry.

'I think it's hungry,' murmured the Doctor. 'The poor thing hasn't been fed in hours.'

Trelaw gazed down at the child in awe. 'What do we feed it?' he whispered.

'Milk,' the Doctor picked up the baby and handed it to Peter and Emily. 'You two had better find some. Call her Ishtar. It'll mean some problems in the playground, but', and he glanced back to Ace, 'some of us benefit through adversity.'

Emily stared at the baby in her arms. The infant reached up and gripped the Doctor's finger.

He smiled a giddy smile.

And then he fell over.

The Epilogues: Getting Away With It

*It's not where you're from,
it's where you're at.*

Ian Brown.

The Doctor woke up. In the vicarage, a comfy place full of dusty furniture and gauche china ornaments. He was lying on a sofa under a tartan blanket. Trelaw was peering down at him in concern.

'Is everything all right?' the Time Lord muttered.

'Everything's fine,' the reverend assured him. 'You try to sleep.'

'Yes.' The Doctor lay back, the muscles of his face relaxing. 'Used the Timewyrm's power to restructure reality. Never happened. One casualty. That's too many.'

'Doctor,' Trelaw adjusted the pillow underneath the sleeping man's head, 'it could have been so much worse.'

And for a moment, Trelaw glimpsed a dark figure out of the corner of his eye. A hooded man, vanishing into shadow. He was nodding, his one eye gleaming with approval. His hard lesson had been taught. It was almost something that Trelaw could have put into a sermon.

War knows no morality.

Trelaw crossed himself. Glancing at the calendar, he hoped

211

that the Doctor would recover soon.

The reverend would be busy tomorrow.

In his dreams, the Doctor saw a table, a big oak thing in a banqueting hall. The third Doctor was entertaining the Ferryman, who as they both knew was actually the fourth Doctor, should he have wished to keep his proper name.

'Spacious,' declared the fourth Doctor, his eyes twinkling over a glass of wine. 'Tell me, don't you feel lonely, living here all by yourself?'

The third Doctor sipped from his glass thoughtfully. 'No, old chap,' he muttered. 'I rather enjoy the solitude.'

In his sleep, the Doctor nodded gently.

Ace was wandering through the snow-covered churchyard, wrapped in one of Peter's overcoats. It had been eight hours since she had returned to the land of the living, and the Doctor had still been asleep when she left him, two hours ago. It was good to have real time back. From the dense white clouds, the first flecks of new snowfall were swirling down, stinging her face and lips.

She suddenly dived forward on to the ground, and kissed the snow, tasting it. All these snowflakes − all different, all so short-lived, but all beautiful. From a distance, they all looked the same, but close up, they were all so complex and different. The creeps she had invented in her comfy old fantasy of ordinary life would never have bothered to notice that.

A child would bundle these snowflakes up and throw them at another child. And that was cool if you were a kid, no harm in that. But she wasn't a child any more.

She had come back.

She stood up, brushing the snow off the coat. She wouldn't have come up here if she hadn't known the Doctor was going to be all right. Known it in her bones. Did he know how she was going to die? Had he looked it up on one of those dark nights?

Did it matter?

Looking down at the village, at the Christmas trees glimpsed through windows and the colourful lights that illuminated the frontage of the Black Swan — a very modern pub now — Ace wanted to run down to a phone and call everyone that she loved, and tell them. She wanted to eat a massive bacon sandwich, to arrange a vast explosion of fireworks, to dance and snog her head off.

One day, she would die. Taken suddenly and sweetly, she hoped. That was okay. Even better if she didn't, mind. Like a character at the end of her book, she would stop doing things. What she had achieved, for good and bad, would have to do.

What she did, what she was going to do in this astonishing world, would be as strong and beautiful as a snowflake.

Ace grinned up at the rising moon, pushed her hands deeper into the pockets of the coat, and ran down the hill towards the vicarage, blowing kisses at the sky.

Peter Hutchings stood watching from the door of the spare bedroom as Emily fed Ishtar from a bottle.

Ishtar. It sounded like a sneeze.

The Doctor, while he was drinking lots of tea and burning crumpets at the vicarage, had explained that the Timewyrm would always exist, as some sort of basic universal principle, but it would remain unconscious, at least until the Time of Darkness. The human portion, that which had created the creature in human time, was now inhabiting the baby's brain. To do so, it had had to jettison much of its memory, its personality, everything but bare life.

Ishtar Hutchings would grow up exactly like any other baby, give or take the odd nightmare.

Emily was over the moon, of course. Yeah, now there was an expression that Peter wouldn't be able to use straight-faced again. His wife had coped with the whole experience better than he had, handling it with her usual practicality.

She glanced up at him, smiling. He smiled back, and wandered in to say hello again to his new daughter.

He stood at the base of the hill on which St Christopher's stood, his back to her as she descended.

Maybe he was thinking, going over the terrible experiences they'd gone through. Or maybe he was planning again, constructing another elaborate campaign to rid the universe of evil. Ace decided that she would probably never know what he thought, or even how he thought.

The Doctor turned round as she tripped down the hill behind him. His eyes sparkled in the first dark of evening, and his face held an expression of sad wisdom. He looked at her for a long moment. Ace noticed that his eyes had returned to their normal brilliant blue.

'Hello,' he said finally. 'I'm the Doctor. And this is my friend Ace.'

The two adventurers held each other for a long time. And then, wrapped about each other still, they tramped back to the vicarage.

Far above them, Saul was sounding the first bells of Christmas Eve.

The evening was a blur of food, drink, and song, both at the Hutchings household, and the bar of the real Black Swan, which the Doctor had entered with some trepidation.

Ace spent ages on the vicarage phone trying to discover Johnny Chess's home number, without success, and the Doctor treated everyone to an improvized rendition of 'The Holly and the Ivy' on the spoons. Ishtar Hutchings cried a lot.

Ace woke in the middle of the night on Christmas Eve, suddenly afraid. There was a noise in the room.

Reaching for her rucksack, she switched on the bedside light.

The Doctor was filling one leg of her tights with apples and oranges.

'Tradition,' he smiled uncomfortably. 'Or are you too old for that sort of thing?'

'No . . .' Ace smiled, turning over and going back to sleep. 'Wicked.'

On Christmas Day, after an enormous dinner that the Hutchingses had prepared, Ace tiptoed out into the hall, and looked at their telephone.

She'd never forgotten the number.

After all she'd been through, maybe she should just call home, say that she was still alive.

Maybe they'd care.

She lifted the receiver and dialled. The phone rang once. Twice. Somebody picked it up.

It might have been a man's voice on the other end of the line, or it might not. Ace had put the phone down again before she heard more than a syllable.

Emily stepped out into the hall, and tried to step back into the lounge again, instantly aware that something was wrong.

'I was just,' Ace spoke to her and Emily stopped. 'I was just looking at your phone. It's a great phone. It really is a bloody wonderful phone, that ...'

The tears were running down her cheeks painfully, her face screwed up against the hurt inside her.

Emily gently led her along the hall, to the room where Ishtar was sleeping. They sat down on the bed, and Ace reached out to tuck the baby in where she had pushed the cover aside.

'I thought I was okay now,' Ace whispered. 'After all that, I thought I could face anything.'

'Family's different,' Emily stroked her hair, fixing strands that had gone astray back in place. 'Maybe that's something that the Doctor will have to deal with eventually, too.' She looked seriously into the eyes of the woman from Perivale. 'I've been meaning to say ... I know you're a bit old for this, and it's a bit of a cheek, but I feel like I've known you for a very long time ...'

'Please.' Ace rubbed her brow. 'Please say it anyway.'

'You could stay here, with us. I wouldn't mind another daughter, or a long-lost younger sister, if the neighbours start to do their sums.'

'I know,' said Ace, hugging Emily. 'But I don't like to think what would happen to the Doctor without me. He needs somebody to take care of him. He really does. 'Sides, you've already got one new mouth to feed.'

Ace stood up, purposefully wiping her tears on her sleeve.

Maybe there were some pains that made you, that defined what you were.

She turned back to Emily as she reached the door. 'Thanks for asking,' she blurted, and left before she started again and woke the baby.

The Doctor and Ace made quite a few short trips in the TARDIS during this time, doing what the Doctor called 'looking after the details with hindsight'. They broke into a genetics lab in the twenty-second century, and stole a female baby, grown artificially, without sensory input, to leave her a mindless husk. This, the Doctor told Ace, was so the doctors involved could experiment on her with a clear conscience.

Ace wanted to duck inside St Christopher's on that fateful Sunday with the baby, but the Doctor insisted that since Emily remembered him doing it, he'd better go through the whole process, just to make sure. He bundled the baby that would become Ishtar up, closed his eyes and dashed inside the church. Crossing timelines always made him feel uncomfortable.

As Saul mentally called to him, he steeled himself not to say that everything would be okay.

He didn't want to go through the whole business again.

They placed an advert in the NME of the far future, and the Doctor mentioned that he had indeed read Ace's copy when she'd lent it to him, noticed the warning contained in it, and realized that eventually it would mean something.

'It pays to advertise,' grinned Ace, looking at the brand-new copy of the paper outside Ladbroke Grove hypertube station. 'Hey, what's this, Professor? Wanted, short man with bizarre dress sense, extreme lifestyle and police box. Must play the spoons. No time-wasters.'

'What?' the Doctor grabbed the paper and Ace ruffled his hair.

'Got you,' she laughed.

The Doctor frowned at her.

The brick was cold, gritty and hard through Chad Boyle's mitten. His raised hand was silhouetted against the low sun, so perhaps it was the sudden shade that made the girl turn.

She screamed.

Boyle savagely swung the weapon down.

A hand caught his wrist, and twisted the brick out of it. Chad managed a fleeting glimpse of a beautiful young woman, a scarf wrapped round her face, who pushed him over and then ran through the playground, diving out of the gate into the road.

There a man waited for her. A man that Chad recognized from somewhere, maybe from a dream. He met the little boy's eyes, and smiled a satisfied smile.

Chad Boyle glanced back to see that Dotty had been surrounded by other girls, who were glaring at him, saying that they'd tell on him to Miss Marshall, and how could he think about hitting a girl with a brick?

Chad didn't know. Stupid idea. Got him in trouble for nothing.

When he looked back to the road, the strange man was gone.

'Yeah,' muttered Ace, pulling the scarf from her face in the console room. 'I remember now, I heard about Chad Boyle from Midge a long while back. His family moved up to Barnet before he reached Seniors, and he went on to be editor of a local paper. According to Midge, he'd got his act together and was really nice. Why didn't I know that back in dreamland?'

'It wasn't true then,' murmured the Doctor. 'You just made it happen.'

Greenwich Park shone white above London's grey towers. The Doctor and Ace stood on either side of the meridian. The Doctor's expression was thoughtful, as it had been for the last few days. The TARDIS had become increasingly difficult to control. Ace hardly dared to ask about the night-time scratching at her door.

'What year is it, Professor?' she asked instead.

'1976,' answered the Doctor. 'And no, you can't go and tell Sid Vicious to be more careful. He wouldn't listen, anyway.'

'We're going to have to leave Cheldon Bonniface soon, aren't we? I mean, permanently?'

'We can always pop back,' muttered the Doctor. 'Old friends are like old china. Very valuable, very fragile.'

'But you're off? To do something else?'

'Yes.' The Doctor looked at her suspiciously. 'Do you want to come?'

Ace looked at her trainers for a minute.

'Yeah,' she finally grinned. 'What have I got to lose?'

They walked off, beginning a conversation about Newton's rose garden, and the Doctor's lack of belief in the *I Ching*, and all sorts of things. Behind them an awkward undergraduate, wheeling his bicycle up the hill, collided with a beautiful young woman.

'Oh, excuse me,' blurted Peter Hutchings, grabbing for the books the woman had been carrying. 'I was just looking at that girl's jacket. Those badges . . .' He waved his arms vaguely.

'Yes,' Emily West nodded, smiling. 'I was thinking exactly the same thing.' She gathered up her belongings, and was about to walk off.

Then she turned around.

'You look cold,' she grinned. 'Fancy a cup of coffee somewhere?'

The Reverend Ernest Trelaw wiped away the final traces of the Doctor's chalk pattern from the floor of St Christopher's. The Time Lord and his companion had departed that bright January morning after the burial of Rupert Hemmings' head. The Doctor had stood by the grave like some dark angel, his face deep in thought.

Perhaps he had learnt something after all.

For himself, Trelaw was puzzling over how to write up the whole business for the church records. Perhaps Emily's novel would, indeed, be a better solution.

'I think I'm starting to see it, Saul,' began Trelaw. 'The Doctor was playing a game to ensnare the Timewyrm, using us all as his pawns . . .'

'He particularly took advantage of my ability to focus human psychic power,' Saul chorused, sounding a little hurt. 'Myself, Emily, and the baby seem far too perfect a combination to be

218

the creation of mere chance, and too diabolical a conception for divine grace.'

'Indeed.' Trelaw finished his work and stood up. 'And the Timewyrm had a game planned too, to use you to help seize the Doctor's form, to consume the Earth. But above and beyond both their plans, someone had decided to teach the Doctor a lesson about conscience, and the weakness of a warrior. I think that's all I'll write in the records.'

He moved to the door, and glanced around the church, checking that everything was safe.

Centuries in the past, humans had come to worship in the plot where Saul now lived. From the Celts, through the Romans and into the Saxons, men and women had bowed their heads to something far above, something grand that was made of what the universe was made of, and yet was part of their care and concern. With each religion, the specific belief had varied, but the faith had eternally been there. The Saxons brought stone and etched its dust into their hands with the heavy task of construction. The Normans had added their own architecture, and every age had laid its mark on the work in some form. All of them knew one thing, that there was something beyond themselves out in the night, something good.

Trelaw made his way to the vestry door and, as he touched the ancient wood, looked up at the billions of stars that glittered overhead in a holy arc of distant magic. He made small supplication to his God. Somewhere, sometime, there was a man among those stars who would fight for, and die for, the principle behind all this wonder. And in that moment, a star detached itself from the cosmos and dashed down to touch the Earth below. Trelaw chuckled and closed the door.

'You seem happy tonight,' Saul sang into the still night air.

'I went to see the Hutchingses. When I left little Ishtar, she was sleeping so quietly . . .'

'That is good. Now you must sleep quietly yourself.'

Trelaw leant heavily on a pillar. 'Yes, old friend, I must. I don't know if I can reach the vicarage, I'm so tired . . .'

'Then sleep here,' Saul murmured. 'I will keep you warm.'

Trelaw curled up in a pew, pulled over a prayer mat for a

pillow, and closed his eyes.

'Goodnight, Saul.'

'Goodnight. All is quiet. Sleep with pleasant dreams ...'

And, smiling, the reverend did so.

Long ago in an English winter.